The Cats of Queens
A Tale of Extraordinary Cats

James Randall Miller

For Emma, bright and beautiful,
May your life be a brilliant, sparkling adventure.

I have lived with several Zen masters—all of them cats.
— ECKHART TOLLE

1

HIS ACUTE HEARING DETECTED the threat before he saw it: Panting. Then, a deep, menacing growl cut through the stillness, freezing Cosmo mid-step. The battle-scarred street cat of dubious lineage stood rigid, his amber eyes narrowing as he scanned the alley for escape routes. The dog was close—too close—its rancid breath detectable even through the bitter cold of a Queens winter.

Street-smart from years of survival, Cosmo knew better than to confront a creature three times his size—especially since it could easily swallow him in just a few bites. His muscles tensed beneath his rough fur, ready to spring toward a nearby leafless maple tree—his only chance for survival.

The beast lunged from the shadows, massive jaws snapping. Cosmo sprang upward with a burst of desperation, claws sinking into the rough bark as he scrambled just beyond the dog's reach. The creature snarled, its massive form prowling around the tree, its eyes gleaming with hunger and frustration.

"Damn hundfang," Cosmo muttered to himself, the term cats used for these fearsome creatures. Only after the hundfang drifted away did Cosmo allow himself a moment to relax. Though, in a world filled with threats like hundfangs, rats, and other stray cats, relaxing was a relative term.

He perched on a high branch, his fur still bristling as he surveyed the sprawling borough of Queens, New York. The skyline stretched before him, a maze of concrete and steel. This place had been home to him and his ancestors for generations.

The air, usually thick with the pungent odors of human activity, now smelled subtly different. His whiskers twitched. Something was wrong.

Even the pigeons had gone quiet, replaced by an eerie silence that spoke of approaching danger. His fur prickled as the stillness unnerved him.

Then, a gust of wind swirled through the alley, kicking up debris that blasted grit against his eyes.

Back on the ground, Cosmo prowled down the alley, sticking to the shadows like any streetwise cat. His dirty fur and the jagged scar on his cheek reflected his feral existence. Ignoring his growing unease, he focused instead on appeasing the gnawing hunger in his belly. Whatever he could scavenge now might be his last meal for days, especially if the storm brought the snow he anticipated.

He crept toward an overflowing trash can behind his favorite eatery with every sense on alert. The half-open lid offered a tantalizing glimpse of the contents inside. With a low growl of anticipation, Cosmo jumped onto the can, causing the lid to slip off. It hit the ground with a loud clatter, echoing off the eatery's brick walls.

Inside the bin, a multitude of smells assaulted him—day-old rice, spoiled fish, wilted vegetables. Yet, cutting through the stench of decay, a familiar aroma caught his attention: cooked meat, his favorite from this eatery! His eyes gleamed as he clawed through the discarded remains until a generous portion appeared—still warm, still inviting.

The first bite burst with flavor—sweet, savory, and spicy. Cosmo tore into the meat with unrestrained hunger, savoring a meal free of mold. After devouring every morsel, he leaped off the trash can. There was no time to waste.

The temperature plummeted with frightening speed, and the air carried a sharp, salty tang. Though he knew every shelter within his territory, something about this approaching storm made his usual hideouts feel woefully inadequate.

Thomson Avenue stretched before him, eerily empty. The street, usually teeming with two-legs—what cats called humans—now lay silent and still. A sudden realization struck him: the steam heating pipes beneath LaGuardia Community College would offer the warmth he needed to survive what was coming.

A violent gust knocked him sideways as he paused at the corner of Van Dam Street. Above him, the sky had darkened to a heavy, leaden gray, the kind that foretold a storm unlike any storm he'd known.

Cosmo's instincts proved accurate. To the north, a monstrous nor'easter battered New England. Boston lay paralyzed under three feet of snow as the storm surged south, bringing a bitter wave of Arctic air that threatened every unsheltered creature in Queens.

As Cosmo darted across Van Dam Street, he spotted Aura, his sibling, strolling past a bodega, seemingly unaware of the danger. Beside her was a young, brilliantly white cat, clearly unfamiliar with the streets. The cat moved with uncertain steps, her pristine fur starkly contrasting with the gritty concrete beneath her paws.

"Aura!" Cosmo's sharp cry cut through the wind. "Wait up!"

He scurried across the street to them, tail lashing with urgency. "Aura, a big storm's coming. A really big one. We'll die if we don't find heated shelter soon!"

Aura's fur bristled at his words. Before she could respond, Cosmo's gaze shifted to the young white cat beside her. His expression hardened.

"Who's this... this pampered cat?"

"Go easy on her, Cosmo." Aura stepped between them, her ears flattening protectively. "This is Zuzu. She's my friend."

With a dismissive twitch of his whiskers, Cosmo turned back to Aura. "A coddled friend. Brilliant."

A blast of wind swept debris past them, as if highlighting his sarcasm.

Aura ignored his comment. "You're right about a storm coming. I can feel the temperature dropping, but will it really be that bad?"

"Yes!" Cosmo's eyes darkened as he glanced at the roiling clouds above. "I'm heading to the heating pipes beneath LaGuardia Community College. The two-legs there keep them running day and night. Without heat, we won't survive this storm. You're welcome to come with me." His gaze flicked dismissively to Zuzu. "As for your pal here, I suggest she head back to whatever fancy digs she came from—and fast."

Aura's tail twitched with irritation. She pressed close to Cosmo's ear, her whisper fierce. "She can't return to her home. It's a long story—one I'll tell you later. For now, she's with us." The look in her eyes made it clear this wasn't up for debate.

A bitter wind screamed down the street, forcing them to huddle closer despite themselves. Cosmo hesitated, then gave a resigned nod. His gaze shifted to Zuzu, his voice still hard but no longer outright hostile. "If you want to live, follow us. Stay close and keep up. If you can't, you're on your own. Got it?"

Zuzu's eyes locked with his, and she nodded. For a brief moment, Cosmo caught something in them—not just fear but a flicker of resolve.

"All right, let's go," Cosmo said. "I know a place by the steam pipe corridor at the college where we can slip in. Follow me. We need to move fast."

They hurried down Thomson Avenue toward Court Square, passing storefronts where two-leg shopkeepers were closing up early. The wind grew stronger with each block, threatening to sweep them off their feet. Suddenly, Aura stopped.

"Why are we stopping?" Cosmo asked, his lashing tail conveying his irritation.

Aura's face contorted with sudden worry. "Cosmo, I know Murphy and Josephine will be okay, but what about Karma? He moved so slowly yesterday—I know his joints are bothering him. That abandoned building he lives in has no heat."

Cosmo's ears flattened against his head as guilt washed over him. How could he have forgotten about Karma? His eyes widened. "Damn. You're right."

He glanced at the dark clouds rolling in from the north. Around them, street signs creaked and swayed, their metal moorings groaning against the strengthening gusts. "It won't be long before everything gets ugly. Hopefully, we can convince Karma to come with us."

Aura turned to Zuzu, her voice gentle but urgent. "Karma, Murphy, and Josephine are our best friends. Murphy and Josephine have heated homes to live in, but Karma... he's a street cat like us. He's old and frail, and he raised Cosmo and me—we owe him everything." She paused, studying Zuzu's face. "I know you're tired, but can you keep up while we go to him? He lives about four blocks from here."

Zuzu looked down at her paws, now raw and bleeding from the rough concrete, then back up at Aura. She inhaled deeply, steeling herself. "Let's help your friend. I think I can do it... but maybe not as fast as you're walking now. Is that okay?"

Zuzu's pluck and concern for their friend earned her a grudging measure of respect from Cosmo. "Zuzu," he said, his tone softening, "I'll slow down a bit, but we need to move fast. Our lives depend on it." He glanced at her delicate paws. "When the snow comes, try to step where we step—it'll make walking easier."

She nodded, her eyes bright with gratitude at the subtle positive shift in his tone. "I understand. Thank you, Cosmo, for helping me."

He gave her a brief nod and turned to lead the way. Snow had begun to fall, sporadic flakes dancing in the strengthening wind. By the time they reached the dilapidated garment factory where Karma lived, the temperature had dropped sharply. The wind relentlessly buffeted them, making each step challenging as the chill cut through their fur. Even Zuzu's thick Persian coat offered scant protection against the bitter gusts.

The building loomed before them, its broken windows like dark eyes staring down at their approach. Cosmo led them around to a partially boarded-up doorway, moving quickly but carefully. "The entrance is over here!" he called over the wind. They slipped through a gap between the warped boards and into a space thick with the scent of dust, abandonment, and—faintly—Karma.

"Karma, are you in here!" Cosmo shouted, his breath visible in the cooling air. His voice echoed off the bare walls, bouncing between old machinery covered in years of dust.

A flicker of movement caught their attention. From his den—a room that had once been a women's restroom—Karma emerged, slow and deliberate. He moved like a ghost, blinking as he adjusted to the dim light. "Cosmo," he murmured, "is that you?"

"It's me, old friend," Cosmo replied, his voice warm. "Aura's here with me." They stepped closer, allowing Karma to see them. "And this is Zuzu. She's with us for a while."

Karma's stooped posture spoke of his years, but his eyes still sparked with intelligence as he studied them. His gray-streaked fur seemed dull in the weak light, but his purr of greeting was strong and welcoming. "Welcome to my home," he said, gazing at Zuzu. "You're young, pretty, and clean. Why are you with this rabble?"

The playful lilt in his voice brought an unexpected warmth to the cold room. Zuzu hesitated before answering. "Well, I, uh, well... I'm homeless now, too." Her smile faded as the words left her mouth, replaced by embarrassment.

Karma sat slowly, his joints stiff from the cold. "Young one, don't equate homelessness with worth. A cat's true value comes from the content of their character." His eyes sparkled with warmth. "From what I can see, you're quite rich."

Zuzu nodded, touched by his kindness. "Thank you, Karma. I see why Cosmo and Aura call you their friend."

Karma's whiskers twitched with amusement, but the slight shiver running through him hinted at the toll the cold was taking. He smiled and turned to Cosmo and Aura. "I like this one."

A violent gust rattled the building's remaining windows, making them all instinctively huddle closer. Snowflakes drifted through the broken panes now, dusting the floor. Cosmo glanced at Aura, then back at Karma. "I wish we could stay and chat, but a fierce storm's approaching, and it's nearly here. This one's different—like nothing I've ever sensed. The temperature's going to drop to deadly lows. Without heat, we won't make it. We're heading to the steam pipes under LaGuardia Community College, and we want you to come with us."

Aura pressed closer to Karma, her fur brushing against his. "Karma, you know Cosmo has a knack for predicting the weather, and he's never wrong. Please come with us."

Karma sighed, his eyes darkening with thought. "My friends, that's a long walk for this tired old cat. I'll stay here and ride out the storm."

Cosmo's tail swished with frustration. "Karma, this storm will kill you. You have to come with us."

Before he could speak further, a gust of wind, so powerful it felt almost alive, slammed into the building, shattering another window. They scrambled for cover in one of the bathroom stalls as the glass shards danced across the floor.

Snowflakes spiraled through the broken window, a preview of what would come. Aura moved closer to Karma, her voice gentle but urgent. "Karma, your building won't keep out this cold, and the temperature's dropping fast."

"She's right," Cosmo added. "This isn't like other winters. The storm that's coming—" Another violent gust interrupted him, and the old walls groaned in protest. "Listen to that wind. It could be like this for days."

Unable to deny the deepening chill that made his old bones ache, Karma's whiskers twitched as he considered their words. This had been his home for three winters—a luxury for a stray cat. Leaving it felt like surrendering a piece of himself. "Perhaps I could find a warmer corner in the basement," he suggested, though his voice lacked conviction. "One of the rooms down there might block the wind..."

"The basement will be just as cold," Cosmo insisted. "Maybe colder. But the steam pipes under LaGuardia never stop running. Never. We'll be warm there—all of us. Together."

Zuzu, who had been watching silently, suddenly spoke. Her voice trembled, but a strength in it surprised them all. "Karma, I know we've just met, but... would you consider coming with us for my sake? I'm new to all this, and your wisdom..." She hesitated, then continued softly, "I'd feel safer knowing you were there."

Something in the young cat's plea seemed to pierce Karma's resistance. In turn, he looked at each of them—Cosmo's determined face, Aura's concerned eyes, and Zuzu's hopeful expression. Another gust tore through the building, bringing down a shower of ancient dust from the ceiling pipes. Cosmo glanced up nervously, wondering if the roof might take flight. "We need to go. Now."

"Okay," Karma whispered, his voice heavy with resignation. "But if I can't make it, promise you'll leave me."

"We will," Cosmo said softly, "but that's not going to happen. Hopefully, the buildings will help shield us from the wind. Aura and I will walk on either side of you. We can do this, Karma."

Karma rose slowly to his feet, his joints creaking in protest. He paused, his gaze sweeping over his sanctuary one last time—the familiar shadows, the dripping faucet that had been his water source, the corner where he'd spent so many nights. So much to leave behind, he thought.

"I know it's hard to leave your home for a place unknown," Aura said softly, lovingly brushing her cheek against his.

"Okay," Karma sighed. "Let's go."

Outside, the storm's full force hit them, nearly stealing their breath away. They arranged themselves around Karma—Aura on his left, Cosmo on his right, with Zuzu close behind. Snow fell in earnest now, thick flakes driven sideways by the wind, stinging their eyes and coating their fur.

"Everyone, stay close," Cosmo shouted, his voice barely cutting through the storm's howling fury. "We'll move as fast as Karma can manage. Let's try not to stop until we reach the college."

Before his home vanished, Karma took one last look over his shoulder, watching its dark silhouette fade behind the curtain of snow. With a sigh, he turned forward, hoping they'd make it to the refuge that promised heat... and life.

As they pushed into the storm, the world around them disappeared into a white void, erasing the familiar landscape of Queens—the buildings, the streets, even the elevated train tracks above. Ice crystals formed in their whiskers and froze their eyelashes together. Between Cosmo and Aura,

Karma moved with determination, but each step drained his strength. His paws, numb beyond feeling, scrambled for purchase on the treacherous ground.

Back on Thomson Avenue, the wind shifted, funneling between buildings and hitting them head-on. Zuzu moved in front of Karma to help shield his face while Cosmo and Aura pressed closer to him, forming a living barrier against the cold. The wind howled through the gaps, its icy fingers slipping beneath their fur, stinging their skin like needles. Their snow-laden coats offered less protection with each passing minute.

"We're doing fine," Aura shouted, though her voice shook with more than just the cold. "Just two more blocks." She tried to sound confident, but fear threaded through her words. She'd seen cats frozen solid after storms less severe than this—their bodies discovered only when the snow melted weeks later.

Zuzu's legs trembled now, both from the cold and muscle fatigue. Her paws, unused to such harsh conditions, felt like blocks of ice attached to her legs. Each step was an act of pure will. Still, she kept pace, drawing strength from the determination of her companions.

Another gust roared through the urban canyon, bringing a wave of snow that struck like a white wall. This time, Karma stumbled, his legs buckling beneath him. Ice had formed between his paw pads, turning each step into agony.

"I need... I need to rest," he gasped, his breath coming in sharp, labored bursts.

"No!" Cosmo bellowed, his voice sharp with fear. "If we stop now, we're dead—all of us! The cold will seize our muscles, and we won't be able to move again. We have to keep moving!"

Aura pressed her body closer to Karma's side, sharing what little warmth she had left. "Lean on me, Karma. We're not leaving you behind." Her voice carried a firm, urgent edge.

Through sheer force of will, Karma found his footing. His movements were jerky now, mechanical—as if his joints were freezing solid. Slowly and lethargically, he stepped forward. Cosmo and Aura matched his halting pace while Zuzu remained in front, her head lowered against the wind, looking back often to adjust her pace to match theirs.

The wind shifted, and for a brief moment, the snow fell straight down, creating an illusion of calm. But the temperature continued to plummet, and ice crystals formed even more in their whiskers. Undaunted, the cats pushed forward in near-blindness, guided only by Cosmo's uncanny sense of direction. The cold bit deeper with each passing minute.

"There!" Cosmo called out suddenly, his voice muffled by the storm. Through the whiteout conditions, the dark bulk of LaGuardia Community College loomed ahead. "The maintenance entrance is near here. Stay close to the wall—it'll block some of the wind."

As their paws sank into the snow, they crept along the building, which provided some shelter from the fierce gusts. Completely exhausted, Karma's legs trembled, and his tail dragged limply.

"We're almost there," Cosmo urged, pushing through the storm. He nudged aside a snow-buried grating, barely visible in the dark. Warm air from the steam pipes greeted them. "You go in first, Karma!" Cosmo shouted over the wind. "It's a three-cat drop—be careful!"

With the last reserves of his strength, Karma squeezed through the opening and landed with a heavy thud on the concrete floor. He looked up at his friends and, with a voice rasping from exhaustion, beckoned them to follow. "Come join me. It's lovely in here."

They dropped into the underground corridor one by one, leaving the howling storm behind. The warm air wrapped around them like a comforting blanket. The snow on their fur transformed into rising mist, creating an ethereal dance of water vapor around them.

As the storm raged above, turning Queens into a frozen wasteland, they lay exhausted and motionless, thankful for a reprieve they could scarcely have imagined moments before. The steady hum of the steam pipes soon lulled them to sleep, a mechanical lullaby promising warmth and safety through the long night ahead.

2

THE NEXT MORNING, AURA awoke with a sharp intake of breath. She glanced at Karma, still sleeping soundly beside Zuzu. Even in his slumber, his presence brought a sense of calm—though the memory of his stumbling steps through the snow lingered in her mind.

As the steam pipes filled their underground refuge with warmth, the storm above raged, muffled by concrete and soil. She noted how the warm, humid air contrasted sharply with the cold that had nearly claimed them.

Sitting up, Aura scanned the corridor for Cosmo. Her gaze landed on him further down the hall, standing like a silent sentinel. As she watched him, a wave of admiration and gratitude washed over her. Even after their grueling journey through the storm, he stood guard over them all, a steadfast protector.

With a stretch, she moved toward Cosmo, weaving around condensation that pooled on the concrete floor. She brushed her cheek against his when she reached him, a tender gesture of love. "Thank you for watching over us. Get some rest—I'll take over."

Cosmo didn't respond to her words. His muscles were taut, and his eyes locked on the shadows. "I've scouted the place," he murmured, "and found another potential exit along with a few defensive positions." His whiskers twitched at the sound of scratching in the dark. "Aura, there are rats in here. Big ones."

The fur along Aura's spine bristled. "Those horrid creatures..." she hissed, her voice thick with anger. Cosmo pressed closer to his sister, sharing her hatred. They both bore the scars of that day in the den—the day they lost their mother and littermates to a swarm of rats. Karma had found them, nursed them back to health, and raised them as his own. Such care for orphaned kittens was nearly unheard of in the harsh and unforgiving world of street felines.

Karma joined them then, moving with careful steps. His joints seemed looser in the warmth, though his movements still carried the weight of age. "Good morning, my dear friends," he said softly. "I hope I'm not interrupting."

"Never," Aura replied, her words carrying a warmth that came effortlessly from all their years together. "Did you sleep well?"

Karma chuckled. "Never better. My old bones love the warmth of this extraordinary place, and I have you two to thank for that." His eyes held the same kindness that once gave two terrified kittens a reason to live.

As Karma spoke, a large rat darted across the corridor, alarmingly close. Then another. And another.

Cosmo's ears flattened against his head. "They're getting bolder. This must be their territory."

"The warmth draws all creatures seeking shelter," Karma observed with a sigh. "Even those we abhor."

With her fur still bristled at the sight of the aberrant vermin, Aura's stomach rumbled. "Sorry. I haven't eaten in two days, and after yesterday's ordeal getting here, I'm feeling light-headed."

Cosmo nodded grimly. "We all need to eat, and I have a perfect, high-protein entree in mind."

"Do you want help rounding one up?" Aura asked, their shared history making them natural hunting partners.

Cosmo nodded. "Stay close," he replied. "Those wretched rats get vicious when cornered, and if they band together to attack me, I'll need your help." He turned to Karma. "Could you keep Zuzu company? With her pampered upbringing, she's probably never seen a rat. Some are nearly her size, and she'd be defenseless against them."

Karma's eyes widened with concern. "She's that unaware?"

Aura nodded. "Until recently, she lived her whole life indoors."

As Karma returned to be with Zuzu, Cosmo and Aura followed the path the rats had taken. The corridor stretched before them, its shadows hiding unknown dangers. They crept forward until Cosmo spotted a target. His muscles bunched, hunter's instinct taking over. His attack was swift—a blur of fur and claws and teeth. The rat fought ferociously, but years of street survival had honed Cosmo's skills. When it ended, he stood over his prey, chest heaving, blood matting his fur.

While Cosmo tended to his minor wounds and cleaned his fur, Aura carried the rat back to Zuzu and Karma. Roused by the commotion, Zuzu stared in horror at the bloody carcass Aura dropped at her feet.

"What's wrong, princess?" Cosmo snarled, approaching her with deliberate steps. "Is this rat beneath your lofty culinary standards?"

Zuzu's ears drooped with shame. "I... I've never..."

"Never what?" Cosmo interrupted, his voice dripping with contempt. "Never had to eat something that didn't come in a fancy bowl? This is survival."

"Cosmo. Enough!" Karma's voice, though gentle, carried an edge and the weight of earned authority. His eyes locked with Cosmo's. "You were once young, unaware, and helpless. Do you remember?"

The tension in Cosmo's face eased. He nodded, his expression softening. "I do remember," he whispered. "And I'll never forget what you did for me and Aura."

With a deep sigh, Cosmo turned to Zuzu. "Forgive me. The streets have a way of hardening you, and my anger toward you is unjust."

Zuzu nodded, meeting his gaze with unexpected steadiness. "I know I disappoint you, and I'm sure you see me—and probably others like me—with contempt. But if you give me a chance, I hope to make you proud of me. Proud enough to maybe one day call me your friend."

The maternal side of Aura emerged. Her voice softened as she looked between them. "Zuzu, despite Cosmo's often surly nature and impatience with others, he has a heart of gold. And he'll give his life to protect those he calls friends." She looked at Cosmo with love and pride. "Brother, I suggest we show some compassion for Zuzu and teach her to survive, just like Karma did for us. Can you do that?"

"I'll try," Cosmo replied, his voice softening. "I guess it's our turn to pay it forward, like Karma did for us."

Karma nuzzled his cheek against Cosmo's. "You're a good cat, Cosmo. Like Aura, I see your kind heart, too." He turned to Zuzu and spoke in a soothing but firm voice. "Young one," he said, "I understand that eating a dead creature is difficult for you. But survival requires us to step beyond our comfort. Your body needs sustenance—not just for you, but to help us all endure the days ahead. Like us, you must eat what nature has provided."

Zuzu looked at the old cat, then at the rat, her stomach churning with revulsion. "I want to, Karma," she whispered, her voice trembling. "But... I've never had to. I don't know how to eat unprepared food like this."

Cosmo chuckled, but this time without malice. "Your first lesson on how to be a real cat will be learning what your fangs are really for—other than making you look pretty. Watch me tear off a hunk of meat with mine."

He sank his teeth into the rat's thigh, twisting his head to rip off a piece of flesh. After chewing and swallowing it, he looked at Zuzu. "Your turn."

Zuzu swallowed hard, her life of sheltered domestication at odds with her survival instinct. She leaned down and gave what could, at best, be called a tentative nibble on the rat—one that didn't even break the skin.

Cosmo dropped to the floor in fits of laughter. After composing himself, he smiled at the embarrassed feline, his eyes holding more amusement than scorn.

Aura stepped in, her voice encouraging. "Zuzu, try again and give it your all. Watch me." Like Cosmo, she deftly tore off a chunk of meat, her fangs sinking in with practiced ease.

This time, Zuzu rose to the challenge. She squared her shoulders and sank her teeth into the rat with all her might, frantically twisting her head. The effort paid off with a big chunk of meat. She chewed and swallowed the surprisingly tasty morsel, her hunger fueling the effort.

"Excellent, Zuzu!" Karma bellowed, his voice warm with approval. "We're all proud of you!"

"We are," Cosmo added, impressed by the dainty, pampered cat's near-primal effort. "Okay, everyone, let's all dig in."

After huddling around and consuming their meal, they all lay on the warm concrete floor of the building, basking in the satisfaction that comes from having a full belly. The steam pipes hummed overhead, their constant drone a reminder of their sanctuary from the storm.

"A mighty tasty meal, that was," Karma said contentedly. "Even with a storm raging above us, life is good."

"It is," Aura agreed. She looked around the corridor and smiled at what she saw. "You know, this place could be a permanent home for us. Karma, don't take this the wrong way, but you're getting to the point where you'll need our assistance more."

"No offense taken," Karma replied, his voice carrying a note of acceptance. "I know my years are showing."

"I agree with Aura, Karma," Cosmo said softly. "It's our turn to help you now."

"I'll be happy to help in any way I can," Zuzu added. She hesitated, fear flickering in her eyes. "If... if you all let me stay with you."

Aura sat up and looked at her, a soft smile tugging at the corners of her mouth. "Zuzu, I'm sure I speak for all of us when I say you'll be welcome here."

Karma nodded and looked at Cosmo, his eyes silently seeking his concurrence.

Cosmo took a deep breath, his eyes narrowing as he considered her words. "Okay, but as long as you're with us, don't expect any of that pampered cat crap you left behind." His sharp tone reflected his no-nonsense demeanor.

Zuzu nodded quickly. "I'll pull my weight, Cosmo. Just watch, and you'll see."

Cosmo flicked his tail as he replied. "Good. So, what's your story, Zuzu? How did you end up on the streets?"

Zuzu sat for a few moments, gathering her thoughts. The warm air from the steam pipes wrapped around them as she began to speak, her voice soft but steady.

"I used to live in a place called Skyline Towers. It's not far from here. I was just a kitten when Mrs. Chen brought me home. She was elderly and frail but kind. Her apartment was huge—soft carpets, comfy furniture, and see-through things that let in the sun. She never went out, not once that I can remember. Once a week, her groceries were delivered, and a cleaning two-leg female came to tidy up the apartment. She never liked me much—she'd complain that I shed too much, making her job harder."

Her voice softened with memory. "I spent most of my days curled up on Mrs. Chen's lap or playing with little things she'd leave out for me. She loved to talk to me, but I could never understand her language well. It was always soft and soothing, so I liked hearing her. I'd sit on her lap as she looked out the see-through things. We watched the two-leg creatures like her rushing around below, or we'd watch the sky changing colors."

Zuzu sighed, her gaze distant. "The world outside was always beyond my reach. I never thought much of it, though, because being inside all the time was just... normal. I was safe, and so was she. That's all that mattered to me. Still, I sometimes wondered what life would be like on the other side of the see-through things."

Her voice caught slightly. "But then... one day, she didn't wake up after an afternoon nap on our couch. No matter how hard I tried to rouse her, she remained still. The days turned into an endless wait as Mrs. Chen lay there, her hands folded gently on her chest as if she were simply sleeping.

But a gnawing feeling settled in that something was wrong. Each day, I'd gently nudge her, hoping for a response, but she never stirred, never opened her eyes. A strange odor began to emanate from her. Loneliness washed over me, a cold, dark emptiness. And the hunger... I'd never known hunger like that before."

The others listened intently, the steam pipes hissing softly in the background. Aura's eyes softened with sympathy, and even Cosmo's usual hardness seemed to soften in the presence of her vulnerability.

"The cleaning two-leg came on the fifth day after Mrs. Chen didn't wake from her nap. She screamed when she saw Mrs. Chen. Soon, other two-leg creatures came and took Mrs. Chen away. They grabbed me and brought me to a place full of different-looking creatures—some like us—who made all sorts of loud, unceasing noises."

"I was put in a cage, alone and terrified. I didn't understand what was happening. All I could think about was how much I missed Mrs. Chen." Zuzu's voice trembled slightly. "The two-legs there fed me, but they never paid attention to me. I was just another creature in a cage to them."

Her eyes hardened with the memory. "Then, one day, they made a mistake. A smelly, hairy two-leg male forgot to lock my cage after bringing me a bowl of dreadful-tasting pellets and water. When no one was near, I dashed out, running down the aisle. I saw the door swing open, and before I knew it, my instincts kicked in. I darted into the street and nearly got hit by a big moving box. In a panic, I ran, terrified. The outside world was nothing like I'd imagined—so unlike the safe, peaceful existence I'd known. The noises, the smells, the two-legs, the moving boxes with two-leg creatures in them, the other animals—everything was bigger and louder than anything I'd ever experienced. I didn't know where to go or what to do, but I knew I couldn't go back to that cage. I'd rather be dead than return there."

Her eyes softened as she looked at Aura. "And that's when I saw you."

Aura smiled and nodded, remembering their first meeting.

Zuzu paused, her voice thick with emotion. "You saved me, Aura. And then Cosmo joined us, and we came here. You both helped me. I love you both... and you too, Karma."

Karma nodded and let out a slow, thoughtful exhale, his whiskers twitching as if trying to stifle a chuckle hidden beneath his weathered exterior. "Love, eh?" he said with a hint of tongue-in-cheek amusement. "I remember the days I used to chase it, but now I'm too old to remember why I bothered. But seriously, I've learned that love comes in many forms. Not always the kind you expect... not always the kind you think you want."

He looked at Zuzu with a twinkle of wisdom in his eyes. "But I can tell you this: those who have family—whether by blood or by choice—are the lucky ones. You've found yours here, Zuzu, and that means more than you might realize."

He paused and then looked at her with a knowing light in his eyes. "The world is full of risks, loss, and loneliness, but being part of a family makes it all easier. You're part of us now, Zuzu, and that's enough to make your world look better." He leaned back, feeling his old bones creak softly. "If there's one thing I've learned, it's that love doesn't always need words. It's in the things we do for each other." His eyes softened. "You'll see. You'll see..."

"I do see, Karma," Zuzu replied. She paused, thinking. "Last night, as we braved this terrifying storm coming here... I felt so close to all of you, and... odd as it sounds, I found it all exhilarating."

Her remark amused Cosmo. "If you're looking for more exhilaration, I'll teach you how to take out a rat."

While the others chuckled at his quip, Zuzu felt a warmth spread through her. It was the kind of teasing that made her feel accepted into the group. "Um, I have something to ask," she said, her ears flattening with embarrassment.

"What's that?" asked Aura.

"Um... do you think they have a litter box in here?"

"What's a litter box?" Cosmo asked, his ears tilting back in confusion.

"It's a small box filled with soft clumping material where you... you know... whiz... and the, um, the other thing."

Cosmo burst out laughing. "Zuzu, for a street cat, the whole world's our litter box."

Zuzu's embarrassed expression touched Cosmo, reminding him of Karma's earlier words about being young and oblivious. Memories of his own first days on the streets rushed through his mind—how overwhelming and frightening everything had felt.

He turned to Aura. "There's a floor drain down the corridor—you can't miss it. It's private and away from where we sleep. Maybe you can take Zuzu there and keep an eye out for rats while she does her thing."

After Zuzu and Aura took care of business, they lingered for a moment in the quiet of the corridor. Aura pressed against Zuzu's shoulder, offering her a comforting smile. "You're doing well," she said softly, her voice filled with warmth and reassurance.

Still on edge, Zuzu's whiskers twitched nervously. "I never imagined life could be so... different," she murmured. "But I'm glad I'm not facing it alone."

Aura's eyes softened as she met Zuzu's eyes. "You can stay with us as long as you like. Believe me, there are calm days, too, even for street cats."

Zuzu offered a tentative smile. "For my whole life, I've had nothing but calm, boring days. I now see the extraordinary gift they were."

3

THE NEXT DAY, THE storm had passed, leaving behind a haunting stillness that seemed to magnify the steady throb of the corridor's steam pipes. In their underground shelter, the air hung thick with humidity—almost unpleasantly so, though still a welcome change from the brutal cold outside. For street cats, however, their sanctuary started feeling more like a prison with each passing moment despite the life-saving warmth of the pipes.

Restless after being cooped up for so long, Cosmo's whiskers twitched with the urge to venture outside again. The warmth from the pipes had kept them alive, but now the reality of their situation settled in: deep snow likely covered their entry point, trapping them below ground, and Karma, frail as he was, could never leap upward to the escape opening, even if Cosmo managed to tunnel through the snow.

Cosmo paced the corridor, his tail twitching with growing anxiety. The distant scurrying of rats deepened his unease. He glanced at Aura. "We can't stay here much longer," he muttered, his eyes locked on the grate above. "We need to see what's out there."

Aura nodded, her gaze fixed on the entry point above them. "I agree. Let me know if you need help."

With effortless agility, Cosmo leaped onto a thick, curved pipe near the grate. Standing on his hind legs, he began clawing at the snow, scraping through what felt like an endless barrier of white. Aura joined him, and together, they tunneled upward.

"Let's hope this is just a snowdrift blocking the opening," Cosmo whispered, his voice laced with tension. "If it's like this everywhere, we're in deep trouble."

At last, they broke through, the frigid air stinging their lungs as Cosmo's breath came out in a visible cloud. He poked his head out of the opening and gasped. The world outside was unrecognizable—what had once been their familiar territory was now buried beneath an endless white expanse.

He looked down at Aura. "It's not good. Let's join the others and figure out what to do."

They dropped back onto the hard, concrete floor of the corridor and walked to Karma and Zuzu, who were waiting anxiously, their eyes filled with concern.

Cosmo sighed heavily. "From what I could tell, everything's buried under more snow than I've ever seen."

"Uh, oh," Karma said softly. "How much snow?"

"At least a cat length. Maybe more in some places."

"What do you suggest we do?" Karma asked, his voice tired and tinged with dread.

Cosmo's tail twitched as he considered their options. "Aura and I should scout around to see if the snow's packed enough to walk on its surface instead of sinking through. If that's true, we'll be able to move around more easily."

Zuzu's wide eyes reflected her fear. "Will you... will you two come back soon? Can I come with you?"

Aura noticed Zuzu's distress and moved closer, her voice soft but firm. "Zuzu, we may decide that staying here is the best option, but we need to eat. There probably aren't enough rats in here to feed all of us for long. We'll have to find more food beyond here. For now, I need you to stay here with Karma."

Zuzu's whiskers drooped, and she nodded meekly.

"We'll be fine, Zuzu," Karma replied, his voice warm with tenderness and assurance. "With your sore paws, staying here is best for you, too." He smiled and winked at her. "While they're gone, I'll regale you with stories of my youth."

Despite her anxiety, Karma's lightheartedness and animated expression eased her tension. "Okay," she murmured.

Cosmo affectionately touched his cheek to Karma's, admiring how easily the old cat had calmed Zuzu, just as he used to do with him and Aura when they were young. He'd heard Karma's stories countless times and still found them comforting and entertaining. "We'll be back as soon as we can." He turned to Aura. "Ready?"

She nodded. "Let's do it." She looked back at Karma and Zuzu. "See you soon."

She and Cosmo leaped onto the pipe in a flash and scurried up through their newly dug opening.

Outside, they stood in stunned silence, surveying the transformed landscape, now looking alien and hostile. Light snow continued to fall, adding to the growing sense of despair.

With a flick of his head, Cosmo interrupted the silence. "Let's go."

He leaped forward, but instead of landing on the snow's surface, he plunged deep into its depths. Panic surged as the snow swallowed him whole. He clawed desperately, the cold weight of the snow crushing in around him, his paws scrabbling for purchase. The world went white as powdery snow filled his nose and stung his eyes.

Aura gasped in alarm. "Cosmo!"

With a growl of frustration, Cosmo broke the surface, gasping for air. He shook the snow from his fur and staggered back to her.

After catching his breath, Cosmo studied the building. Its eaves had kept some snow from accumulating directly against the walls. "Let's walk along the perimeter of the building," he suggested. "The snow's less deep there."

Aura said nothing, simply nodding in reply.

With each step, their paws still sank several inches as they navigated the narrow strip of shallower snow next to the building. Reaching the building's edge, they stopped, unable to go further. They both stood on their back legs, surveying the white wilderness. Cosmo sighed. "Even if we could get to it, our territory is buried in snow. My guess is we'll be stuck here for several days."

Aura sighed, feeling the gravity of the situation. "I agree. Let's go back and tell the others."

A gust of wind sent a cascade of snow tumbling from the building's roof. They pressed their bodies against the wall to avoid being buried by the avalanche and waited for it to pass.

Cosmo turned to Aura, his expression grim. "We need to face facts," he said quietly. "Even if we find food, getting Karma out of that corridor... we'd never be able to get him up to the escape opening..." He trailed off, unable to finish the thought.

Aura's ears flattened against her head. "I know. But we can't leave him down there forever. And Zuzu's paws need time to heal before she can handle this frigid cold."

Back in the corridor, Zuzu pressed herself close to Karma, seeking comfort. "I'm scared," she admitted in a whisper. "What if something happens to them?"

Karma's eyes softened with a warmth that only he could provide. "Cosmo and Aura are capable cats, little one. They've faced challenges that would have broken others. They'll be fine."

A sudden scurry of rat feet shattered the silence. The rats had been watching, biding their time, waiting for this moment. Now, they emerged from every crack and crevice, their numbers far greater than before. Converging on Karma and Zuzu, they saw their chance to strike with Cosmo and Aura out of the way.

"Zuzu," shouted Karma, his voice urgent. "Follow me!" He dashed to a corner. "Let's wait here—in this corner. They can only come at us from one direction when they attack."

In the corner, a terrified Zuzu stood next to him, trembling. "What should I do, Karma?"

"Fight with all your might, young one," Karma commanded. "Bite them hard—like you bit into that dead rat we ate. Swat them with your claws. Aim for their eyes and noses to make them back off. Do everything you can not to let them overwhelm you!"

The rats surged forward, their claws clicking against the concrete. The lead rat, a hulking creature with a jagged scar running down its face, bared yellowed teeth and charged first. Karma leaped at it with surprising agility, his claws flashing. He scored a deep gash on the rat's face, and the creature hissed in pain, recoiling. But Karma was relentless, striking again and again, forcing the rat back.

Zuzu's heart hammered against her ribs as a rat lunged toward her, its rancid breath hot on the air. She struck out instinctively, her claws slashing across its face. The rat screeched, its sharp teeth bared, but Zuzu didn't hesitate. She swiped again, harder this time, and the rat bolted, blood dripping from its eye as it disappeared into the shadows.

Karma faced off against another rat, barely dodging its snapping jaws. From muscle memory from countless street fights, his claws raked across the rat's nose, and the creature recoiled, hissing with pain.

Another rat charged at Karma, but before it could reach him, Zuzu leaped, her body light as air. She landed a powerful swipe across the rat's side, sending it skittering away.

"Good job, Zuzu!" Karma called, his voice sharp with praise. "Keep fending them off like that!"

With a quick nod, something fierce and primal stirred inside Zuzu, an instinct she'd never known she had. Her pampered past felt like a distant memory as she lashed out, striking another rat as it lunged.

The rats retreated and regrouped quickly, realizing they couldn't overpower them without changing tactics. This time, they charged as a pack. Knowing they couldn't survive this onslaught, Zuzu shrieked in terror.

Above ground, as they neared the opening, Cosmo and Aura heard a terrified cry.

"That's Zuzu!" Aura wailed, panic lacing her voice.

"Follow me!" Cosmo shouted as he dove headfirst into the opening. He landed on something with a thud, and when it squealed, he knew what it was—a rat! With a flash of claws and teeth, he tore into it, sinking his teeth into its throat and severing its jugular with practiced precision.

Aura landed next to him, unleashing a frenzied battle cry when she saw a dozen rats attacking Karma and Zuzu. To her amazement, Zuzu stood her ground, her once-pristine white fur now streaked with rat blood as she defended Karma with a fierceness Aura found stunning for such a pampered, supposedly defenseless cat.

She and Cosmo leaped in unison at the surprised rats. Cosmo pounced on the alpha rat, a massive creature, and fought it fiercely in a flurry of paw strikes and gnashing teeth until it collapsed. As his foe fell, Cosmo tore into two more rats that had been overpowering Aura, giving her the opening she needed to dispatch one swiftly. Despite the mounting losses, the rats refused to retreat.

"Keep at them!" Cosmo yelled. "We need to push them back!"

Next to him, Aura's claws flashed in the dim light as she lashed out at another big rat who charged her with savage aggression. Her claws caught the rat's snout, forcing it to retreat. Next to her, Zuzu fought off another rat charging at Karma.

Cosmo darted from rat to rat, striking at their faces and making them recoil in fear. Every swipe kept the biggest threats at bay, sending them scattering back into the shadows.

Finally, the rats retreated, their squeals of defeat echoing through the corridor. The family huddled around Karma, all panting from the ordeal. They were fortunate—Karma had a few minor scratches on his face, but otherwise, he was unscathed. Zuzu, her fur now stained with grime and blood, had only a small cut on her upper lip. Cosmo and Aura were unharmed.

Cosmo looked at Zuzu with newfound respect, seeing not the pampered house cat she once was but someone who had earned her place among them. "You did well, Zuzu," he said with surprise in his voice. "Very well."

A weary Karma gave Zuzu an appreciative look. "You fought like a true warrior. I'm quite grateful."

Zuzu, still shaken, felt a strange sense of pride and nodded at Karma. "I—I did it." She paused for a moment, looking at the others with alarm. "I feel funny—light-headed."

"Just breathe deeply for a while, and you'll feel better," Aura said, nuzzling against the young cat. "I'm so proud of you."

Later, when calm returned, they dined on the rats they'd dispatched. This time, Zuzu showed no hesitation about eating their foe.

When they all had their fill, Cosmo looked at them. "We need to be hyper-vigilant from now on. Zuzu and Karma, don't wander around the corridor without Aura or me being with you. I'm going to scout around to see what the rats are up to."

"Can't we just talk with them and work something out?" Zuzu pleaded.

Aura shook her head. "First of all, we don't speak their language. Rat-ese is nothing but a series of crude grunts and shrill chirps. They're far too dim-witted to comprehend cat-ese, our noble tongue. And even if we could communicate, those vile creatures are untrustworthy to the core. They're a blight upon the world."

"They smelled awful—both their fur and their breath," Zuzu said with a frown. "They sure have sharp teeth."

Cosmo chuckled at her appraisal of them. "You're right, but they're a tasty meal when you're hungry, so I suppose they serve some purpose."

Aura smiled at Cosmo's quip but then noticed the concern on Karma's face. She frowned. "Are you okay, Karma?"

"It's clear to me that I'm a burden to you all," he replied with a voice filled with heaviness. "I remember Magnus, a dear friend who couldn't pull his weight anymore. One day, during a winter storm much less severe than this one, he quietly wandered off... and we never saw him again."

"Stop!" Aura interrupted firmly, her voice urgent. "We're family. We don't leave family behind."

Karma's eyes glistened with emotion as he gazed at her. He simply nodded, lay down, and rested his head on his paws.

As Karma and Zuzu slept that night, Cosmo approached Aura after surveying the area. The steam pipes creaked above them, their mechanical rhythm a constant reminder of their underground prison. "The rats are gathering again," he whispered. "We can't hold out much longer against repeated attacks." He sighed deeply. "We need to leave this corridor soon..."

Aura nodded, understanding the implications. "We need to find another way out of here for Karma." Her voice caught. "Remember when he found us after the rat attack that killed our mother and siblings? The idea of him losing his life in such a way makes my heart tremble..."

"That's not going to happen, Aura. We'll protect him." Cosmo said with a tenderness that blunted his usual gruffness. "Tomorrow, I'll look closer at the other potential exit I spotted when we first got here."

Later, while on guard duty, Cosmo looked at his sleeping family. The sound of rats reminded him that time was running out. They needed to act soon. As he watched over Karma, memories of the old cat finding him and Aura, two terrified kittens, flooded back. Now it was his turn to protect, to lead.

His whiskers twitched at an uncomfortable truth: he had always cherished his solitary existence. The freedom to roam, to care only for himself. Now, here he was, standing guard over others who needed him, each indifferent ways. The weight of responsibility pressed down on him like the snow above their heads.

The steady pulse of the steam pipes filled the dim corridor as Cosmo settled into his vigil. Tomorrow, they would face the rats, the snow, and whatever else threatened his family. But for now, he kept watch, alert to every shadow, every sound.

4

THE NEXT MORNING, ZUZU woke, gasping for air, her throat burning and painfully constricted. Each shallow breath was a struggle, and panic clawed at her as a terrifying pressure gripped her neck. Her limbs grew weak, and each rasping breath dragged her deeper into a dizzying darkness.

Alarmed, Aura gaped at her. "What's wrong, Zuzu!"

"I can't breathe... this thing around my neck is choking me. I think it's why I felt light-headed yesterday." Her voice came out as a frightened wheeze, barely more than a whisper.

Aura's whiskers twitched with concern as she moved closer and inspected Zuzu's fancy sequined strap. She tugged at it gently with her paw. "I see why you're having trouble breathing—this strap is far too tight. As you've grown, it must've become increasingly constrictive."

She turned to Cosmo, her voice sharp with urgency. "Brother, come look at Zuzu's strap—she can't breathe because of it."

Cosmo padded over and examined the strap, noting its thinnest point beneath her neck, where there were no sequins. "Why did you let those two-legged creatures put this on you? I pity the two-leg who ever tries to put one on me."

Zuzu sighed. "The two-legs like wearing them. Mrs. Chen had several around her neck. Some were made of shiny white balls that I liked playing with when I sat on her lap." Her voice caught with the memory.

"Unbelievable," Cosmo muttered. He touched the strap with his paw, tugging it with a claw. His ears flattened as he assessed the situation. "Hmmm... I think we can chew through this. It feels a lot like a rat's skin. Do you want me to try?"

"Yes, please," Zuzu replied, her eyes bright with hope.

"Okay, lie on your back so I can get to it better."

When Zuzu complied, exposing her vulnerable throat in a gesture of complete trust, Cosmo felt an unexpected surge of protectiveness. He sprang into action, nipping at the strap with his incisor teeth. His usual impatience gave way to focused precision as he carefully nibbled at the material, removing tiny bits, one piece at a time.

After several minutes, he paused and looked at Aura. "I'm about halfway through it. Do you mind taking a turn?"

"Sure," Aura replied, her voice warm. "Good work, Cosmo."

He stepped back for Aura to resume the work. She followed Cosmo's lead, chewing off tiny bits of the collar. After a while, like Cosmo, she also grew weary from the effort.

Karma stood and moved toward her. "Let me take a turn."

"Thanks for your help, everyone," Zuzu murmured, her whiskers trembling with each labored breath. "Do you think you can get it off?"

Karma leaned in, assessing the progress. "Oh my, little one, it's nearly cut in two. I'm as good as a rat at gnawing on things, so I'll get to it."

With the steady patience that only years of experience could bring, Karma carefully chewed through the final strands of the strap. It fell from Zuzu's neck, clinking softly as it hit the floor.

Zuzu rose slowly, her body trembling with relief as she took a deep, unrestricted breath. "I can breathe again!" she purred, stretching her neck in all directions. "Thank you, everyone!"

Cosmo laughed, enjoying Zuzu's delight. "The next time one of those two-legs tries to put one of these on you, go for their throat."

They all laughed at Cosmo's remark and settled into an easy conversation. Cosmo stretched out near the warm pipes, pondering the two-legs. "You know," he said thoughtfully, "the two-legs are interesting creatures. I marvel at how they keep themselves upright on their big back legs, especially in the snow where they wobble along. Can you imagine a cat trying to walk on just two paws?" And with their shorter, nimbler front legs, they use them to carry things and hold each other's paws."

"They do fall sometimes," Aura added with amusement. "Especially when it's icy. I love seeing how awkwardly they land—so unlike us cats." Her eyes glinted with a spark of humor.

"They are unusual creatures," Karma added, his eyes growing distant as memories of countless observations drifted through his mind. "Equally wondrous is how they build massive artificial dens that reach into the sky, filled with those peculiar see-through things they use to see outside."

Zuzu's ears perked up as she offered her observations of the two-legs' dens. "The air in their dens stays the same—not hot, not cold—even when the seasons change outside. I never understood how they do that. And they have water that appears like magic from shiny metal pipes."

Aura frowned, her tail flicking in distaste. "I don't like the two-legs' language. They often make harsh sounds at each other that hurt my ears. It's nothing like the elegant simplicity of cat-ese."

Everyone nodded at her comment except Karma. He lifted his paw thoughtfully. "Since cats are always around the two-legs, some of their language has filtered into our vocabulary. Some would say poisoned it. We now use many of their words—rat, duck, and so on."

"You're right, Karma," Aura said. "Especially the cats who live with the two-legs. Sometimes, it's hard to understand them."

Zuzu nodded, adding her thoughts to the conversation. "All the two-legs who came to our place always referred to the female I lived with as Mrs. Chen. And she always called me Zuzu." Her voice softened with fondness at the memory.

A sudden scuffling in the shadows made them all stiffen, but it was just debris shifting in the draft. Cosmo smirked, brushing off the tension as he returned to their conversation. "What really baffles me," he continued, "is that most of their fur is on the tops of their heads. So, to make up for it, they wear these ridiculous, often brightly colored layers that they change daily—as if they can't decide what they want to wear."

Aura burst into laughter. "And get this—they even cover the paws on their big hind legs! Can you imagine us covering our paws?"

The group's laughter echoed through the corridor, momentarily drowning out the constant hum of the steam pipes. They all marveled at the sheer absurdity of the upright creatures.

Karma sighed, his gaze distant as he pondered the peculiar beings. "Odd as they are, no one can deny they're highly capable and adaptable. I mean, just look around—there are countless numbers of them. And, oh, what I wouldn't give for one of those noisy moving boxes they use to get around."

Cosmo nodded in agreement, his tail swishing thoughtfully. "Here's something else they're good at—dealing with snow. They have these clever devices to push the snow aside and make paths. Then they use those big, noisy moving boxes to take the snow away."

With grudging admiration, their heads bobbed in agreement.

As they huddled near the warm pipes, Aura suddenly bolted upright, her eyes wide with excitement. "Cosmo, what you just said—that's it! That's what will save us!"

Cosmo tilted his head, his tail flicking with curiosity. "What do you mean?"

"The two-legs, like they always do, will soon be making paths through the snow. Once they do that, we can move around easily again!"

Cosmo's ears shot forward, his whole body tensing with sudden hope. "Aura, that's brilliant!" But as soon as the words left his mouth, his enthusiasm dimmed.

"What is it?" Aura asked, puzzled by his sudden change in mood.

"Two problems," Cosmo responded, his tail drooping. "First, Karma—and probably Zuzu—can't leap up to the pipe to get out of here. Second, even if we find a way out, where would we stay in this brutal cold?"

The steam pipes hissed overhead as Karma raised his paw, his eyes solemn. "As I said before, I will not be a burden to you. If Zuzu can leap to the pipe, then you should all go and leave me here."

A heavy silence fell over them.

Aura broke it with renewed energy. Her tail shot straight up as inspiration struck. "I know where we can go. Murphy's place! The two-legs he lives with have a building behind their house they use for storing things. Remember? Murphy gave us a tour of it last summer—he bragged about how it's his cat cave, the one he retreats to when the two-legs get too bothersome. It's not heated, but we'll be warm enough if we huddle together."

"Okay, that could work," Cosmo replied thoughtfully. "It's near the eateries on Thomson Avenue, so we could get food. But we still have my first problem: Karma can't fly, so what do we do?"

"Simple," Aura responded, her whiskers twitching with determination. "We check out that other possible exit you found and see if it works for Karma. If not, we keep looking until we find a way out."

Cosmo nodded, his expression serious. "When I try to find another way out, the rats might attack me all at once, so you'll need to come with me, Aura. This will leave Karma and Zuzu exposed again."

Zuzu rose to her feet, her once-pristine fur now bearing the proud battle marks of a street cat. She stood tall, chin lifted with newfound confidence. "If you two aren't gone for long, Karma and I can stay in the corner again. If the rats attack, I'll scream as loud as I can so you can come to our aid."

"Good idea, Zuzu," Karma said warmly, touching his nose to her cheek. "You proved you can handle yourself if the rats return."

A sudden roar from above made them all freeze.

The corridor vibrated with the thunderous sound.

"What's that!" Cosmo yelled, bounding toward the tunnel. "Everyone stay here while I check it out." He leaped to the overhead pipe and scrambled up toward the surface.

Cold air rushed down as Cosmo poked his head through the opening. He immediately saw the source of the noise—the two-legs were clearing snow with massive machines that growled like thunder, shooting white arcs high into the air and leaving clear paths in their wake.

"Nice!" Cosmo murmured to himself.

He darted back down the tunnel and joined the others. "Just as we thought, they're clearing the snow off the paths. By this time tomorrow, we'll be able to travel again." He looked at Aura. "I suggest we leave now and check out that other exit."

Aura turned to Karma and Zuzu, her eyes narrowing with concern. "Cosmo's right. It's critical we find another way out. But first, let's lap up as much water as we can from the leaking pipe. The last thing we need is for either of you to get thirsty and leave the safety of the corner."

Karma nodded with a glint of admiration in his eyes. "You're always thinking ahead, Aura. It's in moments like these that you shine the brightest."

After they drank their fill of water, with Karma and Zuzu secure in their defensive corner, Cosmo and Aura set out. As they walked further down the corridor, faint hisses echoed from the shadows—the rats were still lurking, no doubt plotting their next move.

The air grew noticeably colder as Cosmo stopped abruptly, his whiskers twitching at the sudden shift. He turned to Aura. "This is the possible exit I found. Do you feel the cold air? It must be coming through some opening." His gaze lifted, drawn to a sliver of daylight near the ceiling, then fell. "Look, Aura! See this concrete ledge? It's about one cat-length high. Karma could jump onto it, then to the overhead pipe. If the opening's big enough, this could be our way out."

Aura's gaze followed his, her tail flicking thoughtfully. "I'm smaller than you—let me check it out." She sprang onto the ledge with a fluid leap, landing gracefully. Then, using her momentum, she launched onto the pipe, her body flowing smoothly from one movement to the next. On the pipe, she stretched up on her hind legs to investigate the source of the cold air.

Her whiskers drooped in disappointment as she dropped back down beside Cosmo. "It's no good. Just a small crack. There's nothing we can do to enlarge it."

"Damn."

"I know. What do we try next?"

Cosmo's ears perked forward, and his eyes brightened with a new thought. "Hold on," he said. "With this many rats down here, there has to be a big source of food somewhere. Maybe there's an eatery in this building. And every eatery has entry points—that's how the rats would've gotten in here."

"Good point, Cosmo." But then she sighed, frustration seeping into her voice. "We've been gone too long. Let's head back and work out a plan for how to proceed. Since the eatery could be far away, I think all of us should move as a group."

"I agree," Cosmo said. As they turned to head back, they froze—a half-dozen rats had gathered, blocking their path.

"Great. Here we go again," Cosmo growled, his muscles taut and his fur bristling in anticipation. "Ready?"

"More than ready!" Aura's battle cry rang out, echoing off the walls as she lunged forward.

The two feline warriors pounced on their enemies, their claws flashing in the dim light as they struck with deadly precision. Soon, four dead rats lay on the ground while the survivors limped into the shadows, their labored breaths mixing with the heavy scent of blood in the air.

"We'll feast tonight," Cosmo said with grim satisfaction. "One juicy rat each. Let's get them back to the others."

Each of them grabbed two rats by their tails and returned to their waiting family.

After feasting on their fresh kills, they huddled together, planning their next move. As they talked, above them, the two-legs continued clearing paths through the deep snow.

In the morning, Cosmo's keen sense of smell caught the unmistakable scent of cooked food wafting through the corridor. "Hey, everyone, let's follow this scent!"

He and Aura took the lead as they crept down the corridor, their keen eyes scanning the shadows for rats. The scent of food grew stronger until they found themselves beneath what could only be the college's eatery, where the tantalizing aromas of freshly cooked food drifted down from above.

When they spotted a rat darting through an opening, they followed its path and suddenly emerged into the kitchen's fluorescent glare. The unexpected brightness made their eyes involuntarily squint. Nearby, a two-leg pushed open the heavy door to take out the trash, and they seized their chance. Without hesitation, they darted outside, leaving the startled worker gaping in their wake.

Outside, snow transformed the world into a dazzling white expanse. After the humid warmth of the tunnel, the cold air stung their lungs, but they tasted freedom—sweeter than any meal or the comfort of their underground shelter. With exhilaration in his voice, Cosmo turned to his family. "This way—follow me!"

The winter sun bathed the freshly cleared path as they moved toward Murphy's place, leaving the rats—and the dark corridor—behind. Karma walked carefully while Zuzu, marveling at the crystalline landscape she had only seen through windows, kept close beside him. For Karma, winter was nothing new; for Zuzu, it felt as though she had stepped into another world...

5

As the four cats journeyed through the snow-covered landscape, sticking to the cleared paths, Zuzu, nestled between Cosmo and Karma, could hardly contain her curiosity. "Who is Murphy, Cosmo? Have you known him long?"

Cosmo's whiskers twitched with amusement, his eyes sparkling as he glanced at her while speaking. "Not long after I left Karma and Aura to live on my own, I met Murph in an alley not far from here. He was a street cat, just as naïve as I was about survival. We became fast friends, hunting together and chasing all the cute cats around Queens. As free-spirited males, we were terrors." His eyes sparkled with the memory. "A couple of winters later, Murph met a little two-legged girl and her mother at the Sunnyside Gardens Park. He followed them home and settled on their porch. The girl took a shine to him, started feeding him, and eventually her family let him sleep inside. Once that happened, Murph bragged that he'd found paradise. If you ask me, he traded his freedom for a warm house and regular meals."

The wind picked up, sending swirls of loose snow dancing around them as they trudged on. The cold cut through their fur, and Karma's steps grew heavier. His breath came in labored gasps, and despite the gusts, vapor clouds billowed from their mouths with each exhale, briefly lingering in the air before being whisked away by the wind. Without a word, just a shared glance, the others instinctively huddled closer to Karma, offering warmth and silent support.

After a mile and a half, they reached 43rd Avenue, where Cosmo led them to an elegant house nestled between two similar homes. The late afternoon light cast a golden glow on the two-story structure, built in the early 1920s. Though showing signs of age, it retained its charm—red brick on the lower level and stuccoed upper floors that reflected the grace of the era. Two large urns flanked the dark oak front door on the expansive porch, likely filled with flowers in the summer.

"Welcome to Murph's promised land," Cosmo smirked. His tail twitched with barely contained mirth.

Zuzu's eyes widened as she gazed up at the structure. "It doesn't rise as high as where I lived," she mused, "but I like how the sun reflects off the see-through things."

Cosmo nodded at her comment. "C'mon, everyone, let's head to Murph's cat cave behind the house."

It didn't take long to reach the alleyway that led to it. The two-legs hadn't cleared the snow here, but the ruts left by their moving boxes formed narrow paths down the alley. Cosmo flicked his head to signal the others to follow and moved forward. They marched single-file down a rut, their paws crunching softly in the snow, until they reached the back of Murphy's house.

An unscalable snowdrift stood between them and the garage. Cosmo paused, eyeing the obstacle, then turned to the others with a wry smile. "Your mighty leader will now demonstrate his tunneling skills," he said, his voice laced with playful arrogance. "I'll dig through it, and then you can all follow me."

Without waiting for a response, he dug his claws into the snow, his muscles straining as he burrowed through the dense barrier. Snow flew outwards with every determined thrust of his claws. A few minutes later, with a triumphant flick of his tail, he emerged in front of the garage, relieved to find the eaves had kept the snow from touching the building. One by one, the others followed through the tunnel he'd created.

The four of them quietly observed the humble, detached garage, their breath forming small clouds in the cold air. Aura eyed the hole in the rotted door. "This is the opening we went through when Murphy showed us his cat cave. Follow me, everyone, and let's get settled in."

Karma's whiskers drooped as he examined the hole with a frown. "Looks a bit snug for a cat of my stature."

Cosmo shook his head. "You'll fit just fine, Karma. If not, I'll give you a good push from behind. Just... please try not to pass gas in my face, alright?"

Karma's eyes crinkled with mischief. "Passing on that opportunity will be a challenge."

A fond smile crossed Cosmo's face, and he paused momentarily, deep in thought. "You all go inside. I'll let Murph know we're here—I'll try to summon him with our secret call." He glanced at Aura, his expression turning serious. "Let's hope there aren't any rats in the garage, too. If there are, yell, and I'll come running."

Cosmo crept to the opposite side of the garage and stood on his hind legs, surveying the snow-covered backyard. Although small, it seemed like a pleasant retreat, featuring a large tree and several bushes along the fence.

He paused for a moment, listening to make sure the others were okay. Then, with a deep breath, he let out a blood-curdling scream—just long enough to send a message, but not so long as to attract every two-leg in the area.

A few tense moments passed, and then, with great effort, Murphy squeezed through a cat door near the bottom of the house's back door. His considerable bulk made the flap groan in protest as he waddled onto the covered porch, scanning the area for Cosmo.

Cosmo's whiskers quivered from suppressed laughter at the sight of his rotund friend. He waved a paw. "Murph, over here!"

Murphy's face lit up, his eyes sparkling with relief. He dove into the snow and met Cosmo in the middle of the yard.

"Coz! I've been worried sick about you surviving this storm. How are you, and how's Aura and Karma?"

Cosmo's tail twitched as he smiled, knowing Murphy was really asking about Aura. Since the day they met, Murphy had a crush on his sister. An unrequited crush.

"They're fine. We made it to the heated underground corridor at the college and rode out the storm there. Murph, you won't believe this, but rats have completely infested the place. They attacked the four of us in droves."

Murphy's ears perked up as he flashed Cosmo a sly grin. "The four of you? Does this mean you've finally given up your nefarious ways and settled down?"

Cosmo shot him a look that only a hardened street cat could perfect—a look that questioned Murphy's intelligence, blended with sheer disdain.

"No, Murph. Aura found an uptown cat who ended up on the street. We've been taking care of her."

Clearly enjoying the moment, Murphy's voice took on a teasing edge. "We?"

Cosmo's fur bristled slightly. "Yeah, me too. Her name's Zuzu, and she's not a pampered house cat like you. She showed her mettle when the rats attacked us."

"Is she cute?" Murphy asked, a twinkle in his eye.

The absurdity of the question made Cosmo's jaw drop. "Forget it, Murph. You're twice her age, and let's face it—you're no longer what I'd call a hunk of burning love."

Murphy pretended to look hurt. "I'll have you know I just finished a brutal diet—and let me tell you, it was one rough afternoon."

Cosmo couldn't help but chuckle at his friend's farcical humor. "Damn, Murph, you're the first belly-scraping cat I've ever seen."

"So, did you come here just to razz me?" Murphy quipped.

Cosmo's smile faded, replaced by a serious look. "We need your help, Murph. The others are in your cat cave. Karma's age is catching up to him, and we need a solid shelter until it warms up. Do you mind if we stay for a while?"

Murphy's whiskers twitched as he nodded. "Stay as long as you need. Just keep quiet and don't draw attention." He gave Cosmo a mischievous grin. "I'm looking forward to seeing Aura again and meeting Zuzu. Is Aura still unencumbered?"

Cosmo playfully swatted his friend. "Murph, you'll have to meet them outside because there's no way you'll fit through the cat cave opening. And yes, Aura's unencumbered, and she's still feisty as ever, so consider yourself warned."

Murphy laughed heartily. "Do you remember when I tried to, well, you know, be romantic with her? She almost killed me."

Unable to contain himself, Cosmo burst into laughter. "If Karma and I hadn't heard the commotion and rescued you, we wouldn't be having this conversation right now."

Snow crunched beneath Murphy's paws as he shifted his weight. "Those were the days, my friend. Anyway, before my two-legs come looking for me, let's head to my cat cave so I can say hello to everyone."

"Sounds good. Karma will be thrilled to see you again." Cosmo eyed him, and the levity lifted from his tone. "Murph, hear me: Aura's had a rough few days, so dial back the charm offensive with her. And she's extremely protective of naïve Zuzu. If you don't want to get skinned alive, consider Zuzu off-limits."

"Party pooper," Murphy replied with a wink. "I'll be on my best behavior."

They tramped back to the cave's entrance, following the trail they had made in the yard. Cosmo popped his head in and called out, "Hey, everyone, come out and meet Murph!"

One by one, they emerged—Karma first, likely pushed from behind by Aura and Zuzu—followed by Aura, and then Zuzu, her white fur a rare sight among street cats.

When Aura laid eyes on Murphy, beaming at her, her jaw dropped in shock at his corpulence. "Damn, Murph—did you eat all the two-legs in your house?"

Murphy's belly jiggled as he chuckled, unfazed by her overt disparagement. "It's good to see you again, too, Aura." He gave her a mock bow, a grin spreading across his face.

Unlike Aura, Karma's eyes twinkled with diplomatic grace as he deftly masked his astonishment at Murphy's ballooning size. "It's been too long, Murphy. Great to see you again. You look... fit and healthy." In the background, Aura failed to stifle a chuckle at Karma's titanic understatement.

"Karma, Karma, Karma—you're right, it's been far too long since we've all gotten together. I'm so delighted to see you all again." His gaze shifted, and his eyes softened as he turned his attention to little Zuzu, fighting to keep his tongue in his mouth. "And you must be Zuzu. Welcome to our group. I'm sure we'll become fast friends."

Intimidated by the sight of the largest cat she had ever seen, Zuzu's whiskers trembled. "It's nice meeting you, too, Murphy," she shyly replied.

Aura's fur bristled as she stepped in front of Zuzu, shooting Murphy a menacing look. Cosmo leaned in, whispering in his ear. "I warned you, Murph."

When Murphy chuckled at Cosmo's caution, it clicked. Cosmo's tail twitched with understanding—Murphy, ever the rascal, was tweaking Aura with his Zuzu comment. Murphy, he concluded, still liked living on the edge.

"Hey, everyone, you're welcome here, but stay out of sight from the two-legs. They don't want this place becoming a haven for street cats."

"We'll be careful, Murph," Cosmo replied. "But we'll need to venture out for food."

Murphy's eyes gleamed with enthusiasm. "Less than a mile from here, there are eateries where the leftovers are downright tantalizing. Trash can food at its finest! I'll give you the lowdown when you're ready to check them out."

"Thanks, Murph," Cosmo said. "You're a true friend."

Murphy nodded thoughtfully, his eyes narrowing as if weighing something important. "If you want, later tonight, when my two-legs are asleep, you can come inside for a meal." Murphy lowered his voice conspiratorially. "But you'll have to be very quiet—like mice. Can you do that?"

Their ears perked forward as they all nodded, tails swishing with excitement.

"What kind of food, Murph? Rats?" Cosmo's stomach growled in anticipation.

Murphy's whiskers twitched. "No rats. The two-legs hate rats more than we do. What we'll eat will be a surprise." His tail flicked back and forth. "I'll come get you when it's clear."

He paused, his eyes widening. "But before you come into the house, I need to teach you something."

Aura's head tilted. "What?"

"If one of my two-legs wakes up and sees all of you in the kitchen, don't scatter, and don't attack them. Instead, sit down and stare at them like this." Murphy settled onto his haunches, his bulk making the snow crunch beneath him. He leaned back, staring at his friends with wide, pitiful eyes that seemed to demand sympathy. "When you look mournful like this, you'll melt the hearts of my two-legs, and they'll want to help you. I don't know why, but it always works." He paused and added, "Now, everyone, try it—just like I did. Remember: pathetic is the key!"

Except for Cosmo, they all sat and stared at Murphy with woeful expressions. Murphy scanned each of them, nodding in approval. "Good. Very good."

Cosmo's tail lashed with skepticism. "Damn, Murph. Teeth and claws are the only way to go if you ask me."

Murphy's eyes narrowed. "I'm not asking you, Coz! Damn it, I know two-legs. If you can't agree to this, then stay out of the house and go hungry."

"All right, all right. Relax, Murph. We'll do it your way," Cosmo grumbled.

Later that night, well past midnight, Murphy exited the home's cat door and stealthily slinked toward the cat cave. His breath formed small clouds in the frigid air as he poked his head through the opening. "Cosmo, it's me!"

Moments later, the four cats appeared. As they stood looking at him, Murphy whispered, "Okay, when we get to the house, I'll go in first. You all follow me. Remember, no talking, and don't bump into anything. I'll show you where the food is, and you can take turns eating. Got it?"

They all nodded.

Moving like shadows across the snow, Murphy led the silent feline pack to the house. The biting wind seemed to intensify, sinking into their fur with each step. At the cat door entrance, Murphy stopped and faced them. "Watch how I go through the door and do it like me," he whispered. When he nudged the flap open, warm air poured out. The heat hit them like a wave, and for a moment, each of them paused, savoring it, especially Karma with his stiff limbs. Cosmo's and Aura's tails swished in satisfaction, and Zuzu's senses felt overwhelmed by the sudden change in temperature.

With great effort, Murphy squeezed through the cat door. Aura almost laughed at how he struggled to fit through the small opening. Once inside, the warmth of the house felt like a splendid, warm summer night.

Murphy touched his paw to his face, signaling them to stay quiet. He padded over to a contraption on the floor, and the others followed closely behind.

His whiskers quivered as he pointed to a bowl filled with small, round pellets. "Here's the food," he whispered. "When you eat what's in the bowl, more comes out from up here." He gestured toward a container filled with more of the same pellets. "Who wants to eat first?"

"Karma goes first," Aura whispered with authority, motioning for him to go to the bowl.

Karma's nose wrinkled as he neared the bowl, sniffing the odd, ball-like pellets. The scent was faint and foreign—nothing like the pungent trash can food he was accustomed to. His whiskers twitched with uncertainty as he cautiously picked up one of the pellets and took a tentative bite. It crunched loudly in his mouth, the sound sharp and unfamiliar. The dryness of the pellet made it hard to swallow, and he chewed slowly, unsure.

After downing several of them, he looked at the others, trying to sound upbeat. "Better than moldy trash can food," he whispered, though his throat begged for water. He finished a few more pellets and yielded the bowl toward Aura. "I desperately need a drink of water."

Her tail swished skeptically as she nudged one of the morsels with her paw, eyeing it suspiciously. "What is this stuff?" she whispered, sniffing it before giving it a hesitant lick. Cosmo, always the bold one, leaned down and snatched a stray pellet near the bowl. Surprise flashed in his eyes as it crunched loudly in his mouth. "Murph," he whispered, "are you sure this is food? It's hard and dry as dirt." He grabbed a couple more pellets and flinched as they crunched in his teeth. He shot Murphy a contemptuous look. "Don't even tell me you like this better than a big, juicy rat."

"Shhh!" Murphy cautioned, glancing around. "And by the way, unlike rats, the pellets don't bite back when you try to eat them. Keep eating, Aura," he whispered. With a satisfied grin, he gestured toward a pile of food balls a short distance away. "Cosmo, since you're a big eater, I made a separate pile just for you. Enjoy!"

Aura continued eating, grimacing with each unsavory bite she swallowed. Once she finished, she looked back at Zuzu, who stood behind her, nervously swishing her tail. "Go ahead, Zuzu. It's your turn."

Zuzu's ears flattened against her head as she eyed the "food" with disdain. "I hate pellets," she grumbled. The others knew why—after Mrs. Chen passed, the two-legs had fed them to her while she was locked in a cage. Her voice wavered as she glanced at Murphy, hope flickering in her eyes. "Do you have anything else to eat? A rat, maybe?"

Aura's expression softened, and she leaned close to Zuzu, touching her cheek to the smaller cat's. "Zuzu," she whispered, "we don't know when we'll get our next meal. These food balls are easier to eat than your first rat. You need to eat."

Zuzu's shoulders drooped in defeat. She picked up a pellet with reluctance, bit into it, and grimaced at its disagreeable taste. She continued eating in a daze, as if she were chewing on old, unpleasant memories instead of food.

As Cosmo devoured the pile of food balls Murphy had made for him, Karma joined in and ate with gusto.

When Zuzu finished, Murphy motioned toward his water bowl. "After those dry balls, I always drink a lot of water," he murmured. "Trust me, you'll want to do the same. There's no water in my cat cave."

After such a dry meal, the water felt cool and refreshing on their tongues. Each of them took a turn lapping it up, grateful for the relief. Once they'd all had their fill, Murphy led them back to the cat door.

"Well, my friends, I hope you sleep well. I'll say goodnight here instead of wrestling to get out through that skinny door again. Cosmo, if you need anything, give me our secret call, and I'll be there in two shakes of a dead cat's tail."

Cosmo chuckled at Murphy's dead cat remark and gave him a playful nudge. "I won't forget this, Murph. We owe you."

"Hey, that's what friends are for." Murphy's gaze lingered on Aura as he said it, and he winked. This time, she smiled back and nodded.

As they returned to the cat cave, the cold air hit them like a slap. Inside, they huddled in the corner furthest from the opening. Their fur brushed together comfortingly as they huddled close for warmth. Karma purred contentedly. "There's nothing like falling asleep with a full stomach, feeling cozy, and surrounded by friends. I'm grateful."

"I'm grateful, too," Aura said, her voice softening with emotion. "Thanks, brother, for everything you've done these last few days. We wouldn't have survived the storm if you hadn't found Zuzu and me."

"Nor I," Karma added.

Cosmo's usual gruffness melted away. Praise for a street cat was rare, and he appreciated their words more than he let on. "I'm also grateful for all of you—and Murph. Friends like you are hard to come by."

The cold wind whistled softly outside, and soon, they drifted off to sleep, each finding comfort in the communal warmth and the strength of their bonds.

6

IN THE WEE HOURS of the morning, a storm to rival the one they'd just weathered brewed in Cosmo's belly. With quiet urgency, he abruptly rose and darted out of the cat cave, burrowing into the nearest snowbank to conceal what was about to happen: his gut was about to violently reject the food balls Murphy had so generously provided for dinner.

A thunderous eruption followed. Then another.

"Damn you, Murph," he muttered. "Your food balls are passing through me like crap through a goose..."

Cosmo smirked, thinking that if he weren't buried in the snow, he would've woken up every two-leg in the area.

After what felt like an eternity, convinced that every trace of food balls had evacuated his system, Cosmo made a sharp U-turn to avoid trekking through the foul-smelling aftermath of his own doing. Emerging back into the open, he glanced at the twinkling stars scattered across the dark sky like countless fireflies. Despite the cold, he paused to admire their brilliance.

A sudden thought struck him, and he burst out laughing. Given Murph's prodigious size, he must eat his weight in food balls every day, likely resulting in an impressive amount of outflow exiting his rear end. After what he'd just experienced, Cosmo was sure a massive pile of Murph's dung was buried somewhere beneath the snow in the yard—probably big enough to be called Mount Murph. He chuckled to himself as he returned to the cat cave.

As Cosmo neared the opening, Karma shot out, causing him to spring upward instinctively, as cats do when startled. When he landed, he saw the same wide-eyed look on Karma's face as when he'd first darted out.

"Burrow into the snowbank before you go, Karma! It'll pass before you know it."

A half-hour later, Karma returned and nestled beside Cosmo, who was lying near the others. He leaned in close and whispered, "Boy, those food balls went through me like crap through a goose..."

Cosmo chuckled at Karma's use of the same metaphor to describe their ordeal. "Let's get some sleep," he said with a flick of his tail. "I purposely lied down here so I wouldn't block the path of Aura and Zuzu if the same affliction we had visits them."

Soon, he and Karma settled back into a deep sleep. Thankfully, the wrath that had struck them didn't affect the females.

Later, as the sun crept up, its rays filtered through the small, grime-streaked window of the cat cave, illuminating the dust particles in the air.

Aura stirred, yawned, and surveyed her surroundings. The cat cave, a shadowy, forgotten corner of the world, was cluttered with broken furniture and cardboard boxes strewn haphazardly across the floor. Cobwebs stretched between the rafters, and a faint odor of mildew and old wood filled the air. The old walls creaked in the wind, but amidst the mess, there was a strange comfort—a place to curl up and escape the sharp bite of the cold. It wasn't much, but for now, it was their refuge.

A loud, repetitive barking jolted the other cats awake. Instinctively, Cosmo arched his back as the unwelcoming sound echoed through the garage. With each passing second, it seemed to draw nearer.

Zuzu pressed closer to Aura, seeking protection. "What is that horrible sound?" she asked, her voice trembling.

The others, alert and on edge, knew all too well what it was. Cosmo moved toward the hole in the garage door. Without peering out, he could hear the heavy paws approaching, accompanied by the relentless barking. His muscles tensed. The sound grew louder as the beast drew closer.

Karma moved to the other side of Zuzu, placing her between Aura and himself. "That, little one," he whispered, "is a hundfang. And by the sound of it, a big one. Don't make a sound..."

A massive hundfang head—almost as big as a full-grown cat—thrust through the opening. Its hot breath steamed in the cold air, and saliva dripped from its snarling jaws as it sniffed the air, eyes wild with predatory intent.

Cosmo struck without hesitation, his claws raking across its sensitive nose. Blood sprayed as the beast jerked back with a howl of pain.

Before anyone could breathe a sigh of relief, the hundfang started clawing at the opening with its huge paws, trying to enlarge the hole to get in. When its head shot through the opening again with jaws snapping, Cosmo unleashed an even more savage attack, his claws tearing at the beast's eyes and muzzle.

The creature screamed in pain, retreating as its heavy paws crunched through the snow. Soon, its high-pitched cries faded into the distance.

Satisfied that the threat had eased, Cosmo returned to his frightened friends. "They might be big, but hundfangs can be bloodied, too," he said with a smirk and a hint of swagger. He sighed deeply. "Well, I guess we've traded a killer storm and hordes of rats for a killer hundfang."

Trembling, Zuzu looked at the others. "I've never seen anything so scary and vicious. Are there lots of hundfangs out there?" Her eyes conveyed sheer terror.

Aura pressed her cheek to Zuzu's, offering comfort. "I'm afraid there are. Lots of them, and they come in all sizes and colors."

Zuzu swallowed hard at the thought.

"Zuzu," Cosmo said, his voice softer than usual, "you've got much to learn about surviving on the streets. After what just happened, we'll start with hundfangs." He turned to Karma. "You're the best teacher among us. Why don't you tell her about them—and don't hold back, okay?"

Karma nodded, settling into a more comfortable position, his expression growing serious. "Zuzu, there are many kinds of hundfangs, and you must learn to recognize them all." He paused, locking eyes with her to make sure she was listening closely. "What attacked us just now was a demon hundfang—the most dangerous kind. They're huge, powerful, and they kill cats without mercy."

"Even skilled fighters like Cosmo?" Zuzu asked, her eyes wide.

"Even me," Cosmo confirmed. "I once had a friend—Ajax—who was the meanest, toughest street cat in Queens. A demon hundfang caught him, Murph, and me out in the open... Ajax stood up to the hundfang to give Murph and me time to escape up trees. There wasn't much left of Ajax after that hundfang finished with him..." His voice trailed off, the memory still raw and painful.

"And here's the most important thing you need to remember," Aura added urgently. "Hundfangs can't climb. If you ever see one, especially a bushy-tailed or demon hundfang, get high off the ground immediately. Your life depends on it, Zuzu."

"What are bushy-tailed hundfangs, and what other kinds are there?" Zuzu asked, her voice barely above a whisper.

"Bushy-tailed hundfangs have reddish-orange fur, while others appear more brownish," Karma explained. "They're elusive, never associating with two-legs, and they tend to stay far from the places we inhabit. They're usually smaller than demon hundfangs, but they're just as deadly—and far more cunning. Then there are the puny hundfangs—yipping little creatures with high-pitched voices, no bigger than we are. We could fight them if we had to and likely come out on top, though it's also wiser to avoid them when possible."

"Just remember," Cosmo added, "any hundfang bigger than a cat is more dangerous than a rat. And that's saying something."

Zuzu's whiskers drooped, and her ears flattened against her head as she absorbed the frightening information. "Are... are there many hundfangs around here?"

"Too many," Aura replied softly. "The two-legs keep them in their artificial dens or yards. They often get out and roam our territory. That's why we must be especially cautious when searching for food." She paused, her gaze distant. "Why two-legs would want a hundfang instead of a cat is beyond me. But then again, we've already established that they're peculiar creatures."

"Will the demon hundfang that attacked us come back?" Zuzu asked, her voice trembling despite her best efforts to sound calm.

Cosmo shrugged. "Maybe. But he got a taste of what happens when he messes with a capable street cat. I doubt he'll try poking his nose through our opening again."

"Still," Karma added thoughtfully, "we must be cautious, especially since demon hundfangs often hunt in packs."

"That's a good point, Karma." Aura's gaze softened as she looked at Zuzu, her eyes filled with confidence. "It's not all doom and gloom on the streets, Zuzu. We're just saying you can't ever get lazy or lower your defenses. You always have to be vigilant and aware of what's around you—like in the corridor where Karma picked out a defensive corner in case rats came. His quick thinking probably saved both of you."

"I understand," Zuzu replied, her voice steadier than before.

There was a brief silence as Zuzu processed the conversation, her wide eyes flickering with uncertainty. Aura pressed against her, offering a soft smile. "Don't let all of this scare you, Zuzu," she said gently. "Out here, we stick together. You'll learn quickly, and we'll teach you everything you need to know to survive. It's not about being fearless—it's about being smart and prepared. Remember, even the toughest cats have to respect the streets."

Cosmo nodded in agreement, his usual smirk returning. "Speaking of survival," he groaned, rubbing his belly with a paw. "Murph's food balls were like a demon hundfang in my gut. They cleaned me out, so now I'm starving. Later today, let's visit some local eateries for some real food. On the way back, we can stop at a park and teach Zuzu how to climb a tree."

Karma chuckled. "Little one, you'll see that climbing a tree is easy—especially if a demon hundfang is nipping at your rear. Going down, though, that's the hard part."

Cosmo laughed. "You got that right, Karma."

7

HAVING SCORED EXCELLENT, MOLD-FREE scraps from a local diner, they headed to Sunnyside Gardens Park—not far from Murphy's house—as the sun reached its peak. The park lay silent under a blanket of snow, with crisscrossing paths nestled between rows of snow-dusted trees. Although some paths were cleared of snow, few two-legs were there, so it was a perfect, peaceful setting for the cats. Cosmo spotted a tall maple tree beside their cleared path, its branches reaching out like an open invitation. As they walked to it, the snow crunched softly under their paws.

At the base of the tree, Cosmo turned to Zuzu. "This one's perfect," he said, his voice filled with energy. "Watch me." He bounded onto the tree and raced up to the first branch. There, he paused and looked down at Zuzu. "Your turn. Use your claws to grip the bark and pull yourself up. Don't think about it—just do it. If a demon hundfang were chasing you, you'd have to move fast, right?"

Zuzu nodded, took a deep breath, and scampered upward, but it was nowhere near as graceful as Cosmo's smooth climb. She joined him, her heart pounding in her chest. Fear washed over her as she looked down, realizing how high they were. Her paws felt slippery against the rough bark, and her breathing came in quick, cold bursts.

"How... how do I get down now?" she asked, her voice trembling.

Cosmo chuckled. "You go down like you came up, with your head facing the sky. Take a few deep breaths first. When you're ready, turn around and dig your claws into the bark to control your descent. Keep your body steady and don't look down. Trust yourself."

From below, Karma watched intently. "C'mon, little one, you've got this! It's fun once you get the hang of it!"

Zuzu inched downward, each movement slow and deliberate. Her claws scraped the rough bark, fighting to find purchase. Every step dragged on, but she kept at it, her shallow breath quickening, her nerves buzzing. Finally, she reached the bottom.

Karma cheered, his tail flicking with excitement. "Bravo, Zuzu, you did it!" he called, his voice full of pride.

Looking both relieved and exhilarated, Zuzu beamed with satisfaction. "You're right, Karma—I did it!"

She glanced up at Cosmo, expecting to see him climb down. Instead, he called down to her. "Not bad. Now try it again!"

Zuzu's mouth fell open in shock. "Again? Are you sure I need to do it again?"

"Practice makes perfect!" Cosmo boomed. "Now get up here!"

Aura's whiskers twitched with amusement as she watched Zuzu—wide-eyed and tail quivering—strive to impress Cosmo. After a few moments, she shifted her gaze to Karma, studying him thoughtfully, reflecting on how he had aged.

His coat had become thin and patchy, and gray fur now dusted his once-vibrant face. His movements had slowed with age, yet he still carried himself with quiet dignity.

Earlier, during their foraging, she had noticed more concerning signs—his confusion by the trash cans, how he would nibble at the food, pause, and then look around as if he were lost. His frequent drinking of water worried her, too. Equally troubling was how the stories he once told with such grace now seemed scattered in his mind, like leaves in the wind.

Yet, she marveled at how he never complained. No matter how tired or aching he felt, Karma always kept a positive attitude, inspiring them all with his unyielding spirit. Proud of his determination to keep moving, even as it became harder for him to keep up, a bittersweet smile tugged at her lips.

The difficult journey to the underground corridor and then to Murphy's house had made Karma's deterioration painfully clear. Aware of his decline, he had repeatedly urged them to leave him behind. Yet he persisted—for now. But Aura could sense the inevitable approaching. The mere thought of a world without him weighed heavily on her heart.

Also weighing on her was being Karma's caregiver—especially with the added responsibility of caring for Zuzu. Cosmo was still Cosmo—an independent, free-range street cat with no interest in looking after anyone long-term. The thought of shouldering the weight of both Karma and Zuzu alone overwhelmed her.

The park's winter silence cloaked her like a blanket until the sudden sound of paws crunching through the snow jolted Aura from her troubling thoughts. She spun around and spotted a dear friend coming her way.

"Josephine! What are you doing here?"

The big cat bounded over to Aura, tail flicking behind her, an air of confidence about her. "I been cooped up with my two-legs fo' days thanks to the storm. Had to get out befor' I loses my sanity."

Her gaze shifted menacingly to the unfamiliar young cat, causing Zuzu to freeze, her whiskers quivering at the imposing presence. The big female's eyes flicked up to Cosmo in the tree, then back to Aura, narrowing with suspicion.

"Y'all ain't told me that Cosmo be teachin' kittens how to climb trees," she growled. "What be next? He gonna bathe her, too?"

Cosmo's tail twitched as he chuckled. "Jojo, you know Zuzu's not a kitten. And I'm not giving her or anyone else a bath."

A few years ago, Josephine had decided to leave the street life behind and settle down as a house cat, just like Murphy. The two-legs who took her in were a lively family—loud and active, just like her. For Josephine, it was a perfect match. Except for one thing: it ended her romantic relationship with Cosmo, who felt she'd abandoned him for a life of comfort. A pang of regret tugged at her chest as she gazed at him. How many times had she imagined returning to him when things with her two-legs turned difficult? But Cosmo had moved on. He didn't need her anymore. Not in the way he had before. This explained her immediate dislike of poor Zuzu.

Josephine blinked, shaking the thought off as quickly as it came, but the slight tightness around her eyes betrayed the moment of vulnerability. Her eyes narrowed as she fixed her gaze on Cosmo. "I sees you gots a thing fo' young ones now." Her voice, filled with disdain and suspicion, continued. "Feel like yesterday when we was out gettin' into all sorts of trouble together, and now, here you is babysittin'." Her eyes narrowed further, her voice booming across the snowy park. "I sees how you be lookin' at her. You all 'hero' now, teachin' her 'bout life. Soon, you be havin' her fetchin' you snacks from the trash cans."

Zuzu, feeling more than a little uncomfortable, shifted on her paws. "I... I don't know what you mean."

Josephine's eyes scanned Zuzu, taking in every detail. "Look at you. Cute, white fur, soft paws, and no scars." She flicked her tail dismissively.

"You probably has a fancy pillow at home, huh? All nice and pampered, you is."

For all her bluster, Josephine couldn't help but notice Zuzu meeting her gaze, unwavering, the young cat's courage catching her by surprise.

Zuzu's voice was small but firm. "I'm not pampered. Well, not anymore."

"Mmhmm. Sure you not." Josephine shot Cosmo a glance. "Guess it be easy to forget street hardships when you entertainin' young innocents."

"Jojo, enough!" Cosmo's voice had an edge now, the delight of seeing her slipping away.

Undaunted, Josephine continued. "You ain't be foolin' me, Coz." She flicked her tail in Zuzu's direction. "I knows what be goin' on."

Until now, Karma, standing next to Zuzu, had watched Jojo and Cosmo's banter with silent amusement. "Jo, Zuzu became homeless just before the big storm, and we've been helping her. Nothing unbecoming is going on between her and Cosmo."

Aura joined them, chuckling at Josephine's skeptical glance at Karma. "He's right, Jo. We'd all be dead by now if not for Cosmo lookin' out for us. Today, a demon hundfang tried to attack, so we're here teachin' Zuzu how to climb a tree to escape those horrid creatures." She winked at Jo. "If I see Cosmo trying anything with Zuzu, I'll tear him apart."

Zuzu blinked, confused. "What does 'trying anything' mean?"

Josephine burst out laughing and looked at Zuzu with an impish grin. "Girlfriend, we definitely needs to talk."

Cosmo scurried down the tree and joined them. Josephine brushed her cheek against his, a gesture showing that her anger had passed. "It good to sees you ag'in, Cosmo. I be powerful worried about y'all and went out today lookin' for you."

"It's good to see you, too." Cosmo took a deep breath, then frowned. "Because of the cold, we're staying with Murph until it warms up." He paused, choosing his words carefully. "Have you... uh, seen Murph lately?"

Josephine burst out laughing. "That cat let hisself go! Oh, my, he let hisself go! He a fat cat in every way possible."

Cosmo chuckled and nodded at her response. "Please don't tell me you eat those wretched food balls like him. We tried some last night, and they went straight through me... and Karma, too."

"I eats a whole lot better than Murphy do."

Aura smiled at Josephine's response. "Hey, we're heading back to Murphy's cat cave. Care to join us?"

Josephine shook her head, a playful glint in her eyes. "Love to, but I needs to get back home. How 'bout I sees you some other time?"

"Anytime will work," Aura replied. "But about Murphy—he might not be able to join us..."

"Why?" Josephine's whispers quivered in surprise. "He okay?"

Cosmo laughed, answering Josephine's question. "What Aura's trying to say is that Murph is so enormous now that he might not fit through the cat cave opening. But today, that demon hundfang clawed at it to get to us, so maybe it's big enough now for our ample friend to squeeze through."

After saying their goodbyes, they watched Josephine's confident stride as she headed home. Her visit had brought welcome warmth and laughter to their day, pushing aside thoughts of demon hundfangs and Aura's worries about Karma, if only for a little while.

8

TWO DAYS LATER, AS the sun dipped low in the sky, the foursome of cats got an unexpected visitor. A familiar face popped the cat cave opening. "Yoo-hoo!" Josephine bellowed, "Y'all in here?"

Her sudden appearance startled Zuzu, who stood near the opening. She looked wide-eyed at Aura. "Um, it's your friend."

Aura's face lit up with delight. "Come in, Jo!"

Josephine squeezed through the opening, grinning widely. "How y'all doin'!" She quickly surveyed the place, noting how it was cluttered with various two-leg items, but it provided decent shelter from the elements, which, for street cats, was a luxury.

Cosmo and Karma ambled toward her, both surprised but pleased to see her.

Aura touched cheeks with her. "What brings you here so late, Jo?"

Josephine rolled her eyes. "My two-legs be throwin' a big party. They all actin' loud and crazy, carryin' on like a pack of howlin' hundfangs. After a while, I has enough and left. If you don't mind, I hang with y'all fo' a while."

Cosmo's whiskers twitched with amusement. "I'm surprised you didn't join them since acting wild and crazy is your thing."

Josephine gave him a look—one that said, back off, or things will get ugly. She flicked her tail at poor Zuzu, who shrank back a little. "I ain't no young cat like yer kitten friend here. My days o' troublemakin' and actin' up be behind me." She gave him a sly grin. "But don't you worry—I still retains my youthful vigor."

"Welcome to our temporary residence, dear Josephine," said Karma, his voice warm and cheerful. "Please, make yourself comfortable."

She leaned in, brushing her cheek gently against his, her voice softening. "You still my favorite cat in Queens, Karma. How you is?"

Karma's ears drooped as he sighed. "I'm... fine. Feeling my age, I suppose. But life, as always, is good."

Josephine caught his subtle message, the sadness in his words tugging at her heart. "I glad you haves this safe place to stay." She turned quickly to the others, forcing her voice to be steady. "Where be our hefty friend?"

"Murph's with his two-legs, no doubt parked at his food bowl," Cosmo said with a smirk. "How he tolerates those food balls escapes me, but no one can say he's malnourished."

Josephine laughed at Cosmo's quip. "Them dry balls an acquired taste."

"Hey," said Cosmo, "I'll give Murph our secret call to see if he wants to join us." His tail excitedly flicked as he ducked out of the cave to summon Murphy.

A few minutes later, the moonlight vanished from the opening as Murphy's head appeared, his face contorted with effort. "Push harder, Coz!" he yelled. Behind him, Cosmo grunted and strained, his paws scrabbling against the ground as he tried to shove his well-fed friend through the entrance.

To his relief—and likely Cosmo's as well—Murphy made it through the opening with a smile. "All I had to do was exhale, and I popped right through."

Cosmo, whiskers quivering with amusement, moved next to Murphy to watch Josephine take in the sight of their enormous friend. Her eyes widened in disbelief. "Murphy, Murphy, Murphy! My friend, your belly in danger o' explodin'! You the heaviest cat I ever sees!"

Murphy took her unflattering remarks in stride, giving her a good-natured wink. "Hey, it's always smart to put some meat on your bones to make it through the winter."

His remark earned a collective eye roll from everyone but Zuzu, who had shrunk back into the shadows, feeling like an outsider.

Josephine's tail twitched as she noticed the uncomfortable-looking Zuzu. "Hey, little kitten, don't be standin' off actin' likes you invisible. Get over here." The playful tone in her voice didn't quite reach Zuzu, who froze, unsure how to react to the female cat's commanding presence.

Karma moved to Zuzu, his whiskers twitching with amusement. "Don't be intimidated by Jo, little one. She's just tryin' to tell you, in her unique way, that she likes you."

Zuzu looked at Josephine with sad eyes. "I thought you hated me."

Josephine's expression softened, taken aback by the comment. "Little kitten, I know you be goin' through some rough times. I ain't here to adds to them."

She paused, noticing Zuzu's discomfort, before speaking again. "If my friends calls you their friend, then you be my friend, too. We clear here?"

Zuzu timidly nodded. "Thank you, Josephine."

"Call me Jo," the big cat replied, sealing their friendship with a smile.

Murphy piped up, grinning. "What Jo says goes for me too. Welcome to the gang."

Josephine shot Murphy a dubious look. "Watch this one, little kitten," she said, her tone teasing but knowing. "He always have one thing on his mind. As I tells you the other day, we needs to talk."

Murphy feigned hurt at her remark, putting a paw to his chest as if wounded, then quickly changed the subject. He pointed to a corner of the cat cave. "Hey, let's lie on the blankets to stay warm and catch up."

"A splendid idea, Murphy!" Karma chimed in, his voice filled with approval.

Though his girth made navigating through the cramped space difficult, Murphy led the way to some tattered blankets that formed a nest in the corner. With a smile, he plopped onto one of them, blissfully unaware that his large frame took up a sizeable portion of it. "Gather around, my friends—plenty of room for everyone."

As Zuzu started to lie next to Murphy, Josephine erupted. "Oh, no, little kitten, don't sits beside this has-been street cat. No need for you to be traumatized any mo' than you already is."

Murphy rolled his eyes at her remark, which, one could argue, had a bit of merit. Karma lay beside him with a chuckle, fairly sure Murphy wouldn't try to take liberties with him.

Shared memories enveloped them as the group settled onto the blankets. Cosmo glanced at the cave opening and grinned. "Well, we have the demon hundfang to thank for making this evening possible. If he hadn't enlarged the entrance, Murph would literally be out in the cold, looking in." His whiskers quivered with amusement. "I can picture the demon hundfang right now, in a cave like this, with his pack, telling the story of how he lost half his nose to the legendary demon street cat of Queens—the one with a very large friend who can devour forty pounds of food balls in a single meal."

The group burst into laughter, including Zuzu, who started to feel more at ease with Murphy and Josephine. Without thinking, she piped up: "I wish we'd saved my fancy sequined strap and put it on the demon hundfang. He'd have a hard time explaining that to his friends."

Cosmo roared with laughter, imagining the demon hundfang trying to explain to his hardscrabble buddies how a street cat had stolen his dignity and left him with a dainty little sequin strap as his calling card.

Josephine—laughing as hard as Cosmo—reached over and touched her paw to Zuzu's. "Zuzu, I ain't laugh that hard in ages." It was the first time she'd ever called Zuzu by name. Now curious about the young cat, she looked at her, still smiling. "So, what be your story, my friend? How you end up on the streets?"

The cave grew quiet as Zuzu swallowed hard, the weight of her past making her throat tighten as she relived what had brought her to the streets.

"My, my, my..." Josephine inhaled deeply, taking in what Zuzu said. "I knows Skyline Towers. Girl, you be a uptown cat."

Zuzu nodded, her voice quiet. "I was. But not anymore. I've got nothing. I'm nothing."

Aura shot her a cross look. "Don't ever say that, Zuzu. Ever. You're part of our family now. You've got us, and that's something. Not nothing."

"Damn right it is," Josephine added, her tone warm. "Street cat friends—they make the best friends."

Zuzu's ears perked up as she nodded, glancing between Josephine and Murphy. "If that's true, then why did you two leave your friends and go live with two-legs?"

Josephine's easy smile faded. She looked at Murphy, nodding for him to answer first.

The shadows in the cave seemed to deepen as Murphy paused, considering his words. "I don't know if you've noticed, but I walk with a limp. It happened the day Coz, our friend Ajax, and I got attacked by a demon hundfang. It killed Ajax and severely injured my right rear leg. Some two-legs found me, took me to a place with lots of other creatures—including hundfangs—and put me in a cage. But they took care of me."

His ears flattened as he paused, glancing at Cosmo, a faint smile tugging at his lips. "They fed me food balls there, and after a while, I developed a taste for them.

"When I got better, some two-legs came by and looked at me. I liked the attention, and they seemed to like me back. Anyway, they took me to their home and let me live with them. Their little two-legs didn't treat me well, so I ran off... well, more accurately, I limped off. I found living on the streets a lot harder with my bum leg. Finding food got difficult, and I started losing weight—getting dangerously thin. One day, at the park, a little two-leg girl came up to me. She seemed nice, so I followed her home. They let me stay with them, and I like it here." Murphy's whiskers drooped as he gazed at Zuzu. "So, that's my story."

Zuzu nodded, a flicker of amusement crossing her eyes, though the weight of their conversation tempered it. "At the place for creatures, they fed me food balls, too. I didn't develop a taste for them."

Murphy chuckled and turned to Josephine. "Your turn."

Josephine exhaled sharply. "I wish my story is as good as Murphy's, but truth is, I be wantin' an easier life. A life not spent always searchin' fo' my next meal or fightin' off other cats, rats, or hundfangs." She leaned back, her eyes distant for a moment. "One day, as I roamin' the hood, I sees a bunch o' two-legs in their yard, playin', eatin'—everthin' I like doin'. They gives me food, and since I ain't eaten in two days, I thought, these two-legs, they is nice creatures.

"So, I stays with them. And Zuzu, they keeps feedin' me—not them awful food balls like Murphy eat, but real, tasty eats. Zu, I knows a good thing when I sees it, so I plants my royal ass on their soft pillows and stays. Ain't been hungry since. I be a queen in Queens."

Cosmo's fur bristled at her words. "It's nice to know that you traded a life with me for an ass pillow."

Josephine gave him a derisive look. "You seems to enjoy that pillow too when you come a-callin' regular-like, curling up with me through the night."

She paused, reflecting for a few moments before speaking again, her voice a little softer. "Cosmo, livin' be mo' important than lovin'."

"I'd argue against that." His tail lashed once as he stood. "I need to get some fresh air."

The air grew heavy after Cosmo left the cave. Aura looked at Josephine. "He's right, and we both know it. I see the sadness in your eyes every time we get together and you look at Cosmo. It's plain to see that you still love him, and your decision to live with the two-legs haunts you."

"He still loves you, Jo," Murphy said gently. "You broke his heart."

Josephine's ears flattened against her head as she sighed and nodded. "You both right. My heart broke just as bad as his. Just as bad." She paused, her eyes flickering between them, the sadness evident. "I can'ts go back to what was. I done got fat, lazy, and pampered—that be a death sentence on the streets..."

She sighed again, her tone lighter, almost as if to break the tension. "But don't y'all worry, I still gots a little fire in me. Ain't no two-legs ever goin' to domesticate me."

Zuzu nodded, her eyes full of sadness. "Thank you both for sharing your stories. I understand why you made your choices now. I—I liked my life where everything was easy, and I see now how I was pampered beyond belief without even realizing it, but..."

Josephine finished the sentence for her. "But you felt emptiness with them material comforts, huh, Zu..."

"I did. I always longed for something more meaningful, but I didn't know what that might be. Until now. I know street life is hard and dangerous, but I love how exhilarating it can be, and..." She looked at Aura. "The wonderful feeling of having good friends who care for you."

Cosmo slid through the opening, looking less grumpy than when he left. He plopped down on his spot on the blanket. "Did I miss anything?" he asked, his tone surprisingly anger-free.

Josephine inwardly sighed, relieved that the potential for more hard words seemed to have passed. "Zuzu been tellin' us 'bout her life. She done good meetin' y'all." She looked at Cosmo with sincerity in her eyes. "Thank you for bein' who you is, takin' care of Zu. You a good cat, Cosmo. A good cat."

Cosmo's tail flicked, but he said nothing. His eyes lingered on her, the space between them charged with something unspoken. The silence stretched on, heavy.

"Thank you for your kind words, Jojo. You're a good cat, too."

Josephine softened at Cosmo's words. A rare moment of heartfelt sincerity crossed her lips. "I mess up, Cosmo. If I could do it ag'in..." She hesitated momentarily, her eyes glistening as she looked at Cosmo. "You know... I ain't proud o' how I left, Coz. I knows I hurt you."

Cosmo's tail flicked, his whiskers twitching with a rare vulnerability. He glanced away, his voice quieter than usual. "It hurt, Jo. But... you did what you had to do."

There was a heavy silence. The others exchanged glances, but no one spoke.

Josephine let out a short breath, her expression softening just a little. "Well, I ain't gonna sit here and cries about it. That your job, Coz."

Cosmo smirked, sarcasm flickering in his eyes. "I see you're back to being you."

Murphy, sensing the need for levity, broke the silence. "Well, now that we've all had our deep emotional therapy session, does anyone want to talk about food?"

Grateful for Murphy changing the subject, Cosmo gave him a slight nod and a half-smile.

A comfortable yet quiet air settled over the cat cave.

The soft rumble of Karma's breathing drew Aura's attention, and she suddenly realized his voice was absent from the cave. She turned to find him sleeping soundly, his breathing slow and steady. A slight twitch of his paw betrayed a faint dream, and her heart tightened.

She remembered how Karma had once thrived in moments like this—he was the heart of their gatherings, captivating everyone with his wit and charm. Tonight, he displayed none of this.

Cosmo caught her looking at Karma. His eyes met hers, and his tail twitched slightly. An unspoken heaviness filled the space between them.

She turned to the others, her ears drooping as a wave of dread washed over her. "I can't stand the thought of losing him. The idea of facing the world without Karma's steady presence—it's overwhelming."

Josephine sighed and nodded. "Karma... he always be the strong one," she said quietly. "He be a rock for us all."

"I know," Aura replied, her voice trembling. "But he's getting weaker every day, and I can't... I can't imagine being alone..."

Cosmo shifted uncomfortably, but his voice remained steady. "What do you mean 'alone'? You've got me, and you've got everyone here."

"I love you, Aura," Zuzu added, her voice filled with warmth. "I'll always be with you if you need me."

"Me, too," said Murphy. "You can live here in the cat cave if you need to."

"And it go without sayin' that I be here for you," Josephine added, her voice warm.

Aura shook her head, her eyes clouded with emotion. "Thanks, everyone. Your love touches my heart. But I don't mean being alone in that way. Karma was always my confidant, my mentor, my... well, my everything. When he's gone, I won't be anyone's little kitten anymore."

"He's been the same for all of us, Aura," Cosmo quietly added. "Each of us relies on him as much as you."

Everyone nodded in agreement.

"So," said Cosmo, his voice steady, "what's our way forward?"

"What do you mean?" Aura asked, puzzled.

"I mean, how do we make Karma's life as comfortable as possible?"

Aura sighed, the weight of the situation sinking in. "I thought that would fall on me—and only me."

Josephine reached over and affectionately touched Aura with her paw. "Well, girlfriend, you gots that wrong. I be helpin' you any way I can."

"Me, too," Murphy said with a wink. "If I soak my food balls in water, they're much easier to eat. I'll gladly go on a diet and keep Karma in food balls forever."

Cosmo smirked. "Damn, Murph, don't give him a reason to stop living." His quip lightened the mood, but then his expression changed. He grew serious, glancing at Karma with a rare tenderness before turning his gaze back to Aura. "I love him, Aura. Not in your tender, maternal way, but in a way that never forgets all the kindness and love he's shown me. I won't abandon him. Ever."

Aura's heart swelled, touched by his sincerity and the love of her friends. She looked at Zuzu with affection in her eyes. "I hope you see now what I meant when I said being part of our family is something. As you can see, those weren't just empty words."

Zuzu leaned in and touched her cheek to Aura's. "I see, and I love being part of this family."

As the evening wound down, the group settled into the quiet of the cat cave. Sad parts of the conversation still lingered in the air, but so did the sense of belonging. They were a family in their own way, bound together by the trials they had faced—and those yet to come.

With a mischievous twinkle in his eye, Murphy couldn't resist one last jest. "Well, you know what they say—the more cats in a room, the worse the smell."

Everyone but the sleeping Karma erupted into laughter, the sound echoing softly against the cat cave's walls. For just a moment, the worries of their world faded away.

After Josephine and Murphy left for their homes, the remaining cats curled together in their blanket nest, their fur brushing softly against each other.

Unable to fall asleep, Zuzu lay still, her eyes flicking to Karma as he rested. She could feel the quiet worry that seemed to hang over the group. They all seemed so focused on him—his frailty, his slowing movements, and the other changes that had come with age. As a former house cat who lived nearly her whole life with an elderly two-leg, she had no inkling of the concept of a cat family. Until now. She marveled at how one cat could mean so much to a group of cats—the way they all watched him and how their voices softened when they spoke of him. There was love between them, a deep bond—and a fear of losing something precious. Zuzu didn't know what the future would hold for Karma, or her, but one thing was clear: whatever happened, this family would hold on to each other through it.

9

A PALE WINTER DAWN crept through the cat cave's tiny window, casting a dim light on Aura's closed eyes. She stirred, blinking groggily, and stretched, the morning chill making her shiver despite her fur. Her breath puffed in soft clouds, lingering for a moment before dissipating into the cold air. She let out a long, slow yawn, savoring the quiet moment before glancing at the others. A pang of dread gripped her heart when she noticed Karma wasn't there. His usual spot beside Cosmo was empty. Her breath caught.

He's probably just outside, relieving himself, she told herself, trying to quell the panic that flared in her chest. She padded toward the cat cave entrance, stepping out into the biting cold. A shiver ran through her body as the chill penetrated through her fur.

The winter air nipped at her nose and lungs as she inhaled. She blinked a few times to adjust to the light, and when her eyes focused, she scanned the area for any sign of Karma—or any potential threats. The area around her, lightly dusted with snow, was peaceful and quiet. Too quiet.

Fear gripped her insides. Since their winter ordeal began, Karma had never wandered off without telling someone. He knew the dangers of doing this. And then it hit her—was he, in some way, fulfilling his earlier words, urging them to abandon him because of the burden he thought he was placing on them?

Zuzu joined her. "In the cat cave, I saw your worried look. What's wrong, Aura?"

Aura fought to keep her voice steady. "He's gone, Zuzu. Karma's not here."

Zuzu's fur puffed with alarm. "But... but he's always here."

"I know." Aura's gaze swept the area again, her heart racing in her chest. She tried to steady her breath, forcing calmness into her trembling limbs.

Time was slipping away, and she needed to act. "Since I can't see his tracks in the new snow, he's been gone for a while. We need to find him—quickly. I'm going to wake Cosmo."

Aura darted into the cat cave. She jolted Cosmo awake with a swift tap of her front paw, breathless as she explained what had happened. His eyes widened in alarm, mirroring her concern. Without a word, he scrambled outside to check. When he returned, his tail twitched nervously, and the tremor in his voice emphasized the seriousness of the situation.

"You know how Murph and I always prank each other, right?" Cosmo asked, his voice thick with anxiety.

"Karma's missing! How is that relevant right now?" Aura snapped.

Cosmo flattened his ears, his tail drooping in shame. He sighed, his voice trembling. "Last night, after everyone fell into a deep sleep, I snuck into Murph's house and peed in his food bowl. When I came back, Karma was still asleep." He inhaled deeply and sighed. "I don't know... maybe that woke him up, and he went out to relieve himself. If... if I'm the reason he left... I'll never forgive myself."

Aura's frown deepened. "You can't control his bladder. If he had to go, he had to go. Cosmo, he fell asleep early last night, so he probably just needed to relieve himself." She paused, thinking. "This makes the timeline clearer. He left after you went to Murph's place and before the snow started falling. So, he's been gone for two or three hours."

Relief softened Cosmo's features when Aura didn't blame him. "That makes sense, Aura. Given his slow gait, he can only be about four or five blocks from here."

Aura nodded. "I agree." Her gaze hardened, and she leveled a withering stare at him. "While I don't think you caused Karma to wander off, you do realize that if the two-legs had caught you in their house, your little prank could've gotten us found out and chased off. Stop acting like an immature young cat and think of the consequences before you act!"

He glared at her, ready to respond angrily, but then caught himself. His whiskers drooped, and he sighed, looking chastened. "You're right, Aura. You're right. It won't happen again."

Aura nodded curtly, accepting his heartfelt apology. "Good. Now, call Murph. We need him to help find Karma."

With Aura and Zuzu scampering behind him, Cosmo dashed around the cat cave and loudly called for Murph. Moments later, he squeezed through the back cat door and found Cosmo, Aura, and Zuzu near the cave, frantically waving for him to join them.

"What's wrong!" Murphy shouted as he neared them, his voice sharp with panic.

"Karma wandered off during the night!" Cosmo cried. His worry hung heavy in every syllable. "We can't find him."

Murphy's bulk quivered as his face tightened with concern. "He's not in my house, either. How far have you searched?"

"Just around the immediate area," Aura replied, her gaze drifting up to the falling snow. "Cosmo and I figured out he's been gone two or three hours, so with his slow gait, he can only be about four or five blocks from here."

"Damn," Murphy muttered. "That's still a big search perimeter. I have an idea—you three start looking for Karma, and I'll head to Jo's house to get her. The more eyes we have, the better."

"Good idea, Murph," Cosmo said. "Aura, how about you and Zuzu check the alleys behind the restaurants? I'll cover the streets around here."

"Let's do it." Aura agreed. "And we'll meet back here in two hours."

They all nodded and scampered off. As they scattered, the snow began to fall faster, threatening to cover any tracks left by Karma.

A block away, Aura suddenly halted, her gaze fixed on some partially covered tracks in the alleyway.

"Why'd you stop, Aura?" Zuzu asked, surprised.

"Look here, Zuzu—there's... something strange." Aura's paw trembled as she traced the partially buried paw prints. "If these are Karma's, he's walking in circles... like he doesn't know where he's going."

Zuzu's tail curled anxiously. "Oh my," she exclaimed, her eyes widening as she saw what Aura pointed out. "That's not good, is it?"

"In away, it is," Aura replied. "It means he's not moving as far as we thought. That gives us a better chance to find him."

"We'll find him," Zuzu said, though her voice lacked the conviction she hoped for. "Where do we search now?"

Aura flicked her head toward the path ahead. "We stick with the plan and head to the alleys behind the eateries."

The snow crunched beneath Murphy's heavy paws as he trudged toward Josephine's house on Roosevelt Avenue, just two blocks away. His breaths came in ragged, labored gasps. He stopped after only two hundred feet, panting. *You can do this, Murph. Catch your breath and keep moving,* he thought. In his street cat days, covering such a short distance—even at full speed—would have been effortless. Now, it felt like a marathon. His legs trembled beneath his bulk as he pushed on again.

By the time Murphy reached Josephine's house, he was spent—too winded to even call for her. After what felt like an eternity, he finally caught his breath enough to let out a short, raspy call, the kind Cosmo used to summon him.

Josephine heard it and scampered through a cat door like his. She gasped when she saw him, looking ready to collapse. "Murph, you okay? Brotha, you looks like you gonna die."

Murphy held up a paw, signaling her to give him a moment. His sides heaved as he took several deep breaths before speaking. "Jo, it's Karma. He wandered off during the night, and there's no sign of him. We need your help to find him."

She noticed how he struggled to get the words out and looked at him with concern. "Murph, you be lucky to make it back home. You rest here a while and catch yer breath. I'll go lookin' fo' Karma."

Murphy's eyes clouded with shame as he met her gaze, self-disgust written across his face. "Sorry, Jo. Look at me. I'm a fat mess."

"You is," she replied bluntly. "Murph, this here be yer wake-up call. Yer body can't handle the load—can't handle it. You ain't gonna last long if you don't do somethin' 'bout it."

He nodded. "I know. But, Jo, when food's right there, out in the open, I can't stop myself from eating it. No street cat passes up easy food, and that habit has never left me."

She sighed, glancing down at herself. "I hears ya. Look at the weight I be packin' on." Her fur brushed his as she touched her cheek to his. "We gonna talk later on this. Right now, Karma need us. Where they seachin'?"

"Aura and Zuzu are heading to the eateries, and Cosmo's checking around the areas near my house." Snow dusted his whiskers as he shook off the fresh flakes. "If you can find Cosmo, you two could look for Karma together."

"Good idea. You make yer way home when you ready." Worry darkened her eyes as she looked at him. "Murph, will you be able to climb a tree iffin' a demon hundfang come at ya?"

With sad eyes, he shook his head. "Even if a puny hundfang attacks me, I'm dead."

"Then you be extra careful goin' home. Extra careful, my friend." She touched her cheek to his again, then sped off.

As Cosmo padded silently down 43rd Avenue, his paws sank deeper into the freshly fallen snow, and a frown came to his face. His whiskers twitched with anticipation as he searched for any sign of Karma. The quiet street offered no clues about where his friend might have wandered off. Cosmo strode past rows of houses, his fur ruffling in the gentle breeze, scanning the usual spots where a seasoned, street-savvy cat like Karma might be hiding.

When he reached the intersection with 39th Avenue, Cosmo paused, his sharp eyes sweeping the surroundings. *Maybe Karma went to the park,* he thought, remembering the spot where they'd taught Zuzu to climb a tree. With a flick of his tail, Cosmo darted down 39th Avenue and raced toward Sunnyside Gardens Park. The snow muffled sound and scent, and the flakes annoyingly tickled his nose and whiskers as he ran.

As he neared the familiar sight of the park, the tall, leafless trees—branches weighed down by snow—reminded him just how cruel the timing was for Karma to be lost.

He quickened his pace as he entered the park, heading straight for the tree where Zuzu had learned to climb. His eyes scanned the quiet paths and empty benches. Nearing the tree, a flash of familiar color caught his eye. The unmistakable shape of a cat took form in the distance. His heart leaped in his chest. He raced toward it, bounding forward with joy as the shape came into focus—Karma!

The sudden appearance of Cosmo startled the dazed old cat. Karma hissed, his back arching as he lashed out at the perceived attacker. His claws narrowly missed Cosmo, who dodged with lightning speed.

Stunned by Karma's reaction, Cosmo shouted, "Karma, it's me—Cosmo!" But the words fell on deaf ears. The old cat's instincts had taken over. Like a gray blur, Karma struck again, his claws raking Cosmo's nose in a sharp swipe. Pain exploded across his face, and Cosmo staggered back, stars dancing in his vision as he cried out in agony.

Despite the searing pain, Cosmo's patience for Karma never wavered. He quickly composed himself, his body steadying. Slowly, deliberately, he lowered himself to the ground in front of Karma, adopting a non-threatening, submissive crouch.

"It's okay, Karma," Cosmo said gently, his voice low and soothing. "I'm not going to hurt you. It's me—Cosmo."

Breathing heavily, still poised to strike, Karma's eyes narrowed in confusion. His fur remained bristled, his gaze filled with distrust. But as the moments passed, a flicker of recognition dawned on him. Gradually, the tension began to ease from his body. Slowly, he dropped back onto all fours, his claws retracting.

"Cosmo?" Karma whispered, his voice thick with confusion, his eyes scanning Cosmo's face as if trying to piece together the fragments of his memory.

"It's me, my friend. I'm here to help you," Cosmo replied, pushing through the pain, his voice steady. "I've been looking everywhere for you—we all have."

Like fog lifting, Karma blinked slowly, his confused eyes beginning to clear. He took a cautious step forward and focused on Cosmo's face. "I... I'm sorry," he whispered, his voice cracking. "I didn't—didn't recognize you at first." His eyes flickered to Cosmo's bloodied face. "How... how did you get hurt, Cosmo?"

Despite the crushing pain, Cosmo smiled faintly, his eyes glinting with warmth and humor. "I tangled with a hundfang while looking for you. He got the worst of it, though."

Karma nodded slowly. "I don't like hundfangs."

"I don't either." Cosmo reached out, gently touching Karma's shoulder. "It's cold and snowing. How about we head home?"

Confusion flickered across Karma's face, and for a long moment, his tired eyes scanned Cosmo's face. Then, with a soft sigh, he nodded. "Yes. That would be nice. Home."

Cosmo's voice softened further. "C'mon, old friend. Our home's not far now."

Karma shivered. "I'm cold, Cosmo. Very cold."

"I know you are," Cosmo said with tenderness. "Stay close to me, and we'll be home soon."

Snowflakes danced around them as the snow drifted down in soft swirls. Karma and Cosmo started moving—slow, tentative steps. Each gentle step was meant to reassure Karma, to make him feel like everything was okay. Their paws sank deeper into the snow-covered path, which had been clear just two hours ago. Every heartbeat sent a fresh wave of pain through Cosmo's nose, intense enough that he barely noticed the fierce winter chill. The weight of Karma leaning against him grew heavier with each step, but

Cosmo stayed steady, his gaze shifting between the ground and the older cat.

Ice crystals clung to Karma's fur, now matted with snow. But he didn't notice—a good shake would clear most of it away. His eyes were distant and unfocused, and confusion clouded his expression as if the world around him were blanketed in a soft, white haze.

"Almost there," Cosmo said, trying to offer comfort in his voice, but his words seemed to fall on deaf ears. Karma let out a quiet sigh, his tail dragging behind him.

As they rounded the corner onto 43rd Avenue, a familiar voice cut through the falling snow with a sharp, urgent call.

"Cosmo! Karma!"

Josephine appeared through the falling snow as she ran toward them, her eyes wide with relief. "You find him!" she exclaimed. But when her gaze fell Cosmo's wounded face, her body tensed with shock and alarm.

"What happen?" she asked, her voice trembling.

"A hundfang," Karma answered absently. "A hundfang got us."

"I glad you okay, Karma," Josephine breathed, the tension melting from her shoulders as she let out a sigh of relief.

Confusion clouded Karma's eyes as he blinked at her. "How do you know my name?"

Josephine's tail dropped, and her eyes widened in surprise. She hesitated, unsure how to respond, and glanced at Cosmo.

"Karma," Cosmo said, his voice steady but quiet, "this is Josephine. She's a friend of ours."

Karma's whiskers twitched uncertainly. "I once had a friend... but he... or she... I once had a friend..." His voice trailed off, fading into the cold air like a whisper.

Josephine's face softened with sympathy. She stepped forward and gently touched Karma's shoulder. "It okay, Karma. We bring you home."

Cosmo glanced at Josephine, his face weary, streaked with blood. "Jojo, would you walk on the other side of Karma? We need to keep him warm."

Josephine nodded, still slightly open-mouthed in shock, and moved to the other side of Karma, pressing her shoulder against his. "We make sure you stay warm, Karma. It ain't far from home, okay?"

Karma nodded faintly. "Yes. Home... Yes."

As they headed home, Josephine's heart pounded with concern as she felt Karma's trembling legs, each of his steps a monumental effort.

Though exhaustion and pain gnawed at him, Cosmo kept his gaze on Karma as he walked, glancing at Josephine every so often. He couldn't shake the image of Karma's wild-eyed attack in the park and how he hadn't recognized either of them. As Karma's stumbling steps left an erratic trail in the snow, Cosmo knew that if Karma collapsed, he would die. Even if they made it back to the cat cave, Cosmo wondered if Karma would make it through the night.

Relief washed over him and Josephine as they reached the alleyway leading to the cat cave.

"We're almost home, Karma," Cosmo said, forcing as much excitement into his voice as he could. "Just a few more steps!"

Through the falling snow, the cat cave came into view. Josephine noticed Aura and Zuzu standing in the alley, pacing. "We here! We here!" she called out to her friends.

Joy lit up Aura's and Zuzu's faces as they raced toward them. "Karma!" Aura shouted, her voice flooded with relief.

Karma didn't greet her. His gaze drifted past her as if she were invisible, his eyes distant and unfocused, as though she weren't even there.

"Karma, are you okay? Can you hear me?"

Ignoring her, he turned to Cosmo. "Is she your friend, too?"

A shocked expression spread across Aura's face as she turned to Cosmo in disbelief. Her astonishment deepened when she saw his mangled nose.

"I'm fine, Aura. We just need to get Karma inside and warm him up." Cosmo pressed his cheek to Karma's. "We're home. Come on, let's get you settled." He glanced at Aura. "You go on ahead, and I'll help him in."

Without saying a word, Aura darted into the cat cave with Zuzu following close behind.

With abundant tenderness, Cosmo helped Karma get through the opening.

Inside, Aura greeted him. "Let's go to our corner sleeping spot, Karma. Zuzu and I will warm you up with our bodies."

Karma nodded and collapsed onto the blankets. Zuzu and Aura lay on either side of him, astonished by how cold his body felt. Within moments, he was sound asleep.

Cosmo and Josephine approached them.

"What happened to you, Cosmo?" Aura gasped, her voice quivering as she saw his bloodied face.

His whiskers drooped as he sighed. "I found Karma by Zuzu's tree in the park. He didn't recognize me and attacked me when I got too close. I managed to calm him down, and only then did he remember who I was." He nodded gratefully at Josephine. "Jojo found us while we were walking back. Together, we helped prop him up and get him home. I don't think I could've gotten him here without her."

Aura nodded with concern in her eyes. "Are you okay, Cosmo?"

He shook his head, glancing over at Karma. "This old street cat still packs a wicked wallop. I haven't been hurt this bad in a long time."

Zuzu looked at Cosmo with sad eyes. "I'm sorry he hurt you, Cosmo. He didn't mean to."

"I know, Zuzu. He's just tired, scared, and confused right now. He needs our patience, compassion, and love."

Zuzu nodded and curled up closer to Karma.

Cosmo looked at Aura. "Where's Murph? He must've alerted Jojo, so I want to thank him."

She shrugged her shoulders. "He's not here. We checked for tracks leading to his back door, but there weren't any."

Josephine's fur bristled. "Oh no... not Murphy, too..."

"What do you mean, Jo?" asked Aura.

"When Murphy get to my house, he outta breath somethin' fierce. Couldn't talk to me fo' a long time. Long time. I tells him to take his time and rest, then get home. Somethin' wrong. I best go find him."

Cosmo sighed and struggled to stand. "I'm going with you."

"No, you ain't, Coz. You hurtin' bad, so you stays here. I knows the path Murphy take, so I be findin' him soon."

Too tired and in too much pain to argue, Cosmo simply nodded.

After Josephine left, Cosmo nestled beside Karma, his head near the older cat's face. Like Karma, sleep came quickly. Outside, the snow continued to fall, covering their tracks with a silent white blanket.

10

SNOW SWIRLED AROUND HER as Josephine searched the alley, her muscles tense with worry. Her paws crunched softly through the fresh snow, each step mocking the stillness of the night. The bitter wind cut through her fur, a harsh reminder that she was lucky to no longer be a street cat.

Just as her worry over Murphy's absence began to spiral, a weak voice called out from a nearby backyard snowdrift.

"Jo... Jo!"

The call sent a jolt through her body. She spun, her tail lashing with anxiety as she searched for the source of the sound. A head poked out of the snow.

"Murphy?" she whispered, breaking the silence.

He heaved himself out of the snowdrift, his face etched with exhaustion and fear.

"I'm here," he croaked, his voice trembling with the release of tension.

"Why you be sittin' in a snowdrift when you so close to home?" Josephine asked, her tail swishing as she walked toward him.

Murphy's whiskers twitched nervously as his eyes darted around. "I was on my way home and spotted a demon hundfang. I saw it before it saw me, so I dove into the snowdrift. Thankfully, it didn't notice me. I've been waiting here, hoping it's gone."

Her ears swiveled in alarm, and Josephine glanced over her shoulder, scanning the area. "You be okay now," she assured him. "Ain't no hundfang. I been searchin' fo' you, worried sick."

Murphy let out a quiet sigh of relief, but his fur remained bristled with tension. "Jo, if I hadn't spotted that hundfang first..."

Josephine nodded. "You be okay now. Let's go back to yer home. I gots good news to speak at you."

She matched his slow, labored pace, falling into step beside him.

"We find Karma," she began, her voice low. "He safe, and he be in the cat cave now." Her ears flattened as she stopped and looked at Murphy with sad eyes. "Karma attack Cosmo when Cosmo found him. Attack him."

Murphy's tail shot straight up as his eyes widened. "Why? Is Cosmo hurt?"

Josephine closed her eyes briefly, her heart heavy. "Karma not know Cosmo. He think Cosmo goin' attack him, so he defend hisself. Cosmo, he gots a nasty nose hurt, but he be all right. Karma in bad shape, though. Bad shape. Cold. Tired. He confused, Murph, mighty confused. Cosmo and me barely get him to the cat cave. He sleepin' now, sleepin' heavy."

Murphy gave her a thoughtful glance. "Sounds like you all have your paws full."

"We do. But we all here for Karma. Cosmo restin' now, too. He hurtin' bad." Her eyes softened with relief as she paused and gave Murphy a heartfelt smile. "I glad you okay, too, Murphy."

When they reached the cat cave, Josephine darted through the opening, grateful to be out of the biting wind. Far from darting, Murphy struggled to squeeze through the tight entrance. His bulk filled the entire opening as he pushed through. Too tired to make a joke about failing to exhale as he entered, he simply greeted the others with a weary smile. Aura's and Zuzu's tense muscles relaxed as they saw everyone was safe. Aura scanned Murphy, checking for any signs of injury.

"I'm all right," Murphy said. "I had a close call with a hundfang and hid in a snowdrift until it moved off."

Warmth filled Aura's gesture as she touched her cheek to his. "Thank you for getting Josephine. Without her help, Cosmo wouldn't have been able to get Karma back here."

Murphy nodded. "How are Karma and Coz?"

Aura hesitated, her eyes darkening with concern. "Karma's asleep now. He's been through a lot. Cosmo's resting too... but he didn't come through unscathed either."

"I know. Jo told me—and how Karma didn't recognize him. Aura, how concerned should I be about Karma?"

Her tail drooped as she sighed, looking away for a moment. "I don't know, Murph. I'm hoping he'll be better in the morning after a good night's sleep."

"Me, too. If you want, I can try to bring some food balls for Karma."

A glimmer of amusement lightened Aura's face as she smiled and shook her head. "Your food passes through Karma's and Cosmo's systems in a rather unpleasant way."

Murphy chuckled. "Okay, I get it." His whiskers drooped with exhaustion as he sighed. "If you don't mind, I'll head out now. I'm sure my two-legs are wondering where I've been."

"I don't mind at all. Try to get some rest, too, Murphy. You look like you could use it."

He nodded. "I'll sleep like a kitten tonight." He turned to Josephine. "Thanks for coming for me. I owe you."

"We buds, Murph. Best buds." Her paw touched his shoulder with gentle affection. "When all this blow over, we goin' talk."

Murphy nodded, knowing that the talk would be about his self-esteem and food addiction. His gaze swept over the others. "Give Cosmo and Karma my best when they wake up. Goodnight, all."

He once more struggled through the opening and padded away.

Josephine inhaled deeply. "Well, I best be goin', too. Like Murph, I sure my two-legs be wonderin' where I is."

"Thanks for everything, Jo," said Aura.

After she left, the cat cave grew quiet. Aura turned to Zuzu. "I'm really glad I had your support today. It means a lot. Thank you."

Zuzu nodded. "I hope, like you said, Karma will feel better in the morning. And Cosmo, too." Her whiskers twitched as she paused. "Can I ask you something about Josephine?"

Aura glanced at her, puzzled. "Sure."

"Her words sound different, and it's hard for me to understand her. Why does she talk like that?"

A warm smile spread across Aura's face. "I've known Jo so long that her 'funny' language sounds normal to me now."

Zuzu's ears perked forward, her curiosity deepening as she tilted her head. "So, why do her words sound different?"

"Zuzu," Aura chuckled, "Josephine wasn't born here. She grew up in a faraway place—hot and humid, with no snow. She never even knew what snow was until she came here. Anyway, they talk like her down there. Her mom and dad lived with two-legs who arrived in one of those noisy moving boxes they use to get around. Jo said they were in that box for days before they finally got here."

Her voice softened as she continued. "When Jo got older, she got wild and rambunctious. She spent a lot of time sneaking out to play on the streets. That's when she met Cosmo. Those two were rabble-rousers, and they fell madly in love. Josephine left her mom and dad behind to be a street cat with Cosmo."

"I understand how the street life could be exciting," Zuzu said, nodding thoughtfully.

Aura nodded, but her expression darkened. "Before long, Josephine was expecting. She went back to the two-legs' home to have her kittens—five tiny little things, full of life and energy. For a while, Jo was so happy. But then... her happiness was taken from her."

Zuzu's fur prickled with anticipation. "What happened?" she asked, her curiosity piqued.

Aura inhaled deeply, bracing herself. "The two-legs gave her kittens away. Just like that, Zuzu. Didn't even think twice about it. Imagine what it would be like to lose your kittens—just have someone take them from you without a second thought."

She met Zuzu's eyes, her own filled with deep sadness. "But it got worse."

"How could it get worse?" Zuzu asked, her tail curling anxiously in confusion.

Aura's voice lowered to a near whisper. "The two-legs took her to a place like the one they took you and Murphy—a place where they cage other creatures. Jo said they cut her belly, and whatever else they did—it really hurt. When the two-legs brought her back home, Jo's mom told her she'd never be able to have kittens again."

Zuzu's eyes widened, a rush of disbelief flooding her. "Ever?"

Aura shook her head slowly. "Never, Zuzu."

"When she felt good enough to get around, Jo took off and joined Cosmo. She changed, Zuzu. Cosmo did his best to comfort her, but their relationship was never the same after that. The sadness of losing her kittens lingers in her to this day. And she never forgave her parents—or the two-legs they lived with. Jo said that about a year after she ran away, they got in their moving box, left, and never returned."

Aura hesitated, then added, her tone heavy with emotion. "You can't truly understand Jo until you know what shaped her. The loss of her kittens... it's something that stays with her. That's why she's so protective of those she cares about now. She's had her heart broken in ways I hope you'll never know."

Zuzu stared at Aura, her gaze filled with quiet understanding. "I'm glad Josephine has all of you to love her."

Aura nodded. Her voice was soft but sure. "It goes both ways, Zuzu. Look at what Jo just did for Karma and Murphy."

Zuzu's whiskers twitched in confusion as she thought for a moment before speaking again. "So, what Jo said about moving in with other two-legs to escape the streets—it... it doesn't make sense to me. If the two-legs treated me like they did her, I'd avoid them at all costs."

"I would, too. But Zuzu, regarding Jo, let me share some life wisdom: we shouldn't judge others until we've faced the challenges they've experienced on their journeys. Not every two-leg is the same. There are kind ones for every unkind two-leg. You mentioned the two-leg you lived with was kind, and Jo and Murphy say the two-legs they live with are good, too. Like cats, some two-legs are kind, while others are mean. We should judge others by their actions, not by the actions of others."

Understanding dawned in Zuzu's eyes, and she nodded thoughtfully. "You're right."

Aura smiled softly and touched her cheek to Zuzu's. "Come on. Let's join Karma and Cosmo and get some sleep. Tomorrow might be a hard day, so we need to rest while we can."

The peace of the night comforted them, letting the troubles of the day fade. Wrapped in each other's warmth, the foursome of cats slept soundly, safe from the dangers beyond their shelter.

11

THE SNOWSTORM FROM THE day before had passed, but outside, the world remained frozen in silence. Pale morning light filtered into the cat cave, where the group lay still, pretending to sleep. Their half-open eyes betrayed them, and they exchanged brief, quiet glances, all focused on the sleeping Karma.

A soft groan broke the stillness as Karma stirred slowly. As he sat up, his body protested with stiffness, his muscles aching and his joints creaking with each shift. Blinking, he adjusted to the dim morning light, his gaze first settling on Aura and Zuzu—curled together, unmoving, as if they hadn't shifted all night. He smiled softly, then turned his attention to Cosmo.

His body went rigid.

An ugly gash marred Cosmo's nose, crusted with dried blood, a stark contrast to the pristine faces of the other cats. The sight hit Karma like a physical blow, and his heart pounded, breath catching in his throat. For a moment, he forgot how to breathe. *What had happened to Cosmo?* he thought. *Had a hundfang attacked him? Or had another street cat tried to take over his territory?*

Time seemed to stretch as Cosmo's eyes met Karma's, their gazes locking for a few silent moments...

"Cosmo... what happened to you?" Karma's voice rasped, but his eyes softened with tenderness and empathy for his hurt friend.

Cosmo's whiskers twitched, and he forced a casual flick of his tail. He answered with a crooked smile. "I tangled with another demon hundfang. He got my nose, but I got the part of him that'll raise his voice a few octaves. Are you doing okay, Karma?"

Karma managed a weak smile. "I think so, but I really need to take a whiz."

His legs trembled as he tried to stand, his body stiff with resistance. He paused, swallowing hard as the world tilted and swam before his eyes. For a moment, he stayed still, letting the fog clear before pushing forward. His joints protested with every step. Determined, he forced himself to move, not wanting to reveal more weakness than he already had.

Cosmo sprang to his feet. "Hold up, Karma. Let me go first and check for hundfangs, just to be sure it's safe." Ignoring his pain, he stepped past Karma and darted through the opening. A moment later, he poked his head back inside. "All clear—come on out, Karma. I need to whiz, too."

After Karma left, Aura and Zuzu exchanged quiet glances.

"Karma sounded okay to me," Zuzu offered, her tail curling hopefully. "But Cosmo—I saw him wince in pain when he stood. He's still hurting."

"I noticed it too," Aura replied, her ears flattening with concern. She took a breath, then tried to shift the mood. "Hey, let's put on happy faces when Karma comes back. If all goes well, maybe you and I could head to the eateries and bring back some food for Karma and Cosmo. Or—" Her whiskers twitched with mischief. "I could ask if they'd like some of Murphy's food balls."

A purr of amusement rumbled in Zuzu's throat as she caught Aura's humor. "They'll be doing a lot more than whizzing after eating Murphy's food."

When Karma returned, Aura and Zuzu welcomed him back, rubbing against him and nuzzling his cheeks. The tension in his face eased, and a broad smile spread across his features in appreciation. "My, you two are chipper this morning. You must've slept well."

Before they could respond, Cosmo popped in, looking grim. "Brrr... it's still cold outside. If you don't mind, I'm going to rest some more."

Seeing how much he was hurting, Aura gave him an understanding nod. "Rest easy, Cosmo."

As Cosmo headed back to their sleeping corner, Murphy squeezed through the cave's opening, his enthusiasm making his usual waddle even more pronounced. "Good news, everyone—my two-legs just left in their moving box. They should be gone for a while. If you want, come into the house for some water and food balls!" His whiskers quivered with confusion as he paused, looking perplexed. "I have to warn you, though—I think my two-legs got different food balls. The new ones taste spicy and gamey—nothing like my usual ones."

Knowing what Cosmo had done to "spice" his food, Aura's whiskers twitched with suppressed laughter. She glanced at Cosmo and rolled her eyes as he dove under a blanket, trying to hide his grin.

"Thanks, Murphy—we could all use some water." Aura's eyes shifted to Cosmo again, noticing the blanket trembling with his uncontrollable giggling. "I'm sure Cosmo will take you up on your offer for some food balls, right, Cosmo?"

The blanket rippled with silent laughter, shaking even more. Cosmo raised a paw from beneath it, trying—and failing—to sound serious. "I'll... pass on the food balls... and just have... water."

"What's wrong with Cosmo?" Murphy asked, his tail swishing with concern.

Without missing a beat, Aura replied, "The way he's feeling, I'm sure anything spicy won't agree with him."

Inside Murphy's house, the warmth wrapped around them like a second coat of fur as the group gathered around his water bowl. Aura's ears drooped when she saw it was only half full—not nearly enough to satisfy everyone's thirst.

Murphy's whiskers perked up as he saw her concern. "Don't worry, Aura—there's plenty more water for you all. Come with me, and I'll show you where it is." He waddled down the hall, his bulk swaying, and led them into a small room with a large, white bowl mounted to the floor. Standing on his hind legs, Murphy peered into the bowl, his tail curling with satisfaction at what he saw. He looked back at the others with a smug grin. "This is where the two-legs store more water. Hop on up, Cosmo, and have your fill of the finest water in Queens."

Cosmo's muscles bunched as he leaped to the bowl's rim, looking into it with a satisfied smile. "Nice." He leaned down and lapped up a generous amount of water. Hopping off the rim, he glanced at Murphy. "That hit the spot. Thanks, Murph."

After they all had a long drink, Murphy walked with them to the cat cave. Inside, grief seemed to weigh heavily on Karma. He stood before them, head bowed, his eyes filled with remorse. "I remember what happened yesterday. I'm so sorry I hurt you, Cosmo. When you found me, I... I didn't recognize you. Everything looked strange and threatening. I thought—" His voice caught.

"You were just protecting yourself," Cosmo said gently, his voice soft with understanding. "I should have approached you more carefully."

Zuzu's fur rippled with concern as she moved closer to Karma. "We were so worried about you. What happened?"

Karma sighed deeply, his shoulders sagging. "I went out to whiz—something I've done countless times. But when I tried to return..." He paused, shame darkening his eyes. "The snow made everything hard to see. I kept walking, hoping to recognize something familiar, but everything looked wrong. Then I thought I heard a hundfang. I panicked... and I ran away as fast as I could." He fell silent, unable to continue.

Aura gently touched her cheek to his. "It could happen to any of us in those conditions."

"But it didn't," Karma said quietly, his voice as cold as the winter wind. "It happened to me because I'm old, and my mind isn't what it used to be. You all know this." His gaze met each of theirs with deep sadness. He turned away. "I can't trust myself to go out alone anymore."

The admission hung in the air like a weight none could lift. While heartbreaking, Karma's raw vulnerability and self-awareness also revealed a quiet strength. Admitting this—acknowledging his limitations—was both painful and courageous.

Cosmo's tail uneasily twitched as he shifted uncomfortably, unused to seeing such vulnerability in his mentor. "Karma, we can figure this out. Maybe we could—"

"Mark a trail," Aura interrupted, her ears perking excitedly. "We could create scent markers with our whiz to lead back to the cave entrance. Karma, even in the snow, you could follow them."

Thoughtfulness softened Karma's features as he considered this. "That might work, but..." He hesitated, then admitted quietly, "Sometimes I get confused, even with familiar scents."

"Then we go with you," Cosmo said simply. When Karma started to protest, Cosmo added, "Not to watch over you—to keep you company. That's what family does. Besides, one of us always needs to whiz, too."

"Karma," Zuzu said with heartfelt sincerity, "going out alone isn't safe for any of us right now." Remember the demon hundfang that tried to get into our cave? And Murphy had to hide in a snowdrift yesterday to avoid one."

Murphy nodded enthusiastically. "Zuzu's right, Karma. I was lucky to escape—thinking about what could've happened kept me up half the night."

Karma's ears perked at the news. "I'm glad you're okay, my friend."

Murphy nodded. "I'm glad you are, too. You scared us, Karma—all of us."

Absorbing their words, Karma spoke again, his voice steadier now. He looked at Cosmo and Aura. "I remember teaching you both that survival means constantly adapting to changing conditions. Maybe it's time I started following my teachings."

Murphy's whiskers drooped as he sighed. "My two-legs should be back soon, so I need to go." He moved to Karma and gently touched him with a paw. "We all love you." He looked at the others. "The next time my two-legs leave, I'll come for you so you can get more water. Why all of you don't feast on my food escapes me. Maybe you'll change your minds when your stomachs start rumbling in unison."

Amusement flickered across Cosmo's face as he smirked. "Murph, I'd rather eat tree bark than your damn food balls. Starvation would be my choice over what you dare to call food."

"Yeah, yeah," Murphy replied with a smile. "Like I said, they're an acquired taste."

He squeezed out of the cat cave, leaving the four cats to themselves.

Karma seemed sad to see Murphy leave. He sat, staring at the others, lost in thought. "Cosmo, I used to know these streets better than anyone. I taught you and Aura how to get around. Remember how I showed you two how to trust your noses to find your way? And now..." He paused, his voice cracking. "I get lost only a few feet away from home. I'm just a pathetic old cat now. Pathetic..."

A flicker of memory, tinged with sadness, flashed through Aura's mind—the time Karma had rescued her and Cosmo when they were two young, overconfident cats. They'd wandered too far from their usual haunts, and he'd tracked them down, following their scent and figuring out where they might have gone when the trail went cold.

He'd always been their protector, someone they could rely on, someone to show them the way back, no matter what. But now? That had passed. Karma knew it, and so did she and Cosmo. In a way, he was now their kitten, and they, the protectors.

"Karma, you're far from pathetic," Aura said in a smooth, calming voice. "Everyone and everything ages. It's the way of the world. Now, it's our turn to be your protectors. Cosmo and I owe you so much. We'll be there for you with joy and love in our hearts—the same kind of love you gave us."

A soft wag of Cosmo's tail accompanied his nod. "Aura's right, Karma. All that we are—it's because of you."

"I don't want to be a burden," Karma murmured, his voice barely a whisper. "I don't want to slow you all down, and it's obvious that I can't keep up anymore."

Watching him closely, Zuzu leaned forward and gently touched her paw to his shoulder. "Karma, I need you. You knew what to do in the underground corridor when the rats attacked us. You taught me how to defend myself, and you and Cosmo taught me how to climb a tree. I love having you as my teacher. I hope you'll keep teaching me in the days ahead."

Karma nodded, his eyes softening. "Thank you for your kind words, little one. You touch my heart. I'm glad you're with us now."

He paused, wrestling with his thoughts, then turned to Cosmo and Aura. "The urge to give up is growing stronger... but I'm not ready yet. Maybe soon, but not just yet. I still have something to offer, but when I can't anymore... you all need to let me go. Let me slip away with dignity. Promise me you'll do that."

Cosmo took a long moment, considering Karma's words. Then, he nodded thoughtfully. "When my time comes, that's what I'd want, too. So, I agree." He looked at the others, his eyes steady, silently asking them to agree.

Aura inhaled deeply, her heart heavy. She looked at Karma, her eyes filled with sadness. "Okay, Karma. I agree."

She turned to Zuzu, wanting the young cat to also have a voice in this.

"I... I agree, too," Zuzu said softly, her eyes mirroring the sadness in Aura's.

Karma nodded, his eyes glimmering with gratitude. "Thank you all," he murmured, almost to himself. "My dignity means everything."

Cosmo cracked a smile, his usual brashness returning. "All right, enough of this heaviness. I suggest Aura and I head to the eateries and scrounge for some real food. Karma, I know you're still tired, so how about you stay here with Zuzu?"

"Sounds good to me," Karma replied, though he hesitated. "But don't you need to rest as well? You must still be in pain."

"I'll be fine." Cosmo's gaze warmed as he looked at Zuzu, his expression serious. "Aura and I will feel better knowing Karma's in your capable care."

Zuzu beamed with pride at Cosmo's faith in her. Receiving such praise from him signaled how far she had come. "I'll defend Karma with my life, Cosmo," she said, her voice steady and full of newfound strength. It was a far cry from the naive, pampered cat she had once been.

When Cosmo and Aura slipped out into the cold, the cave felt quieter but not lonely. Karma headed back to their sleeping corner, curling up on the blankets. Zuzu sat near the opening, warmth spreading through her chest as she embraced her new role as a protector. As Karma drifted off to sleep, Zuzu felt a newfound sense of purpose. For the first time, she felt like a true member of the group, contributing something vital, just like the others.

She glanced at Karma's sleeping form and smiled. In the cat cave's silence, as she protected someone she loved, Zuzu understood what it meant to belong.

12

Guarding the cat cave, Zuzu observed the sunlight filtering through the garage window, shifting as time passed. Suddenly, the jarring crunch of paws in the snow interrupted her reverie. Instinct took over—her muscles tensed, her back arched, and she readied herself to strike.

But then, a familiar "Yoo-hoo!" echoed through the air. Relief washed over Zuzu as Josephine's head popped through the cat cave opening.

"Morning, little kitten," Josephine bellowed as she squeezed through the opening. "How ever'one doin'?"

Zuzu motioned at Karma's sleeping form, pressing her paw gently to her face to hush her. "Karma's sleeping," she murmured. "Cosmo and Aura went to find food."

Josephine nodded, settling herself near Zuzu and keeping her voice low. "How Karma doin'?"

"Better, I think. But..." Zuzu hesitated, her thoughts drifting back to the conversation from this morning. "He made us promise to let him go when he feels he has nothing left to offer."

"That sound like Karma," Josephine whispered, understanding. She studied Zuzu's unsettled eyes. "What be troublin' you, girlfriend?"

Zuzu shifted her weight, appearing uneasy. "Aura told me about you last night—about where you came from... and..." She hesitated, unsure whether to continue."

"Abouts my kittens and me and Cosmo?" Josephine asked gently.

Zuzu nodded. "I hope you're not angry she told me."

"No, Zu. That be part of who I is." Josephine gently touched Zuzu. "Family share both the hard and the good, Zu. Our pain and joy bind us together. It how we learns to love and care fo' each other."

Josephine's gaze drifted to the window for a moment before she turned her gaze back to Zuzu. "Did Aura be tellin' her story to you?"

Zuzu shook her head. "No. Other than Karma raising her, I don't know that much about her."

The cat cave grew quiet as Josephine paused, considering her words carefully. "Have anyone told you 'bout Ajax?"

"Nothing but Murphy and Cosmo saying he was their friend, and a hundfang killed him and wounded Murphy."

"Ajax be mo' than Cosmo and Murph best friend. He Aura's mate."

Shock widened Zuzu's eyes. "I didn't know Aura had a mate."

"She carryin' his kittens when he die." Josephine's voice grew soft as memory took hold. "Five beautiful little ones she have: Kiki, Pogo, Mimi, Rolo, and Gizmo. But without Ajax..." She shook her head sadly. "Times be hard. Food be scarce. Aura can't make enough milk to feed all 'em. Mimi and Rolo... they die."

Zuzu sat perfectly still, listening, her heart tightening with sadness. She could hardly imagine the pain Aura must've felt, carrying her dead mate's kittens and then losing two of them. The air around them grew heavy with palpable sorrow, like an unseen presence gripping them. Aura's story quickly turned even more tragic.

Josephine continued. "Pogo die next. Without Ajax and Murphy injured bad, Cosmo struggle hard to defend our territory. A nasty gang o' street cats attack one day. Killed Pogo." Pain cracked through Josephine's voice. "Then Kiki... po' little Kiki..."

"What happened?"

"Karma find Kiki. Told Cosmo a big movin' box runs over her. She so squashed he only recognize her tail. Only her tail..." Josephine swallowed hard. "Karma and Cosmo, they never tells Aura the details. I glad they don't—and don't you be tellin' her neither."

"I won't. I promise," Zuzu said with conviction. "What... what happened to Gizmo?"

Josephine shrugged. "Gizmo leave. He move to The Bronx—so far away it be like movin' to the moon for us cats. We never hears from Gizmo ag'in. The pain of losin' his siblin's too much for him, Cosmo say. That why he leave."

Zuzu moved closer to Josephine, saying nothing, her eyes glimmering with empathy.

Josephine broke the silence with a whisper. "Now you knows the hard times me and Aura have. Hard times, little kitten. Deep pain—deep pain you feels in yer bones... That why Aura and me tight. Real tight. Our sufferin' be our bond."

They sat silently for a while, letting the words settle between them.

Josephine took a deep breath. "Now you understands why Aura be so protective of us. Why she take a shine to you. Why she fight for you, little kitten. You like one of her own now."

Understanding dawned in Zuzu's eyes as she nodded and looked at Karma sleeping peacefully. "It explains why she's so scared of losing Karma."

Josephine nodded. "It do. But that only part o' it. She 'fraid o' losin' Karma 'cause he the one who gets her through the hard times. He get me through the hard times, too. He a special cat, Zu. A mighty special cat. Aura and me, we scared that when Karma gone, who gonna get us through the next hard times?"

Her breath caught, and a deep sigh escaped her as she paused, lost in thought. "Street life—it tough. It hard and unforgivin'. Ev'ry street cat—and former street cats likes me and Murph—carry diff'rent pain—hunger, loss, sadness, injury. But we keeps going. We finds new ways to love and survive. Like Aura do with you, and you does with Aura."

Karma shifted, moving his weight to his other side, but he didn't wake.

With the gentleness she'd learned from watching Aura, Zuzu touched Josephine's paw. "What hurts do you have now, Jo? I mean, besides losing your kittens and parents?"

Something in Josephine's expression changed as she stayed silent for a moment, her thoughts drifting to the past before she finally spoke. Her voice was heavy, like her memories. "Cosmo. He my biggest hurt now."

"Why?" Zuzu asked, her voice filled with curiosity and concern.

Josephine's gaze fell to her paws as she took a long, slow breath. "Oh, little kitten, that be a hard one to answer." She exhaled shakily, her voice dropping to barely more than a whisper. "After they cuts on me, well... I... I ain't got no mo' desire to get physical—no urges that a female cat have. Cosmo try to be patient, but he a healthy, good-lookin' male cat—he got urges too that I can't meet. He get frustrated with me. Powerful frustrated. He start gettin' a wanderin' eye, start satisfyin' them urges he have."

Josephine paused, her eyes distant as if she were trying to distance herself from the memory. "So, I leaves him," she said softly, her words heavy as if they were choking her. "But... I still loves Cosmo. Loves him mo' than I can say. He... he my one true love, Zu. To this day, leavin' him tear me apart..."

She swallowed hard, a flicker of regret passing over her features. "That why I be unkind to you when we first meet. I thinks you another playthin' o' his."

In just a few words, Josephine conveyed a world of hurt, leaving Zuzu reeling with sadness. She touched her head to Josephine's shoulder, a touching gesture of comfort. "I'm sorry, Jo. I see how hard this has been for you."

A deep sigh escaped Josephine, heavy and slow. "It ain't just Karma who fightin' to keep goin'. I been fightin' too. Ev'ry day a struggle to keeps my head up, to keeps from fallin' apart. I don't know how many times I thinks I can't go on. Sometime it feel like the whole world closin' in on me. But then, ev'ry full moon, weather permittin', Cosmo come to my home and sneak in. We curls up through the night, lovin' on each other. It the reason I go on, Zu. He precious to me. Stupid cat he is, but I loves him. So, we goes on fo' each other. We goes on fo' family."

Josephine offered a small, rueful smile. "Life ain't easy, little kitten. Love ain't easy neither..."

"Thank you for sharing your story with me, Jo," Zuzu murmured. Her eyes held Josephine's, and for a moment, she considered the depth of what she'd just heard. "I understand you and Aura better now. You have me now. I'm a good listener."

Josephine smiled softly. "I is, too, little kitten. When you needs to talk, I be here fo' you."

Their words lingered, and the silence that followed, no longer uncomfortable, resonated. In this moment of sharing, a bond formed between the two—a bond that would seal their friendship for years to come.

Josephine shifted on the cold concrete floor, her eyes soft as she gazed at Zuzu. "How you holdin' up, Zu?"

A flicker of surprise crossed Zuzu's face at the question. She blinked, not expecting it, and shrugged, her shoulders tight. "I'm all right."

Josephine's whiskers twitched as she studied Zuzu for a moment, noticing the subtle tension in her movements. "We friends now. We shares things. Even sad and uncomfortable things. What troublin' you?"

Distress rippled through Zuzu as she shifted uneasily. "Everything seems... everything seems to be happening so fast. Scary things." Her voice dropped to a whisper. "I... I have to fight to keep from falling apart, too..."

Josephine looked at her with understanding. "Little kitten, I knows things seem overwhelming and scary fo' you. Street life be so much diff'rent than housecattin'. But we here fo' you." Her gaze softened as she glanced back at Karma. "Likes you, Karma feelin' overwhelmed and scared, too. But we here fo' him, too."

Zuzu nodded. "Thanks, Jo." Her gaze shifted to Karma, then back to Josephine. "What was Karma like... you know... when he was younger?"

Josephine felt a lump form in her throat at the question. "Karma... he amazin' back then. Amazin'. He a deep thinka and he a father to all us. He be gentle, but he be fierce when he have to. That big heart he have touch so many with kindness. So many..."

Her paw touched Zuzu with gentle affection. "Karma be carryin' us fo' a long time, and I thinks he finally feelin' the weight of it." She paused as the memory of his words came back to her—words he had shared with her during her darkest times. The words still echoed in her mind. "Karma once tell me, 'Jo, life have its way o' changin' things. We just haves to learn when to hold on and when to let go.'"

The sunlight seemed to dim as Josephine fell silent, her mind drifting through memories. With his gentle love and wisdom, Karma had once been her anchor—supporting her through the loss of her kittens, parting from her parents, and leaving Cosmo. Now, his words about knowing when to hold on and when to let go took on new meaning as she realized they might soon apply to Karma himself.

13

COSMO AND AURA RETURNED to the cave in a comical fashion. Each gripped a large, half-eaten slice of pizza in their mouths as they squeezed through the narrow opening. They froze when they spotted Josephine sitting with Zuzu, looking at them with an amused smile playing on her face. Their surprised expressions quickly softened into affection as they dropped their pizza and rushed to greet her with enthusiastic nuzzles.

Zuzu, noticing that Karma was still asleep, lowered her voice. "Is that... pizza?" she asked, hopeful.

Josephine grinned and nodded, whispering, "Yep, that be pizza. They gots some serious eats fo' Karma and you!"

Cosmo picked up the pizza slice and set it in front of Zuzu, squinting at it in confusion. "Pizza? That's what two-legs call this stuff?"

The familiar aroma brought back memories of her old life, and Zuzu nodded eagerly. "I love pizza. Mrs. Chen used to get it a lot, and she called it pizza."

Cosmo flashed a playful grin at Zuzu and touched his paw to the slice. "You've earned this for taking care of Karma. Enjoy."

Zuzu didn't need to be told twice. She bit off a large chunk, her eyes sparkling with delight. "This is really good!" she declared, her tail happily flicking as she chewed.

The sight of Zuzu enjoying the simple pleasure made Aura chuckle. They rarely got a treat like this, and seeing Zuzu so overjoyed lightened the day's heaviness.

The raw wound on Cosmo's nose caught Josephine's attention as he looked at her, genuinely pleased that she had come to check on Karma. "Thanks for coming, Jojo. How are things here and with you?"

She frowned. "I don't sleep good worryin' 'bout Karma. Everthin' fine here, so I be be good now. Karma quiet as a mouse. Me and Zu havin' good talk."

Zuzu's ears flicked at the mention of her name, and she glanced up at Cosmo while chewing. "Jo told me about Karma's younger days—and everything he did for all of you."

Moving with the silence she'd learned on the streets, Aura quietly walked to Karma and gently set the pizza slice dangling from her mouth close to his nose. Her tail twitched as she crouched by him, studying him for signs of distress. There didn't appear to be any as he peacefully slept.

Smelling the food, Karma stirred. His eyes brightened like a young cat's as he caught sight of the pizza. A wide grin spread across his face. "I thought I smelled something. This looks tasty."

"Good morning, Karma. Zuzu says the two-legs call it pizza. I hope you like it."

"I'm sure I will." With effort, Karma slowly sat up, his body stiff from the night's sleep. He surveyed the cave and gazed at the others.

"Good morning, my friends. Cosmo, how are you feeling?"

"I'm okay," Cosmo replied. "And how are you?"

"Hungry. This old cat is mighty hungry."

The tension of the morning lifted as Cosmo smiled and motioned to the pizza slice in front of Karma. "Well, quit yapping and dig in—it's all yours."

Karma grinned and took a bite. "Oh my, this is tasty!"

As Karma and Zuzu ate, Cosmo, Aura, and Josephine sat on the floor near the cave entrance. Their voices dropped to a hushed murmur—just loud enough to hear each another.

Josephine studied Cosmo's face, wincing at his raw nose. "Cosmo, I mo' worried 'bout you than Karma right now. Yer nose look painful."

He sighed. "Yeah, it hurts a lot, and being out in the cold doesn't help."

She frowned, her gaze drifting to Karma, who looked content as he feasted on his pizza. His expression softened when he caught her looking.

"I'm all right, Jo," he said, sensing her concern. "You don't need to worry."

Josephine hesitated, then nodded. "I hopes so. You been through a lot, Karma."

Karma smiled faintly, his eyes showing weariness but also something resolute. "We've all been through a lot lately, but we'll be fine."

The morning passed as Josephine chatted cheerfully with the others, but eventually, she knew she had to head back home.

Shortly after she left, as silence settled over the cave, two-leg voices filtered through the thin walls. Footsteps in the snow grew louder, and the cats' hearts skipped in unison. Just then, Murphy burst in, eyes wide and frantic.

"My two-legs spotted all your tracks and are heading this way!" he shouted, his voice high and panicked. "If they open that door, sit and look at them with pitiful eyes. Pitiful eyes, just like I showed you!"

His panic intensified theirs, and they all straightened, eyes fixed on the cave door. Murphy moved beside Zuzu. The heavy crunch of footsteps in the snow sounded deafening. Battle instinct surged through Cosmo's muscles as he clenched his teeth, the urge to fight welling up inside him. He forced himself to remain still, though his taut muscles twitched, poised to spring at any moment.

The big door creaked and groaned as it slowly opened, sunlight flooding the cave.

Murphy whispered, his voice filled with desperation. "Everyone, sit down! Let's melt their hearts and make them feel sorry for us!"

They obeyed without hesitation, settling onto their haunches, eyes wide with sadness and helplessness—including Murphy's.

When the door creaked fully open, the two-leg male and female froze, blinking at the sight of five cats—including their own—staring back at them with woeful eyes. For a moment, both cats and two-legs stared in shock, neither group expecting to encounter the other.

Despite the situation's urgency, Cosmo fought the urge to burst into laughter. Murphy's two-legs were as large as him, their bellies equally prodigious.

The two-legs spoke in their strange language, their heads nodding in that familiar way Murphy knew meant they'd reached some agreement. Slowly, the male two-leg lowered the door, and it shut with a soft thud. Relief flooded through the cats as the sound of the two-legs' footsteps faded away.

Murphy let out a shaky laugh. "See? The pitiful look works every time."

"Damn, Murph," Cosmo said, "your two-legs are as round as you—do you all just sit around gorging on food balls all day?"

Murphy grinned. "We all like to eat."

The brief moment of humor evaporated as Murphy's smile faded, his eyes darkening with concern. He looked at the others, his voice low and grim. "Trouble's coming—trust me. My two-legs will call other two-legs. They'll come and take you—and maybe me—to that horrible place—the one with the cages."

Determination hardened Cosmo's features as he stood. "Then we can't stay here. We need to leave. Now."

The other cats nodded in agreement, but an unspoken question lingered—where could they go, especially with so many unknowns and dangers?

Zuzu voiced her concern. "Are we going back to the underground place with the pipes and rats?" Her voice trembled with worry.

Karma's wisdom shone through in his calm, steady voice. "How about my place?" he suggested quietly. "It's calm and mostly free of rats."

The others turned to him, intrigued but uncertain.

"Karma, it doesn't have heat," Aura pointed out. "Maybe we should go back to the corridor. It's heated there. We could have Jo come with us and help clear out the rats."

Cosmo spoke, his tone firm. "Karma, Aura's right about the heat. And remember how big the rats were there—it's because there's an eatery in the building with plenty of food."

Karma nodded slowly, his gaze distant as he thought. "The rats in that corridor were unlike any I've ever seen—brave, vicious, determined—and so plentiful. Even with Jo, there are too few of us to stand a chance against them."

He paused and looked at them with reassuring eyes. "I know my place is humble and unheated, but there's water and space to move about. I found peace there. As for warmth, like here, we can huddle together, just as we've done before. It's our safest option for now."

After listening to Karma, Murphy nodded slowly. "As usual, Karma makes excellent points. I'm in no shape to fight rats, and Jo isn't used to fighting anymore... except for when it comes to tongue-lashing someone."

Cosmo chuckled at his remark, knowing it was spot-on. His expression turned serious. "Of the six of us, only Aura and I can fight, and right now, my injured nose won't take kindly to rats biting it. So, I think Karma's place is where we need to go." He looked at the others. "Everyone gets a vote. Raise your paw if you think we should move to Karma's place."

He raised his paw, as did Murphy, Karma, and Zuzu. After a moment's hesitation, Aura raised hers as well.

"It's settled, then," said Cosmo.

That evening, the shadows stretched long in the moonlight as they set off, moving through the quiet streets silently and slowly, careful not to overtax Karma. They paused often, letting him rest when needed.

When they reached Karma's place, they saw the damage the storm had caused—the fierce winds had shattered more windows, leaving the building even more exposed to winter's vagaries.

Walking in single file, they entered the secret entrance to the building. Knowing the way, Cosmo led them through the dark aisles, past piles of decaying fabric scraps and forgotten machinery, until they reached Karma's den—the room that had once served as the women's restroom. Dripping water echoed in the darkness as the corroded sink faucet still leaked, its steady sound cutting through the quiet.

Aura's whiskers twitched. Unlike Murph's relatively cozy cat cave, she noted how the broken see-through things let the cold outside air flood in. She couldn't help but worry about how the temperature would affect Karma. Putting on a brave face, she looked at the others. "Let's get settled in."

Weariness showed in Karma's legs as they trembled slightly from their long walk, but his voice remained steady as he gestured to the room's far corner. "From experience, I know it's warmest over here. Come join me, my dear friends."

They settled into the room, the silence hanging heavy between them. Karma looked at his companions, who seemed burdened by the uncertainty of their future. Once more, he offered comfort. "We're safe. We have water. And we have each other."

Aura nodded. "You're right, Karma. We need to focus on the moment and not the future."

The others nodded in agreement.

In the cold of the night, they huddled together, creating a small island of warmth. Gratitude filled them for this brief respite. What tomorrow held was uncertain, but for now, in the stillness, this peace was enough.

14

A SUDDEN, WHITE-HOT LANCE of pain pierced Cosmo, jolting him awake. Stars exploded in his vision as he bit back the urge to wail. Someone—he wasn't sure who—had shifted in the night, their bony limb striking his injured nose. As the throbbing pain gripped him, he glanced at the others, wanting to erupt in anger at whoever had savaged him. But all were lost in sleep, huddled tightly together for warmth, unaware of his suffering. Knowing it was an accident, he retracted his claws. His precarious composure—already strained by the cold and the ordeal of the past few days—was now on the verge of shattering completely. The pain, now beating in rhythm with his heart, echoed the challenges of the past few days.

For a moment, Cosmo fought the urge to slip away from the pile of warm bodies surrounding him. He longed for the peaceful solitude of his old days—days of quiet and freedom from responsibility. But as the cold gnawed at his fur, he hesitated. The warmth of the others, even if it brought discomfort, was something he needed. With a deep sigh, he accepted that no matter how much he craved solitude, tonight wasn't the night to leave them.

He repositioned himself, turning his head away from the others to reduce the chance of another nose strike. With a sigh, he closed his eyes, unclenched his teeth, and focused on his breathing to calm himself. Soon, sleep claimed him again.

The first rays of morning sunlight crept across the concrete floor, gently stirring Aura from her slumber. A soft smile tugged at her lips as she observed the peaceful scene before her: the other cats, curled together in a tight, furry knot, breathed in contented unison, their bodies rising and falling in perfect harmony as they shared their warmth in the cool dawn air. Her throat felt parched, so she padded to the sink, where the lonely drip of the faucet echoed in the stillness. Each breath plumed out before her, a frosty cloud swirling in the frigid air. With a graceful leap, she landed on the sink and lapped at the dripping water, its coldness a sharp reminder of winter.

Cosmo also stirred and quietly moved toward her. They brushed cheeks in a silent, tender greeting, a small gesture reflecting their deep sibling bond.

"I saw you lapping up some water," he whispered. "I'm thirsty, too."

"How did you sleep?" she asked softly.

Cosmo frowned, a brief wince twisting his features. "Someone shifted in the night and whacked my nose. It hurt so bad that I saw stars."

Aura's eyes conveyed sympathy. "Sorry, Cosmo." Her gaze shifted to his nose and face, which were covered with dried blood.

A moment of silence passed, and then she spoke softly. "After you drink, I can help with that. I'll lick the dried blood off. It might sting, but it needs to be cleaned."

Cosmo's ears flattened with dread. "It's crazy tender, Aura. Licking it will put me in agony."

She nodded, her voice soft but firm. "I know, but it's got to be cleaned. You know it's the only way it'll heal properly."

He gave a reluctant nod and moved toward the dripping water.

Aura watched him drink, his movements slow and deliberate, as if savoring each lap of the cold water. But she knew he was trying to delay the inevitable. After quenching his thirst, he let the water cascade down his face, moistening his nose and the surrounding fur to make it easier for Aura to clean. Finally, he met her gaze, a flicker of resigned dread in his eyes. He sighed deeply, then gave a solemn nod for her to begin..

She wet her tongue under the flowing water and then moved closer to him.

"Ready?" she asked, her voice soothing.

Cosmo frowned. "Let's get it done," he said, flicking his tail. He squinted, bracing for the pain that would soon come.

Aura started on Cosmo's face, licking the blood-matted fur. With each gentle stroke, the crimson stains faded, revealing the short, firm fur beneath. She was patient, taking her time to do it right.

Aura's eyes met his. "It's time to do your nose," she whispered, her voice as soft as a caress.

Every muscle in Cosmo's body tensed as he scrunched his face and gave a hesitant nod, his body taut with anticipation.

Aura leaned in, her breath warm against his face. Gently, she licked the dried blood from the non-wounded sides of his nose. The easy part was over.

Now came the hardest part—tending to the wound itself.

The moment her tongue touched the raw, torn skin, a sharp, anguished cry tore from Cosmo's throat, shattering the stillness of the morning and startling Karma and Zuzu.

In unison, Karma and Zuzu sprang to their feet in a panic, fearing a hundfang or rats had found their way in. They quickly spotted the source of the cry—Cosmo.

"Cosmo, what's wrong?" Karma cried. He and Zuzu rushed to his aid.

Aura's eyes met his from above the sink. "It's okay. We're cleaning his wound. It hurts a lot, but it's necessary."

"How much longer?" Cosmo hissed, tormented by the pain of Aura's well-intentioned care.

"Cosmo, I just started on the wound. I'll hurry as fast as I can. Try to keep your breathing steady, okay? Deep breaths. It might help take the edge off."

She worked gently, but a few spots required firmer strokes. Each stroke brought fresh cries of agony from Cosmo.

Knowing he caused Cosmo's anguish, Karma bowed his head in shame. "I'm so sorry, Cosmo. So sorry."

Cosmo didn't answer, likely not hearing Karma over the roar of his pain.

At long last, Aura finished. "Okay, we're done. Cosmo, your face and nose look much better."

Quivering in pain, Cosmo ignored her and leaped off the sink. Panting heavily, he returned to the sleeping area, where he collapsed and curled up.

Horror-stricken by the ordeal, Zuzu looked at Aura with wide, fearful eyes. "Will... will Cosmo die, Aura?"

Aura shook her head. "No, Zuzu. He won't die, but he's in for a few more rough days." She glanced at Cosmo, then back at the others. "Let's give him some space to collect himself and calm down. Karma, if you're up for it, maybe you could show us the best eateries around here. I'd love to find something good for Cosmo to eat."

"Brilliant idea," Karma beamed. "I know a few places not far from here. If there's no trash can food, we can dispatch some rats who dine there, too."

A while later, they returned. Karma and Zuzu each proudly carried a rat by its tail, while Aura held two—ample bounty for all.

Cosmo blinked at them, still a little dazed. "Wow, I see what you all have been up to. We'll be eating good today." His eyes met Aura's, and he chuckled at the two rats hanging from her mouth. "Thanks for what you did. My nose feels better, and having a clean face feels good."

Aura dropped the rats in front of him and smiled. "You're welcome. You look much better without a bloody face." She nudged the larger of the two rats toward him with her paw. "This one's the biggest. It's yours." She turned to the others with a playful glint in her eyes. "Let's eat!"

After feasting on the tastiest rats Queens had to offer, the contented cats stretched out, their bellies full. The factory's quiet settled over them, bringing a rare sense of peace.

Cosmo tilted his head slightly, sensing something. A glimmer of recognition crossed his face as he figured it out—his inner ears detected subtle air pressure changes. "Hey, everyone, it'll be warmer tomorrow."

Karma nodded in agreement. "I feel the pressure change, too. My old bones will welcome even a little bit of warmer weather. I know some places in here where the sun comes through the see-through things and shines on the floor. Lying in the sun there is quite pleasant."

"Maybe there are warmer places in here to sleep," Zuzu added, excitement sparking in her voice at the prospect of exploring the old factory. "Also, on the way in, I spotted some soft old cloth we could drag to our sleeping corner. It might help keep us warmer at night."

Aura's eyes brightened. "Good thinking, Zuzu. Show me where you found it."

Pride filled Zuzu's chest as the others listened to her ideas without hesitation. It made her feel like an equal. Although she knew she wasn't fully one yet, knowing that her thoughts and ideas mattered just as much as theirs brought her comfort.

As Aura and Zuzu collected materials to make their sleeping area cozier, Karma pointed out to Cosmo the best spots in the building for observing potential threats while remaining hidden. Once again, the old cat impressed Cosmo.

The following days brought welcome changes. The air warmed, though it remained far from comfortable. The snow around the city began to melt, leaving wet patches and puddles that made traveling unpleasant on their paws. Still, the thaw brought the promise of an easier life. Karma made the most of the sunlight filtering into the building, finding a new resting spot on the third floor that afforded spectacular views of the two-legs' dens reaching to the sky.

Adventure ignited in Zuzu as she became an eager explorer of the factory, often with Aura by her side. Together, they ventured through the long-abandoned halls, uncovering soft cloth for bedding and other forgotten objects that could prove useful.

The searing pain in Cosmo's nose lessened with each passing day. As the discomfort faded, his mood improved. He prowled the factory, silently assessing every nook and cranny. Here, a discarded pallet could become a barricade; there, a ventilation shaft offered a potential escape route.

For the first time in a while, peace settled over Cosmo. A small, satisfied purr rumbled in his chest. *Maybe this abandoned place, discarded by the two-legs, could be their home,* he thought. More and more, Aura echoed his thoughts about staying at the factory permanently.

With increasing frequency, Cosmo joined Karma at his resting spot to bask in the sunlight warming the concrete floor. They sat in companionable silence, each lost in their thoughts until a memory surfaced. "Remember that time we...?" one would begin, a twinkle in their eyes. To Cosmo's surprise, he found comfort in the nostalgia, caught between bittersweet and heartwarming memories. Often, the others joined them, eagerly asking Karma to share his captivating stories or simple wisdom.

All seemed well with the foursome... until...

15

It began subtly—just a faint throat clearing, barely louder than a whisper, or perhaps only a gentle cough. Not enough to stir the other three cats from their peaceful slumber.

But then, the quiet stillness of the night broke with the harsh sound of a full-throated cough.

Cosmo's ears twitched, disturbed by the foreign, unsettling noise. Another cough came—louder this time—followed by a soft groan. Beside him, Karma shifted restlessly, ragged breaths escaping him.

Cosmo's heart clenched. "Karma?" His voice was low, filled with concern.

Karma's eyes fluttered open. "Nothing to worry about," he rasped, his voice rough. He tried to sit up, but his body shook as another deep, wet cough seized him, followed by faint wheezing. "I need water."

Aura and Zuzu gazed at Karma with concern. Aura gently touched him with her paw. "I don't like the sound of that cough."

Karma forced a smile, but it didn't reach his eyes, which remained clouded with discomfort. "It's just a little cough. Probably just a dry throat."

But Aura wasn't so sure. The old cat had always been tough, downplaying any hardship, but his erratic breathing hinted at something more serious. Her worry deepened, though she remained silent. The thought of something being wrong, especially with the brutal winter finally loosening its grip, gnawed at her like a cruel joke.

Karma rose unsteadily, swaying for a moment before slowly shuffling toward the sink, each step measured, his body wracked with another deep, wet cough. The others followed, their faces etched with concern.

At the sink, Karma paused, looking up at it. "I'm not sure I can jump that high..."

Zuzu's eyes brightened. "We can make a mound with the stuff I've gathered. It'll make it easier for you to get a drink!"

Aura touched Zuzu's cheek. "Let's do it."

While Karma sat, fighting off coughing fits, the other three cats worked together to move several things into a pile that soon reached halfway to the sink.

"Try it now, Karma," Zuzu beamed.

Despite his discomfort, a smile softened Karma's time-worn face. "Thank you, little one. I do believe this will work."

He hopped onto the pile and then climbed onto the sink. Before bending to drink, he gazed down at the three concerned cats below. "Thank you all for looking after me," he said softly, his voice barely a whisper.

Aura nodded, her eyes softening. "Drink as much as you can. It'll be good for your throat."

Karma tilted his head and lapped at the water, each cool swallow providing some relief to his raw throat. Despite his best efforts to contain them, coughs still seized him between drinks, forcing him to pause and catch his breath. But sadly, the water failed to relieve the weariness gripping him.

Aura watched in tense silence, her worry deepening as Karma's coughing persisted. A cold dread crept through her—this was far more serious than a simple cold or dry throat.

After finishing his drink, Karma eased down from the sink onto the mound, then finally to the cold concrete floor. He trudged back to their resting spot, curling up into himself. As the minutes ticked by, his coughing gradually subsided, allowing him to drift into a restless sleep.

Cosmo stared at Karma anxiously, fighting back his sense of helplessness. Then, an idea sparked within him—something concrete he could do to help. His expression hardened with resolve as he turned to the others. "Aura, he'll be hungry when he wakes. I'm going to gather food for him. Zuzu can show me where you found those rats while I was laid up with my nose. We'll bring back enough for him and the rest of us."

Zuzu's tail flicked with excitement. "I know exactly where to go!"

"Good thinking, Cosmo," Aura said, her voice warm with approval. She turned to Zuzu, offering a gentle reminder. "Remember what I taught you about ending a rat quickly."

"I'll do it just like you showed me," Zuzu replied. She gazed at Karma's sleeping form. "I hope he's feeling better when we return."

Later, Cosmo and Zuzu returned, each carrying two rats by their tails. Karma and Aura rose to greet them.

"Welcome back, my skilled hunters," Karma purred, his voice stronger than before. "It seems we'll feast well."

Zuzu and Cosmo laid their bounty before them. Cosmo's eyes shone with pride as he glanced at Zuzu. "She dispatched her first rat today." His gaze shifted to Karma. "And you—you look and sound much better."

Karma nodded. "The extra rest did me good. I've enjoyed lying in the sun with Aura."

As they finished their meals, Zuzu looked at Karma with hopeful eyes. "Karma, will you tell us another story?"

Karma smiled and nodded, his eyes twinkling as he thought of a story to share. Then, his gaze brightened. "Zuzu, your first kill reminds me of my own... though mine didn't go nearly as well as yours."

He chuckled, recalling the memory. "I was a proud young cat with a towering ego back then. I'd just left home and made myself comfortable under the porch of a spacious two-leg house. There, I discovered a clever rat—a brazen little thing—who would scurry right past me every morning, practically waving his tail in my face. I'd try to swat him, but he was too fast. After days of enduring this disrespect and torment, I decided I'd had enough."

He leaned forward, caught up in the memory. "So, I devised the perfect ambush. Since I knew exactly when this rat made his morning rounds, I positioned myself in what I thought was the ideal spot—behind a big rock near the foundation wall. You see, rats always prefer running near walls instead of being out in the open. I was so proud of myself—certain I had thought of everything."

Karma's whiskers twitched with amusement. "What I hadn't realized was that the rat was studying me just as much as I was studying him. When I crouched behind the rock, ready to pounce, he set his counter-plan into motion. He snuck up and nipped my rear. I leaped instinctively, only to knock myself out when my head hit the underside of the porch. When I came to, dazed on the ground, I watched the rat strut up to me, looking all full of himself."

Karma paused, his eyes twinkling as he recalled the moment. "I'll never forget the smug look on his face as he doubled over with laughter."

Zuzu looked at him wide-eyed. "What happened then?"

Karma chuckled. "I quickly realized there are some rats you don't mess with. So, with my pride and dignity thoroughly deflated, I decided to cede the porch to him. I moved out that day." His gaze softened as he looked at Zuzu. "But you know what I learned? Sometimes, our failures teach us more than our successes. That rat taught me to respect my prey—to understand they can be just as clever as we are. From what Cosmo said about you today—making your first kill with patience and skill—I'd say you're far wiser than I was at your age."

Zuzu smiled at the old cat's compliment. "I'm lucky to have such excellent teachers—including you."

Karma nodded, his smile gentle. "Always remember, to learn, you must humble yourself. Arrogant cats never learn anything, and many don't survive because they never learned the value of humility and growth."

His gaze softened as he looked at Cosmo and Aura. "The greatest joy of my life has been sharing it with you both. You were exceptional students, and watching you grow into such wonderful, capable cats with kind hearts... My life has been richer for knowing you."

Cosmo touched Karma gently, his voice full of warmth. "We've come far, you and I. Teaching me to be humble was probably your life's biggest challenge. But now, I get it." He took a deep breath. "I'm grateful for all you've taught me, Karma. Grateful for everything you've done for me."

Karma's eyes glistened with emotion, his heart swelling. He looked at Cosmo and winked. "A good teacher also learns from their students." He chuckled softly. "You taught me the importance of cultivating patience—my goodness, did you ever teach me that."

Ancient grief colored Aura's voice as she pressed closer to Karma, speaking quietly. "You were there for me during the darkest times of my life. When I lost Ajax... and then my kittens..." She paused, steadying herself. "I didn't think I could go on. But you sat with me through those endless nights, listening to my grief, helping me find purpose again." Her eyes met his. "You showed me that having a broken heart meant I had loved deeply and that such love was worth the pain. You taught me that surviving honored their memory."

Karma touched his cheek to hers and sighed. "I know my end is near." He looked at Cosmo. "When I'm gone, you two need to look after each other. You are my legacy." His eyes turned to Aura. "Just like with Ajax and your kittens, your surviving and thriving will honor my memory. Don't grieve too deeply for me, Aura. Remember, a part of me will always live in your heart." He turned to Cosmo. "In yours, too."

Zuzu gently touched Karma, her voice filled with sincerity. "You will live in my heart, too, Karma."

Karma's eyes softened. "What a wonderful thought, little one."

His chest rattled painfully as another harsh cough seized him, his breath catching in his throat. Weariness crept back into his eyes.

"If you don't mind, I'd like to get some rest."

"Of course, Karma," Cosmo replied softly. "Rest easy, my friend." He glanced at Aura and Zuzu. "I need some fresh air." With a heavy heart, he padded away.

As Karma's labored breathing slowed, he drifted into an unsettled sleep. A heavy stillness filled the room.

Aura and Zuzu curled around Karma, their faces nearly touching as they silently comforted the old cat. Unspoken fear hung in the air—one Aura dared not voice. Her eyes, full of sorrow and love, met Zuzu's.

"I hope, one day, you will be my legacy," she whispered.

Zuzu touched Aura's cheek with hers, offering the most precious gift a stray cat could give—pure love and the solace of shared warmth on a cold night. Without the need for words, the young cat understood the depth of Aura's wish and the boundless love behind it. In this moment, in the quiet darkness, that was everything.

16

Late into the night, Cosmo returned and settled quietly beside the sleeping Aura.

She stirred, looking at him with concern. "You've been gone a long time," she whispered. "Are you okay?"

He moved close to her ear, his voice thick with emotion. "Sorry. I'm struggling. The thought of losing Karma..." His voice cracked. "It makes me feel so low." He sighed deeply, his eyes searching hers. "How is he?"

"Better, I think," Aura answered, her voice soft. "He hasn't coughed for a while, and his sleep seems peaceful."

"That's good news," Cosmo murmured. He stifled a yawn, his exhaustion creeping in. "Let's get some rest."

Morning arrived, and as always, Aura was the first to rise. Her eyes immediately sought Karma, and a soft smile curved on her lips as she saw him lying still, peaceful, and surprisingly cough-free. Things were looking up, she thought, padding to the sink for a drink.

Cosmo woke shortly after, noting both Karma's and Zuzu's restful sleep. He joined Aura without disturbing them. "Let's give them more quiet time," he whispered. "Care to join me upstairs for some early morning sun?"

She nodded, leading the way. They spent an hour conversing quietly, both finding comfort in Karma's apparent recovery.

But then Zuzu appeared, her white fur almost glowing as the sunlight played across it. Her steps were quick and deliberate, her tail twitching with anxiety—an unmistakable sign of trouble.

Aura's ears pricked at the young cat's distress. "What's wrong, Zuzu?"

"I've been looking everywhere for you," she replied, her voice trembling. "Karma—he feels cold. He usually feels warm against me, but now..." She swallowed hard, her eyes wide with concern. "I didn't want to wake him, so I tried looking for you."

"Cold?" Cosmo's expression conveyed bewilderment. "What do you mean, cold?"

"You know what she means, Cosmo!" Aura bolted away, her urgency clear as she rushed to check on him.

Cosmo and Zuzu chased after her. In their sleeping room, Karma lay still.

"Karma!" Aura touched him gently, but he didn't stir. His body felt unnervingly stiff beneath her paw. "Karma! No!"

Cosmo touched his nose to his friend's fur, then pressed his ear against Karma's chest, listening for any sign of life—breathing, a heartbeat. Nothing. His eyes, reflecting deep grief, met Aura's. A tension, almost imperceptible, stiffened his frame.

"He... he's gone. Karma's gone..."

The words hit like a physical blow, and in that moment, Aura's world seemed to shatter. Unable to bear the weight of the loss, she fled the room.

Confused and terrified, Zuzu started to follow her, but Cosmo blocked her path.

"Let her be for a while, Zuzu," Cosmo murmured, his voice tight with sorrow. "Let her be..."

A sadness deeper than anything Cosmo had ever known filled him, and he gazed at Zuzu, eyes brimming with grief and uncharacteristic vulnerability.

"Aura and I will need your strength in the days ahead. She, especially, will need your love. Just be with her and listen to her. Don't try to fix her—only time can do that."

Zuzu hesitated, searching for the right words. Then, she nodded with resolve, her voice steady despite the fear in her heart. "Okay, I can do that." She paused and gazed at him. "What can I do for you, Cosmo?"

He looked at her with sad eyes. "I process grief differently than Aura. I find a quiet spot, away from others, and only when the quiet inside me matches the quiet outside do I feel ready to come back." He sighed deeply. "But I can't do that now."

"Why not?" Zuzu asked, confused.

"Because we can't stay here. Soon, Karma's decaying body will attract pests, rats, and mice—and maybe something worse. And I know Aura—she won't be able to stay here, not with Karma here..."

His gaze shifted toward a shattered window, where sunlight highlighted the jagged edges of the glass. Without looking at her, he spoke softly. "So, what you can do for me is be patient with me if I snap at you. Just know I'm not mad at you. I... I'm mad at the winter for being so cruel to my dear friend."

Zuzu nodded. "I understand what you're saying, Cosmo, and I won't take anything you say to heart."

After a long pause, Cosmo finally spoke again, his voice quieter now. "Maybe we can go back to Murph's cat cave, just for a while, until we find somewhere else to live."

Suddenly, anguished wails tore through the silence, echoing through the building. Zuzu leaped at the sound. "That's Aura—I need to be with her!" Her voice cracked with desperation. "She needs me!"

"No!" Cosmo snapped, his voice sharp to catch Zuzu's attention. "Not yet. She needs to release her grief. When she's done, we'll join her."

They waited in silence, each wail tearing at their hearts. Minutes passed like hours as Aura's grief echoed through the building. Finally, the wailing faded into a heavy, aching silence.

Cosmo took a deep breath and turned to Zuzu. "Okay, let's be with her." Before leaving the room, he cast one last lingering glance at his lifeless mentor. His chest tightened with sorrow and disbelief.

They found Aura in Karma's favorite sunspot, curled tightly into herself. The sunlight bathed her trembling form, casting her grief in sharp relief. Without a word, they pressed close, one on each side, sharing their grief in silence.

As Zuzu lay next to Aura, an overwhelming sense of loss settled deep inside her—something she had felt with Mrs. Chen, but this was far worse. She began to understand why Karma spoke of legacies and love with urgency. With him gone, everything felt different now—heavier, darker.

After a long silence, Aura whispered, "I can still feel him here, in this spot where he loved to lie in the sun..." Her voice caught. "He taught me how to find light—even in the darkest places."

Cosmo waited until Aura's trembling subsided, giving her time to breathe before speaking softly. "Aura... I know it's hard, but we need to think about what comes next. I know you can't stay here..."

"You're right—I can't. Karma's presence is everywhere in here. Where should we go?"

He took a deep breath, knowing what he was about to say wasn't a long-term option. "Right now, I think Murph's cat cave is the best option. Since we've been gone for a while, his two-legs will think all his cat friends are gone."

Aura nodded. "I agree. Plus, we have to tell Murphy and Jo that Karma is no longer with us..." The thought of doing that sent a cold shiver up her spine. Telling their friends would make Karma's passing real.

Taking a shaky breath, she looked at Cosmo. "I can't stay here any longer," she whispered, her voice cracking. "I need to leave—now."

Cosmo nodded but then hesitated. "Aura, do you want to say goodbye to Karma before we leave? Do you want to tell him anything?"

She shook her head. "Everything I ever wanted to say to Karma, I've already told him many times." The room's silence felt heavier now—as if the walls mourned his absence. She looked at Cosmo with tenderness in her eyes. "So have you. I've heard you say them as many times as me."

Cosmo didn't say anything for a moment before nodding. "You're right. Okay. Let's go."

As their derelict home faded into the distance, the sun's warmth felt like a promise, though the air still carried a chill. The world ahead stretched out before them—forever changed without Karma. A troubling question lingered, hidden beneath the surface of their grief, but they dared not voice it: *What if the love Karma had planted within them wasn't enough to survive the weight of his loss?* They had each other, but the future felt as fragile as the fading light of the afternoon.

17

THE TRIO MOVED SWIFTLY toward Murphy's house on 43rd Avenue, unburdened by Karma's sluggish pace. Their journey took them through the heart of Queens, the scents of nearby eateries filling the air—spices from the Indian restaurant, garlic from the Italian place, something sweet from the bakery—but none of it tempted them.

As two-legs bustled around them, speaking in different tongues, their voices formed a symphony of sounds that usually fascinated Zuzu. But today, the borough's vibrant life felt distant, muffled by their collective grief.

They passed through Jackson Heights, where young two-legs played in fenced yards while their mothers watched from porches. The sounds of their laughter seemed jarring against their somber mood. Normally, such activity would force them to stick to the shadows, but today, they walked openly, too numb to care about being seen.

When they reached Murphy's backyard, Cosmo paused, the weight of the news he had to share settling over him. With a heavy heart, he let out their secret call—the brief, sharp cry that only Murphy would recognize.

Moments later, Murphy squeezed through his cat door, his usual cheerful expression fading as he saw their solemn faces.

"What's wrong?" he asked, his voice tight with concern.

Cosmo swallowed hard as the words caught in his throat. "Karma... Karma's gone, Murph. He died in his sleep last night."

Murphy's legs seemed to give way beneath him as he sank to the ground. "No..." he whispered, his eyes filling with disbelief. "Not Karma..."

They gathered around Murphy, sharing in his grief. For a long moment, none of them spoke. The weight of their loss hung heavy in the air.

Aura spoke for the first time since leaving their former home. "We can't stay at Karma's place anymore. We were hoping..." She glanced toward Murph's cat cave. "Could we stay here again?"

Murphy struggled to his feet. "Follow me," he said quietly, leading them toward the alley. As they rounded the corner, they saw the hole in the garage door covered with fresh wood.

"My two-legs blocked the opening," Murphy said, his voice thick with regret. "I'm so sorry. I can offer you all some food balls—"

"No damn food balls, Murph—don't add to our troubles!" Cosmo snapped, his voice sharp with a hiss. He paused, taking a breath, fighting to collect himself. "Sorry. I know you mean well. I... I'm struggling."

"I know you are, Coz," Murphy replied softly, his gaze steady on his best friend. "We all are..."

Cosmo placed a paw gently on Murphy's shoulder. "We're tight, and we always will be." He hesitated, his mind churning. "Would you mind if we look for other entry points into your cat cave?"

Murphy's eyes brightened. "Good idea! Let's give the place a hard look."

They circled the garage, searching for another way in—high or low—but found nothing. The cat cave that had once sheltered them offered no respite.

Murphy met their eyes, his expression full of concern. "What will you do now?" he asked softly.

Aura spoke, her voice heavy with sadness. "We need to tell Jo about Karma. After that..." She shook her head, unable to finish the thought.

"I wish I could join you," Murphy said, his tone apologetic. "But the truth is, I'm too fat and out of shape for the walk."

"It's okay, Murph," Cosmo replied with a gentle smile. "Your place is here." He winked at his friend. "Give some thought to eating only half your weight each day, okay?"

"Sound wisdom," Murphy replied with a good-natured chuckle, understanding the playful dig came from a place of love.

The walk to Josephine's house didn't take long, though Cosmo wished it would last forever, given the difficult news they had to share. As they turned onto her street, the city's usual noise faded.

Cosmo paused at the edge of her backyard, taking a moment to gather himself before using the same secret call he had used for Murphy.

Josephine rushed out of her cat door almost immediately. Her well-groomed fur and confident demeanor sharply contrasted with their unkempt and somber appearance. Her face brightened at seeing them—until she noticed their expressions and realized Karma wasn't with them.

"What wrong?" Josephine's shrill voice cracked as her eyes darted from face to face. "Where Karma?"

Aura's gaze met hers, heavy with sorrow. "Karma... he... he's gone, Jo."

For a long moment, Josephine stood frozen, unable to process the words. Then, a low, agonizing wail escaped her throat. She pressed her face into Aura's fur, her body trembling with grief.

"When? How he go?" she gasped between ragged breaths.

"Last night," Cosmo replied quietly. "In his sleep. He left peacefully, with the dignity he always wanted."

Josephine pulled back, struggling to compose herself. "That good, that be good. Karma, he all 'bout keepin' his dignity. I thankful he not suffer."

Aura nodded, her voice soft. "We decided we can't live where we were, not with Karma being there."

"I understands. I completely understands that. Where y'all be stayin' now?"

"Nowhere," Aura sighed, the weight of their situation settling in. "The two-legs blocked the opening to Murphy's cat cave. We looked, but there weren't any other ways in. So, we..." She trailed off, the reality of their situation pressing down on her.

Josephine glanced at her home with a look of aching regret. "If this be my house, then I has y'all livin' here fo'ever with me. But my two-legs—I all they can handle." She knew they all understood she couldn't offer them shelter, but the thought of not giving her best friends refuge stung.

A door slammed somewhere inside Josephine's house, making them all jump. "Y'all gots to go," she said quickly, though her eyes were full of pain at sending them away. "We family, y'all," she added, her words raw but firm. "We always gots each other's back. When you finds a place, you come gets me. We always be family."

They touched cheeks in farewell, sharing one last moment of sorrow before parting. As they turned away from Josephine's house, the heaviness of their goodbye lingered, her soft cries echoing in their hearts as they walked down the street.

With no destination in mind, they drifted through the streets of Queens. The afternoon sun stretched long shadows from the elevated train tracks, casting a patchwork of light and shade across the sidewalks. The familiar screech of the 7 train, which had always helped Cosmo orient himself in the borough, now seemed hollow and distant.

They moved through Woodside, a quieter area with streets lined with maple trees. The peaceful scene only underscored what they had lost—not just Karma, but the sense of belonging that had once grounded them.

Looking embarrassed, Zuzu broke their long silence. "I'm tired... and hungry."

Cosmo glanced at the setting sun. "We should find something to eat." He looked around, getting his bearings. "There's a row of eateries nearby. They usually have good food."

As they approached the eateries, the scent of discarded food grew more pungent. Cosmo's whiskers twitched, his instincts sharp as he remembered Karma's lesson: always check every angle before approaching a food source. "Stay alert," he warned quietly, his battle-hardened instincts kicking in. "Eateries always attract rats, cats, and hundfangs."

Behind an Italian restaurant, they found several half-eaten meals in the garbage bins and even some bread that wasn't too stale.

As they ate, Aura noticed Zuzu trembling slightly. "Are you cold?"

Zuzu shook her head. "No. I just..." She swallowed hard. "I just thought Karma would've loved this food."

"I'm sure he would have, Zuzu," Aura replied softly. "He would've said it was a nice change from eating rats."

Speaking of Karma deepened Cosmo's grief. He pushed a half-eaten meatball aside, his hunger vanishing.

"Let's go to Sunnyside Gardens Park," he suggested suddenly. "Remember the tree where I taught you to climb, Zuzu? We can rest near there while we figure things out."

When they arrived, the park was quiet and dark. The damp grass felt good under their paws—a welcome change from the hard streets. Though cool, the night air was warmer than it had been in days.

In the moonlight, they made their way to Zuzu's tree—a sturdy maple with leafless branches. Zuzu paused beneath it, gazing up at its broad limbs. She smiled. "I still can't believe I climbed it," she murmured, her eyes sparkling with pride.

Cosmo nodded, his expression softening with warmth. "You did great. Now, let's find somewhere to stay for the night."

They moved deeper into the park, weaving through clusters of trees. The soft, steady sound of running water reached them. Following it, they found a small creek cutting through the underbrush. They drank their fill, the coolness a welcome relief after their long day.

Afterward, Cosmo turned, his eyes scanning the dark, moonlit park. His whiskers twitched as he searched for anything that might provide some comfort. He spotted a small, dry culvert, partly concealed by a thicket of bushes.

"I think I found a place for us to spend the night," he said, his voice lighter, relieved to have found somewhere better than the open ground.

As Cosmo inspected the culvert, he sighed. It was no long-term haven—nothing like Karma's old factory or the safety of Murphy's cat cave. The entrance was narrow, and the air smelled of damp earth and the faint stench of rats. But it would shield them from the cold and any two-leg passersby. For tonight, it would have to do.

Cosmo motioned for the others to go in first. He lay closest to the entrance, his low purr a soft reassurance as his eyes darted nervously toward the shadows, ever watchful.

Zuzu's tail twitched anxiously, her eyes wide with uncertainty. "What will happen to us, Aura? Where can we go? Will we be okay out here? What if a demon hundfang finds us?"

Aura touched her cheek to Zuzu's. "When I was young and terrified of everything that could go wrong, Karma once told me something." She waited until Zuzu's nervous flicking slowed. "He said, 'Aura, worrying is like trying to catch your own tail. You can chase it all day, but you'll never catch it. And even if you did, what good would it do?'"

She purred soothingly and nuzzled against Zuzu. "Karma was right. We can't control what might happen, and worrying is like chasing your tail—nothing good comes from it. All it does is wear you out. Instead of worrying, focus on the good we have. Right now, we have a dry place to sleep, we have each other, and Cosmo is watching over us. For now, that's all we need. Tomorrow will take care of itself, as it always does."

Zuzu curled in tighter to Aura. "Okay," she whispered.

Cosmo interrupted the tender moment, oblivious to Zuzu's need for comfort. "What if we leave Queens?" he wondered aloud. "Try somewhere new?"

The question lingered in the air as the others fell silent. Queens was all they had ever known. Every street corner held memories—some with Karma, some without—but all felt like home. The moment Cosmo suggested leaving, he realized he was doing exactly what Karma had warned against—chasing his own tail.

As the trio settled into their new resting spot, the stillness of the night wrapped around them, offering an uneasy sense of peace. In the quiet, the weight of their situation lingered, unspoken but ever present. As Zuzu nestled closer to Aura, her mind buzzed with fear and unanswered questions. She fought hard to push them away. Pressing her ear to Aura's side, she focused on her friend's steady heartbeat. Slowly, it brought her a measure of comfort, and she drifted off to sleep...

18

DEEP INTO THE NIGHT, faint sounds woke Aura from her fragile sleep. Her eyes flicked open, and her ears twitched toward the noise. At the mouth of the culvert, Cosmo sat trembling and whimpering, a dark silhouette against the pale moonlight.

Without a word, she moved to him, pressing her body against his. Compassion swelled within her, and her heart ached with shared sorrow.

As her love enveloped him, the crushing sadness within Cosmo began to ease.

""I miss Karma, too..." Aura whispered.

Cosmo's voice cracked. "Remember how he used to purr when we were scared as kittens? It always made me feel like everything would be all right."

Aura nodded. "I do. Little things like that keep flashing in my mind."

A sigh escaped him. "He was everything to us..."

She pressed closer to him, offering comfort. "Ajax and my kittens were my world once, and with Karma's help, I found a way to heal from that loss. You and Jo overcame your hard times, too. We'll find our way through this... together."

When morning came, they left their makeshift shelter in the culvert to search for something more secure. On the streets of Astoria, a community within Queens, the usual bustle of two-legs barely registered through their fog of grief. Cosmo took point, each step heavier than the last. Leadership weighed on him now, each decision a burden. He wasn't Karma. He wasn't a deep thinker with gentle wisdom and a knack for knowing what to do. Cosmo preferred few words and direct action: see a problem and beat the problem into submission—either literally or figuratively. But now, as he glanced back to see Aura and Zuzu trailing behind him, relying on him to lead them to safety, a gnawing sense of unworthiness gripped him.

They prowled through abandoned buildings all morning. One had gaping holes in the roof, letting the wind and rain—or snow—pour through. Another had seemed promising until they discovered a massive rat nest within. In yet another, broken glass littered the floor, threatening their paws with every step.

Each failed shelter frayed Cosmo's nerves further. This wasn't a problem he could solve with force—no tree to climb, no enemy to fight. Finding a safe home demanded patience and wisdom, qualities that had never come easily to him.

"Maybe we should try somewhere else—or go back to Karma's place," Zuzu suggested, her tail drooping low as they left yet another unsuitable shelter.

Aura shook her head. "We'll find something... but not Karma's place. I'm never going back there. Ever."

As evening approached, hunger drove them toward the eateries. As they crept down a familiar alley, a sudden movement ahead made them freeze—a large cat hunched over a pizza shop's garbage bin, gorging on discarded food.

The strange cat's head snapped up, his snarl distorting his features. He dropped to the ground, spitting and hissing. His orange and cream fur bristled along his spine, and his muscular build and battle-ready stance radiated raw menace.

Cosmo surged forward, positioning himself between the threat and his family.

The two males faced off, their furious screams slicing through the air. Neither yielded an inch, and death seemed certain to claim one of them in the coming fight.

"Wait!" Aura's cry pierced the standoff. Both males froze. "I know you!" Recognition blazed in her eyes as she studied the stranger. "I don't remember your name, but that fur—I remember your fur!"

The cat's growl died in his throat. His eyes narrowed, confusion replacing rage as he studied her. Tension crackled in the air as both males held their positions. Aura crept forward, her heart hammering against her ribs. The distinctive orange and cream swirls triggered a flood of kitten memories.

"We used to play together," she breathed. "As kittens."

Bewildered, Cosmo flicked his gaze between his sister and the menacing cat, muscles still coiled and ready to pounce.

The orange cat tilted his head, studying Aura first, then Cosmo. Recognition also flickered in his amber eyes.

He raised a paw. "Hold on—" he rasped, his voice strained from the earlier screaming. "Did you two live with a nice male cat named Carmel... or something like that?"

"His name was Karma," Cosmo replied, his muscles relaxing slightly. "He... he died two days ago."

The orange cat's ears drooped, and his voice softened. "Sorry to hear that. I remember how he always told funny stories..."

Aura's heart tightened with sadness, but she hid it with a quiet question. "What happened to you and your family?"

Pain shadowed his face. "One day, as we feasted in a big box behind an eatery, a dozen masked hundfangs ambushed us. We fought hard, but they outnumbered us. Only my brother and I survived. He succumbed to his wounds shortly after. Our home didn't feel right without my family, so I left it and eventually found a place in Flushing—an old warehouse off Northern Boulevard, hidden behind shops and garages. You'd never spot it unless you knew where to look."

He paused, studying them. "Where do you live?"

"We lived in an abandoned factory nearby," Aura said, her voice heavy with grief. "Like you, after Karma died, we couldn't stay there. Now we're homeless, searching for a new place."

His face softened with understanding. "I understand." His eyes brightened with a sudden thought. "Hey, if you want, you can stay at my place for a while. I could use help clearing out the rats." He extended a paw to Cosmo. "I'm Finneas—Finn to friends."

Cosmo touched his paw. "I'm Cosmo. This is Aura, and that's Zuzu."

"Pleased to meet you all—or should I say, I'm pleased to be in your company again." Finn glanced at the trash can. "I've already had my fill, but there's more good stuff in there if you're hungry."

"Thanks, Finn," Cosmo said, giving him a wink. "I'm glad we didn't tangle—if we had, your demise would've been swift."

Finn's chuckle broke the last of the tension. "That scar on your face tells a different story."

"We'd be an even match," Cosmo responded with an impish grin. "I'm sure you can more than hold your own."

Finn's answering nod spoke volumes.

"What's a masked hundfang?" Zuzu asked, her voice tinged with alarm at yet another danger.

"Zuzu," said Cosmo, "masked hundfangs are smaller than demon hundfangs but just as deadly. They've got dark markings around their eyes like masks, and their claws and teeth are razor-sharp. They're bigger than cats, so they have the advantage in a fight. And they often group together where there's food. So, like demon hundfangs, we try to avoid them."

"The two-legs call them raccoons," Finn added with a grin. "Strange name, if you ask me."

After Cosmo, Aura, and Zuzu had eaten their fill, Finneas motioned with a paw. "Follow me—I'll show you the way to my place."

"Thanks for your kindness, Finn," Aura replied. "We could use a good night's sleep in a safe place."

"Happy to help," Finn replied, warmth in his smile.

Finn set a swift pace as he confidently moved through Flushing. The cool night air carried sounds of the city as they passed rows of small shops and garages, their metal shutters sealed tight until morning. Finn stopped at a metal pole gate blocking a dead-end driveway between two industrial buildings.

"We're almost here," he said, pride warming his voice. They followed him as he ducked under the gate and navigated the narrow, pot-holed driveway.

Before them, a secluded warehouse loomed like a silent sentinel, its brick walls darkened with decades of time and neglect. "Hardly any two-legs ever come back here. To them, it's just another abandoned building. Come on. I'll show you how to get in. I'll give you the full tour tomorrow when it's light."

He scurried through a small opening that had once served as a loading dock door, perfectly placed for quick escapes. "I'll bet you're all thirsty," he said. "I'll show you where you can get a drink." He led them to his water source—a cracked pipe deep inside the warehouse, where clean water dripped steadily into a pool before finding a drain. "Clean and fresh," he assured them.

He glanced upward, whiskers twitching. "The roof keeps rain out except for one corner. And there's a heating pipe running through the building—a lifesaver in winter. I stay toasty warm sleeping next to it."

Cosmo looked around, impressed. "You've got it all here, Finn. Water, shelter, protection, and heat. Incredible."

"I thought you'd like it," Finn said with a grin.

He led them through the building's interior, dimly lit by the moonlight filtering through the windows. Crates and piles of old debris filled the spaces. The air smelled stale, tinged with the faint scent of oil and old wood, but it was far more pleasant than other abandoned buildings. And it was dry and safe—a far cry from their exposed park culvert. Finn stopped at a cozy corner.

"This is my sleep spot," he said, motioning to a bed of old cloth and discarded materials. "It's not much, but it's warm with the heating pipe running through here."

Aura met Finn's gaze with quiet approval. "It's perfect. Absolutely perfect."

His chuckle carried genuine pleasure. "Thanks. I like keeping things tidy."

A yawn escaped her. "Sorry. Do you mind if we rest? It's been a long day for the three of us."

"Absolutely," Finn said with a grin. "Make yourselves comfortable. There's plenty of room for everyone."

Zuzu turned her head slightly, watching Cosmo with wide, earnest eyes, silently asking if it was okay to rest. Cosmo offered her a reassuring nod. He plopped onto the makeshift bed, echoing Aura's yawn. "I'll sleep like a kitten tonight."

His confident demeanor relaxed Zuzu, and a small smile of relief tugged at the corners of her mouth.

She and Aura curled beside him. Once they settled, Finn chose a spot nearby, maintaining a respectful distance from his guests.

Relief flooded through Cosmo as he breathed deeply. They had shelter, at least for now, though Karma's absence still ached in his chest.

"Tomorrow," Finn said, breaking the silence, "I'll show you around, and then we can scout outside. There's always something new to find. But for tonight, rest easy."

"Sounds good," Cosmo replied, his eyes weighed down with exhaustion. He glanced at Aura and Zuzu. Usually full of energy, Zuzu lay quiet now, her tail wrapped tight around herself.

Despite being drained, Aura struggled to sleep. Cosmo noticed. "I know you're thinking about Karma," he whispered. "So am I."

Zuzu, equally tired but restless, spoke softly. "Will we ever stop missing him?"

The question lingered in the air, unanswered. The complexity of their grief could not be easily fixed, lessened, or erased. But they had each other, and in their bonds, there was strength.

Cosmo's voice dropped to a whisper as if speaking louder would disturb the fragile peace of the moment. "Remember what Karma said to us the evening before he died: 'Don't grieve too deeply for me, Aura. Remember that a part of me will still live in your heart.' He said a part of him will live in my heart—and in yours, too, Zuzu." He paused, his voice heavy. "So maybe... maybe we should tell that part of him that lives on in us that we love him."

He looked at his family—Zuzu's wide eyes, Aura's exhausted gaze—and felt a lump rise in his throat.

Understanding passed between them, deeper than words.

"Aura," he added softly, "we'll always miss him. But we're still here... together. He'd want us to hold onto that."

She released a slow breath, her words barely audible. "You're right. On his last night, Karma also said, 'You two need to care for each other when I'm gone. You're my legacy.' We're living that now—caring for each other."

Zuzu's tail twitched uneasily, and she inched closer to Cosmo, her small body pressing against his side. "Thank you for caring for me, too."

He nuzzled her gently. "You're one of us now, Zuzu."

Silence descended on the warehouse, broken only by the rhythmic drip of water and the steady rhythm of Finn's breathing as he slept.

Cosmo spoke again, his voice firm, his words heard only by the three of them.

"I love you, Karma, and I need to rest."

A beat of silence followed, and then Aura and Zuzu, their voices soft but sure, echoed in unison, "I love you, Karma, and I need to rest."

The words wove a fragile sense of comfort in the dark.

Slowly, sleep claimed them, easing the weight of their grief a little. In the shared warmth, they found solace. Karma's memory, a quiet ember in their hearts, glowed softly in their dreams.

19

Finn, an early riser, woke with the sun. He scanned the sleeping forms of his guests, and a faint smile touched his lips. They looked peaceful, curled together for warmth. He felt a pang of empathy for them, reminded of the path he had once walked. Quietly, he padded to the cracked pipe and sipped the cool, refreshing water. He stretched, then went outside to take care of business. The early morning sunlight felt warm on his face. He stood still, eyes closed, and savored the moment of peace before heading back inside.

To his surprise, Aura was awake and drinking from the cracked pipe.

"Good morning, Aura. Did you sleep well?" he asked, his voice filled with curiosity and warmth.

Aura stretched, and a faint yawn escaped her. "Good morning, Finn. Thanks for asking. We had trouble falling asleep at first, but Cosmo calmed us with the words Karma shared with us before he died. We found them comforting and slept much better after that."

Finn nodded, sighing softly. "I heard what he said. I didn't want to interrupt your tender moments, so I pretended to be asleep." His eyes met hers with deep empathy. "I, too, know deep sorrow, Aura. I lost my family—my whole family—parents and siblings—after the masked hundfang attack. The pain of that has never left me." He exhaled softly. "I love what Karma said about how he lives in your heart. It made me realize my family still lives in my heart, too."

Aura touched her cheek to his. "I see your big heart, Finn. Karma would've liked you."

"Thanks." Finn's gaze softened, but his voice grew heavier. "Sadly, I think the bigger your heart is, the bigger the pain when you lose someone dear." He inhaled deeply. "A year ago, I lost Lola, my partner. She died while giving birth. Neither she nor the kittens survived."

Aura sighed. "I'm so sorry to hear of your loss. I lost Ajax, my partner, to a demon hundfang. I was expecting when I lost Ajax. He and Cosmo were best friends. The hundfang also injured Cosmo's other friend, Murphy, so badly that he ended up living with two-legs. So, without Ajax and Murphy, Cosmo did his best to bring me food, but it wasn't enough. I couldn't make enough milk and lost two of my five kittens early. Later, one was killed in a territorial fight, and another mysteriously disappeared—we think a hundfang or another cat likely killed her. The last one... he ran away. So, in addition to losing Karma, I've also known the pain of losing my partner and my kittens."

Finn grimaced but remained silent for a few moments, letting the shared sorrow settle between them. "We've both known dark times..." He then looked at Aura with curiosity in his eyes. "So, is Zuzu Cosmo's daughter?"

Aura shook her head. "No. Until recently, she was a pampered indoor cat who lived with an elderly two-leg female. When her two-leg passed away, Zuzu ended up on the streets. I found her, dazed and confused, wandering around Queens. She's been with us ever since." A soft smile tugged at her lips. "Zuzu's a special young cat—still so naïve and innocent. I've come to love her as if she were my own. Cosmo feels the same way."

"I see how you and Cosmo look at her—your combined love for her is powerful."

Aura smiled, though a shadow of sadness lingered in her eyes. "She's a reminder that love can brighten even the darkest times."

Finn looked down for a moment before his gaze met hers again. "I understand. The ones we love stay with us even after they're gone. That's what makes it both hard and precious."

Aura touched his shoulder gently. "You're a good cat, Finn. I'm glad we met you."

"Me, too," he admitted, his gaze meeting hers. "Since Lola died, I've been on my own. I've been lonely... very lonely. Having the three of you here feels agreeable. I hope you'll stay, but that's a decision I know all of you will have to make as a family."

Aura's eyes softened. "I'm grateful for your kindness, Finn. All of us are."

He smiled and nodded. "I'm sure Karma wants you all to feel at peace again. If there's anything I can do to help you find that peace, I will."

Just then, Cosmo ambled toward them, stretching with a groggy yawn. Finn glanced at him with a playful glint in his eyes.

"Good morning, my new friend," Finn said with a mischievous grin. "So, how about we catch a few rats for breakfast? I know where they like to gather in here." He paused, giving Cosmo a playful verbal poke. "You do know how to dispatch a rat, right?"

Aura chuckled at Finn's lighthearted teasing, and for a moment, the heaviness of the morning lifted.

Cosmo looked at Finn with a smug grin. "Rats for breakfast sounds excellent. As for whether I can dispatch them—prepare to be schooled."

Zuzu padded over, stretching out the cold-induced stiffness in her limbs. "Cosmo and Aura taught me how to kill rats so I can help."

Finn chuckled, his eyes sparkling. "Well then, let's see what this team can do. After we eat, I'm thinking we could take a walk around the neighborhood. I'd love to show you Flushing Meadows-Corona Park—it's a fun place."

Aura's ears perked up. "That sounds like a good way to start the day—and maybe it'll remind us that there are still good things out there. But first, let's eat."

On the rat hunt, they spread out across the abandoned building's ground floor, each taking a strategic position. Finn pointed out the rats' favorite pathways, and they set their plan in motion.

Cosmo struck first, pouncing on a rat with practiced precision. Zuzu, to everyone's surprise—including her own—caught another that tried to dash past her. Finn and Aura skillfully herded several more rats toward the others, turning the hunt into an impressive display of teamwork.

As they shared in the thrill of the hunt, their bond seemed to strengthen.

After their successful hunt, they sat down to eat and converse. The conversation flowed easily as they shared their meal, with Finn and Cosmo trading friendly jabs about their hunting techniques.

"I believe Zuzu could help you refine your rat-dispatching skills, Finn," Cosmo said with a playful tone.

He replied with a grin. "You're not too shabby yourself, but I'd be hard-pressed to call you an expert hunter."

Although Cosmo was teasing Finn, Zuzu beamed at his subtle acknowledgment of her newfound rat-dispatching skills.

After breakfast, the group made their way through the streets, following Finn's lead toward the park. The air was crisp and fresh, and though the sun was still weak, it continued to melt the remnants of the nor'easter.

Before long, Finn stopped and pointed at the entrance of Flushing Meadows Corona Park. "Here we are," he said. "This is one of my favorite places in Queens."

In the park, the ground beneath their paws felt cold and damp. The trees stood bare, their skeletal branches reaching up to the gray sky, perhaps—like the cats—waiting for the promise of spring.

Finn led them toward a massive globe of the planet that dominated the heart of the park—the Unisphere, as the two-legs called it. Sunlight filtered through a break in the clouds and glinted off its metallic surface, casting shifting patterns on the ground. The structure towered above them, gleaming and mysterious, an inexplicable monument to two-leg peculiarities. Patches of stubborn snow dotted the otherwise clear ground around it. The cool temperature had kept most two-legs away, leaving the cats in peaceful solitude.

Zuzu gazed upward, fascinated by its size, and then turned to Finn, puzzled. "Where in there do the two-legs live?"

Finn smiled in reply. "No one lives in there, Zuzu."

Zuzu blinked, looking even more confused. "Then why did the two-legs build it?"

"Two-legs are odd creatures, Zuzu," he said with a chuckle. "They often build things that serve no purpose."

"I don't get it..." she said, her bewilderment deepening.

Finn nodded in agreement and then moved toward the spot where sunlight reflected off the sphere, casting a warm pattern on the ground. He stretched out, savoring the rare warmth, and looked at the others. "This is a good spot to enjoy the sun, even if it's not quite warm yet."

Aura and Cosmo eagerly joined him, carefully avoiding the remaining patches of snow. Zuzu hesitated momentarily before curling up beside them, conserving her warmth.

"This feels good," Aura said, shifting against the cold ground. "Even with the sun warming my back, winter still claims the earth."

Cosmo chuckled, his tail flicking as he lay back. "Yeah, it's like spring doesn't want to start, but this sure beats that brutal cold we had recently."

A gentle breeze rustled through the area, and Aura's eyes grew distant. "Karma loved days like this," she said softly. "He always said the changing of seasons reminded him that nothing—good or bad—lasts forever."

The others fell quiet, letting her words settle in the cool air. Finn stood and looked at them with mischievous eyes. "I know where to find some good two-leg food around here."

Zuzu perked up at the mention of food. "Really? Where?"

Finn gestured toward a nearby bench where an open paper bag lay abandoned. "Two-legs leave things behind when they're distracted. I'll bet there's something tasty in that bag."

The group padded over, their paws crunching on the snow beneath them as they moved toward the bench. Finn's whiskers twitched as he sniffed the bag. He reached in and pulled out a half-eaten sandwich. Eager to help, Zuzu grabbed the closed end of the bag and gave it a shake, causing a pile of potato chips to spill out and scatter across the ground.

"See?" Finn said with a grin. "Why two-legs throw away such edible things escapes me."

A grin spread across Cosmo's face as he leaned down and snatched up a chip. "These aren't half bad," he said, swallowing with satisfaction. "Definitely better than Murph's food balls."

Zuzu sniffed a chip suspiciously before taking a tentative bite. Her eyes widened in surprise. "Wow, these are good. I've never had anything like this before."

Aura sampled a chip. "Not bad—it's even tastier than our morning rats."

Everything seemed a little brighter as they munched on the discarded offerings. A simple meal in the park, shared with new friends—perhaps that was enough for now.

After finishing the two-leg delicacies, Cosmo licked his lips. "Delicious."

Finn chuckled. "Just wait until summer, when the food carts are by the Unisphere. The two-legs are especially careless with their meals from the carts and leave all sorts of tasty things on the ground."

"I'm looking forward to it," Cosmo replied, eyes bright with anticipation.

"Oh!" Finn exclaimed, turning to Zuzu. "Get this—there are rats in this park with bushy tails. They're always darting around, obsessed with eating nuts, seeds, and anything that smells like two-leg food. They live in the trees and scamper up them so fast it'll make your head spin. And the nerve they have—getting so close like they think we're too lazy to chase them!"

"Are they mean, like skinny-tailed rats?" Zuzu asked, her eyes wide with curiosity.

Finn shook his head. "Other than enjoying toying with us, they seem pretty good-natured. But they'll put up a good fight if you try to have one of them for a meal."

Cosmo chuckled. "They're not just in the parks—they're everywhere in Queens. And though they're hard to catch, I think they're much cuter and tastier than the skinny-tailed ones."

"I agree with you on that, Cosmo," Finn said, smiling. "Hey, everyone, there's more to see around here if you want to take a little walk."

Finn's enthusiasm as their tour guide made Aura grin. "I'm up for that—especially since it's so peaceful here today."

Zuzu, now feeling more at ease, leaned against Aura. "I like it here. It's like the world is napping before it fully wakes up."

Finn smiled, his eyes thoughtful. "That's a good observation, Zuzu. Like us—and all the two-legs—this park is waiting for spring to truly arrive. It always does." He paused, then grinned, "Let me show you what the two-legs call the Queens Botanical Garden. It's on the eastern end of the park. Boy, it's something in the summer—a lush, fragrant place full of flowers, trees, and peaceful pathways. It's one of my favorite spots in Queens."

After visiting the botanical garden, which appeared pretty meager in its winter dormancy, they decided to return to Finn's home.

As he walked beside Finn, memories flooded back to Cosmo—the days when he roamed Queens with Ajax and Murphy—the sleek, muscular Murphy, equal in every physical way to him and Ajax. He remembered how the three of them never competed for alpha status—how they would discuss decisions together and take a vote if they disagreed. They'd known each other so well that even their silences spoke volumes, a language forged from shared experiences. He wondered if he and Finn could ever achieve something similar.

As they turned onto Main Street, the familiar clamor of Flushing's busy streets began to rise around them. The honks of moving boxes and the distant chatter of vendors greeted them as they walked. Cosmo's thoughts wandered again. He wondered about Finn and the easy camaraderie they seemed to share. Could they work together as co-alphas, like he had with Ajax and Murphy? Could they find that same unspoken understanding, that quiet trust that came from knowing each other's strengths, weaknesses, and everything in between?

The steady rhythm of their paws on the pavement matched the flow of Cosmo's thoughts. He sighed when thinking about the heaviness and unease he felt in his role as leader, knowing he'd forever be in Karma's shadow. Being a co-alpha with Finn could lift some of that burden from him. He could focus on what he was good at—hunting and defending—while Finn could use his skills for finding excellent shelters and food sources. Plus, Cosmo mused, Finn's friendly demeanor easily bested his innate gruffness and impatience.

Cosmo glanced at Finn's confident and purposeful strides. Sharing alpha status with him could work, he thought, but relinquishing sole leadership of the family to him was out of the question. He was still a proud cat and would never be subordinate to anyone.

He decided to talk to Aura about the possibility of a co-alpha partnership with Finn. Though she seemed to like him, he wasn't sure how she would feel about the idea. Still, he sensed that bringing Finn into their family would strengthen their chances of surviving in a world that, for a street cat, was inherently hostile.

20

THAT EVENING IN FINN'S warehouse, Cosmo waited by the cracked water pipe while Aura sat with Finn and Zuzu in their resting place. He caught her eye and motioned for her to join him. She rose, her whiskers twitching with curiosity, and padded over.

"What's up?" she asked in a low voice.

"Let's go outside," Cosmo whispered. "I need to talk to you about Finn."

Aura's ears perked up at the seriousness in his tone. She followed him into the crisp night, where they could speak privately. The dim glow of distant streetlights did little to soften the inky blackness of the moonless sky.

Cosmo scanned the area near a secluded corner of the building to ensure they were alone. He exhaled softly, gathering his thoughts. It wasn't easy for him to share his feelings—especially about himself.

"Aura," he began, his voice low but steady, "I've been thinking all day about Finn—and about me." His eyes met hers, filled with concern and uncertainty. "I think Finn could be an asset to our group. He's strong, resourceful, and seems to care about all of us. But... I'm not sure how I feel about it."

Aura tilted her head, her expression thoughtful. "You mean about adding him to our family?"

"Yeah." Cosmo's gaze drifted to the distance for a moment. "It's a big decision. I've been watching him, studying him... and I think he could help us survive and thrive. We've all got our strengths, and Finn—he seems clever. He knows how to find food and shelter. And he's easy to get along with..."

Aura didn't respond right away. She sat, flicking her tail, contemplating his words. When she finally spoke, her voice was soft yet firm. "Cosmo, you're not just discussing his usefulness, are you? I know what's bothering you—it's the alpha issue, isn't it?"

Cosmo shifted uncomfortably, his ears flicking in annoyance. "Damn, Aura. You know me so well." He exhaled sharply, his voice lowering. "As you know, Ajax and Murph never made a big deal over who was alpha. Working together—that's what mattered to us. But I don't know if Finn would be okay with a partnership like that. If he's not..." His tail twitched tensely. "There's no way I'll take orders from another male cat. That's too much pride for me to swallow."

He paused, lost in thought. "Finn's got something I don't—he's a lot like Karma. Friendly, practical, easy to trust. I like him, and... it seems like you and Zuzu like him, too."

Aura studied him for a long moment, understanding crossing her face. "So, are you saying that if he's okay with sharing alpha status, you'd want him to be part of us?"

Cosmo's gaze dropped to his paws, his whiskers twitching. "Maybe. If we bring him in, it'll strengthen our family. His place could be a good long-term home for us. But..." His voice trailed off. "Ajax and Murphy... we were equals, and that meant everything to me. But Finn? I'm just not sure. What if his real side comes out later, and he turns on us?" Cosmo's tail flicked with concern. "I've seen it happen too many times—cats who seem trustworthy but then betray you when things get tough. I can't let that happen to us."

He paused, his voice softening as he gazed at her. "After Ajax... and after everything we've been through... I don't know if I can bear losing someone else, not like that."

Cosmo's tail flicked nervously, the weight of his thoughts making him restless. Aura noticed the shift in his posture, how his body seemed to bear the weight of so many unspoken fears and worries.

She gently touched her cheek to his. "I know how much you've had to shoulder, Cosmo. Especially lately. But you don't have to carry all the burden. I'm here for you, always."

Cosmo glanced at her, feeling a quiet comfort from her words. He knew she was right. Over the years, they'd weathered pain and loss together, their bond forged in the heat of shared struggles. It wasn't just about survival anymore—it was about healing. Together.

"I know," he whispered, his voice filled with gratitude. "I don't know what I'd do without you."

Aura studied him carefully, letting their words settle between them. "I know it's hard, Cosmo. We live in a hard world. But our friendships ease the hardness. My heart's telling me that Finn is someone we need, someone we can trust and rely on..."

Cosmo noticed her pause, sensing there was more. "Go on, Aura..."

Aura remained silent, her eyes fixed on his face. Finally, she spoke again, her tone measured. "Cosmo, I've talked to Finn. Trust me, he has a good heart. He reminds me of Karma in many ways—the same warmth, the same calm strength—and that's saying something. I don't know if he told you, but... Finn lost his partner last year. She died during childbirth, and the kittens didn't survive. He's experienced deep losses, just like we have."

"He didn't tell me that," Cosmo sighed. "We all know surviving hard times builds character... or it can break you. But Finn seems to have weathered it well." His voice softened as he gazed at Aura. "So, I guess I'm right about your liking him."

Aura nodded. "I have to admit, I... I could see myself building a life with him."

Cosmo blinked, taken aback. "Wait—what does that mean?"

She rolled her eyes. "I'm still in my prime, Cosmo. I still have desires. Sometimes, I wish I could have kittens again." A small smile formed on her lips. "I'm not saying I want to rush into anything, but Finn's good with us and seems to have the kind of heart and character that could make things better."

Cosmo gaped at her, whiskers twitching in surprise. "I see you're already ten steps ahead of me regarding Finn."

She shrugged, her tone matter-of-fact. "I'm just saying Finn has a good heart, and he fits in well with us. Zuzu likes him, too."

Her tail swished thoughtfully. "Maybe we should introduce him to Murphy and Josephine. You know Jo—she can spot a disingenuous cat from fifty paces."

Cosmo's eyes glinted with mischief. "Good idea. Before he meets Murph, I'd better prepare him for the shock of seeing a belly-dragging former street cat."

Aura chuckled at his quip. "Let's not say anything to Finn about joining us until we get Jo and Murphy's thoughts about him. They're family, too, so they should have a say in inviting him into our family."

"I agree."

Aura's gaze softened as she met Cosmo's eyes. "You'll always be an alpha cat to me. How you got Zuzu and me through that awful storm—and everything since then... And how you stood by me through those dark days after losing Ajax and my kittens..." Her voice filled with affection. "Brother, you shine just as brightly as Karma, but in your own unique way. So stop tormenting yourself for not being like him. Be yourself. That's something I treasure."

Moved beyond words, Cosmo gently touched his cheek to hers. For the first time since the storm, his burdens felt lighter.

"Hey," he murmured, breaking the moment. "I'm sure Zuzu and Finn are wondering what we're up to. Let's head back in."

Aura nodded. "Again, let's not discuss with him what we talked about. How about telling them we'd like to visit Murphy and Josephine tomorrow, and he's welcome to join us?"

"Good idea. Aura..."

"Yes?"

"You shine just as brightly as Karma and certainly more than me. You're the heart of this family."

Her eyes met his, soft and sincere. "Thanks, brother. I'm glad I'm in this with you."

Back inside, concern flickered across Finn's face. "Is everything all right?"

Aura smiled warmly. "It is. Cosmo and I spoke of our delightful day with you, Finn. You're a wonderful tour guide and host."

"I had a good day, too," Zuzu purred, her tail swaying. "I wish I could've seen one of those bushy-tailed rats."

"Hey, Finn," Cosmo began. "Tomorrow, if you're up for it, we'd love for you to meet the rest of our family. We've already mentioned Murphy, but there's also Josephine. For various reasons, both left the street life and now live with different two-leg families."

"I'm glad you had a good time today. It was fun showing you one of my favorite spots. As for meeting the rest of your family, I'd love it. Are Murphy and Josephine your siblings?"

Cosmo shook his head. "No. Murph and I are best friends, going way back. Josephine, though... well, let's just say she's different—in every sense of the word."

"Jo and I are best friends," Aura added. "Like me, she lost her kittens, too. We got each other through some hard times. Very hard times..."

"Jo talks funny," Zuzu offered. "But I like her a lot."

"One other thing..." A smirk spread across Cosmo's face. "Murphy. Well... Murphy kinda let himself go. My once buff friend traded fitness for an unending supply of food balls. He's plumped up so much that his belly scrapes the ground when he walks."

Finn stared at him, mouth agape. "You're joking, right? His belly actually hits the ground when he walks?"

Cosmo's whiskers twitched with amusement. "Finn, I'm not exaggerating. He's sensitive about his weight, so when you meet him, no fat jokes, okay?"

Finn nodded. "So, what are these food balls that plumped up your friend?"

Cosmo's nose wrinkled in disgust. "Finn, they're ball-like things so dry and hard that after you eat them, you'll need to drink your weight in water just to moisten your tongue." He shuddered at the memory. "One night, Murph had us come into his two-leg house and gave us all the food balls we wanted. Later that night, they roared out my hind end in convulsive bursts. Karma, too. You should've seen him and me squatting in the snowdrifts with food balls shooting out our rears. How Murph can eat his weight in them every day escapes me. His insides must be a wonder of nature."

Finn erupted in laughter, his whole body shaking. "The thought of you stuck in a snowdrift with your ass on fire—how I wish I'd been there to see it."

A rueful grin spread across Cosmo's face. "I got even with Murph. I snuck into his house at night and pissed in his bowl of food balls."

Finn gasped for breath between fits of laughter. "I have to meet Murphy," he said, eyes bright with eagerness.

The others couldn't help but smile at the joy Finn spread.

When he finally caught his breath, Finn turned to Cosmo. "I think I know what the two-legs call the food they give to Murphy."

"What?" asked Cosmo.

"Kibble."

Cosmo's nose wrinkled in confusion. "That's an odd-sounding word. I think the two-legs should just call it 'horrid.' 'Horrid' would be a more fitting description for his food balls."

After a few more moments of easy conversation, the mood settled into a quiet contentment. The air between them was comfortable, filled with the kind of silence that only close companions can share.

Zuzu yawned, tired from the long day. Her yawn proved contagious, and soon, everyone was yawning.

"I suggest we get some shut-eye," Cosmo murmured. "Tomorrow will be another long day."

Finn yawned again. "Whew, I'm spent. I've enjoyed our time together." His whiskers twitched with suppressed mirth. "Sorry, but I can't help thinking about what I'll say when I meet Murphy. How's this: 'I see you spend a lot of time working out—running back and forth to your food bowl.'"

Cosmo burst out laughing. "Please, please promise you'll say that when you meet him!"

"You two are so bad," Aura scolded, though she couldn't suppress her own chuckle.

After drinking from the water pipe, they returned to their resting area. Like the night before, Cosmo, Aura, and Zuzu curled up together, close enough to feel the warmth and heartbeats of each other's bodies. Finn once again lay a respectful distance away.

"Finn," Aura whispered. "You're welcome to join us." She shifted slightly to make room for him.

"Thanks, Aura." After a brief hesitation, he cozied up to the group. No one felt awkward about it. In that moment, the quiet comfort of being together felt right.

The warmth of their bodies and the soft rhythm of their breathing lulled them into peaceful sleep. Their first day as a family had come to a quiet close...

21

AURA, USUALLY THE FIRST to rise, awoke to an unexpected sight: Finn's eyes, already open, watching her with gentle warmth. A faint smile played on his lips as a silent greeting. She returned it, a subtle tremor in her whiskers betraying her intrigue. They remained still, locked in a shared gaze, as the silence deepened between them.

Finn leaned forward and touched his nose gently to hers. Aura didn't pull away.

Zuzu stirred quietly and groggily opened her eyes. Her breath caught as she spotted Aura and Finn in their intimate moment. She watched them, her tail twitching with growing unease, as they gently touched each other's faces. For the young cat, who had never witnessed such tenderness between a male and female, it stirred feelings of both curiosity and something sharper—a faint, bitter knot of jealousy that twisted deep inside her. Her claws flexed unconsciously, a quiet resentment rising within her.

As the silence stretched on, Zuzu could no longer bear it. She cleared her throat loudly, then yawned dramatically as though just waking up.

Aura and Finn broke apart, their shared moment ending abruptly.

"Good morning, Zuzu," Aura murmured, her voice a mix of embarrassment and quiet joy. "How did you sleep?"

Zuzu shrugged, trying to mask the swirling emotions inside her. Her tail swished with resentment. "I guess I slept okay."

Finn smiled at her. "Good morning, Zuzu. If you're hungry, we could rustle up some more rats for breakfast."

A whirlwind of conflicting emotions surged through Zuzu as her ears flattened. *He's trying to replace me,* she thought, frustration bubbling up from Finn's warmth toward Aura. She wanted to lash out, to defend her place. But her growling stomach had other plans, pulling her back to more primal needs.

"Okay," she muttered, her hunger winning out over her jealousy.

Aura caught the sharp edge in Zuzu's voice and the tension in her posture, quickly realizing that she must've witnessed her moment with Finn. She made a mental note to talk to her about it.

Hearing their voices, Cosmo stirred and yawned deeply. "Boy, I slept well."

His cheerful tone contrasted with his usual morning grumpiness. Sensing he had found peace after their talk last night, Aura's whiskers twitched, and a soft smile spread across her face.

"Morning, Coz," Finn said, his tail curling with mischief. "I suggested to Zuzu that we start the day like yesterday—with a nice rat breakfast. We can always wait if you need an hour or two to stretch and get your creaky bones limber."

"Yesterday, you seemed to spend more time chasing your tail than rats," Cosmo shot back with a grin. "It might be better for me to spend my time teaching you how to dispatch a rat more efficiently."

Finn tapped Cosmo's paw with a playful swat. "Touché."

The morning hunt went quickly, and after their meal, the group set out for Murphy's place on 43rd Avenue. Unlike yesterday, Cosmo led the way, with Finn following behind.

Once in Murphy's backyard, near the cat cave, Cosmo let out his secret call to summon his friend. He turned to Finn, whiskers twitching. "Remember—don't look shocked when you see Murph."

"Given the prankster you seem to be, I've been wondering if you're setting me up to expect one thing, only to reveal a skin-and-bones cat."

No sooner had Finn spoken than Murphy's head popped through the cat door. The effort it took for him to fit through the opening proved Cosmo hadn't been exaggerating about Murphy's size.

Finn's ears twitched, and he inhaled sharply, his gaze fixed on Murphy's comical struggle to get through the door. "My, oh my..." he whispered. "Should we try to pull him out?"

Cosmo shook his head. "Why spoil the show? It's way too good to interrupt."

"Stop it, you two," Aura scolded, though her whiskers quivered with suppressed mirth at Murphy's titanic struggle with the cat door.

"Remember to exhale, Murph!" Cosmo called out, thoroughly enjoying the scene.

Finally, an exhausted Murphy popped through the door. He lumbered toward his friends with an affable expression, his belly dragging on the ground as Cosmo had warned.

Finn's jaw dropped as the rotund cat approached them, his belly swaying with each waddle. "I... I'm at a loss for words..."

"No fat jokes, Finn," Cosmo warned. "Remember, he's sensitive about his size."

With his tail held high, Cosmo greeted his friend. "Murph! You fat so-and-so. What's shaking in fat city!"

Finn rolled his eyes. *So much for sensitivity,* he thought.

"Coz! It's great to see all of you!" Murphy's face brightened as he turned his curious eyes to Finn. "Who are you?"

Aura touched her cheek to Murphy's. "Hey, Murph—this is Finneas. We played together as kittens, but we haven't seen each other for a long time. After we left here, Finn took us in, and we've been staying at his place." She paused, then added, "Finn remembers Karma from his kitten days."

Murphy's mouth curled into a grin. "My friends call me Murph, and I consider you one of them now. Thanks for taking care of my family. They mean the world to me." His ears drooped. "Losing Karma... It's been hard for all of us. Real hard."

Finn nodded, his gaze meeting Murphy's with understanding. "Nice to meet you, Murph. My friends call me Finn. Karma was a special cat. He'll never be forgotten."

Sensing the need to lighten the mood, Finn gave Cosmo a subtle nudge and motioned toward the yard, his tone upbeat. "It looks like you're living the good life here."

Cosmo's whiskers quivered, catching Finn's subtle dig.

Murphy, oblivious to their private humor, beamed. "Yeah, life's good. And as you can see, I don't miss many meals."

"No," Finn's eyes glinted, "I didn't notice that."

Cosmo couldn't contain himself and erupted in laughter. "Murph, I told Finn about your wretched food balls. I regret that now, though. I would've loved to see the show after Finn had his fill of them."

Murphy joined in the laughter. "I see Cosmo told you that my food doesn't agree with him."

Finn's eyes danced with delight. "Oh, what I would've given to witness Cosmo's flaming rear end."

"I would've loved to have seen it, too," Murphy chuckled. "Hey, let's move to the side of the cat cave where my two-legs can't spot us. Otherwise, they'll think they've got another cat infestation on their hands."

The group moved to the side of the cat cave, ducking out of sight of Murphy's two-legs. Once settled, the conversation flowed easily.

Finn gave Murphy a curious glance. "So, what's it like living with two-legs, Murph? And what was it like back when you were on the streets with Cosmo?"

Murphy gave him a lazy half-grin, scratching his belly. "Living with two-legs has its perks—food, shelter, and the occasional belly rub. But street life? That's where the real fun was. You learn a lot out there. A lot about survival. And nothing beats the thrill of a successful hunt."

Aura chuckled, her tail flicking with the memory. "You're telling me. Karma—he never passed up an opportunity for food. Once, he swiped a whole fish off a market table. We barely escaped with our lives!" Her voice softened with fondness. "But you should've seen the look on Karma's face while we feasted. He was so proud of himself."

Zuzu's tail twitched, her gaze darting between Finn and Aura. Jealousy burned within her, but before she could react, Cosmo nudged her gently, eyes gleaming with mischief. "Hey, Zuzu, tell Murph about your first rat kill. He's gonna love it."

She hesitated before speaking, but then her ears perked up, her story too tantalizing not to tell. "It was a big one," she said, her voice gaining strength. "I pounced on it without mercy. Aura said my scream probably scared it to death. Either way, that night, I had a full belly."

Her whiskers trembled with joy as the others purred and laughed with delight. Yet, the sound of Aura's laughter felt distant, almost hollow. Zuzu forced a smile, but the unease in her chest lingered, making it harder to participate in the moment fully. Her tail flicked in frustration, revealing the tension within her.

Cosmo glanced at the sun's position in the sky. "I hate to cut this short, Murph, but we need to get moving. We've got a visit with Josephine planned, too."

Murphy nodded, still purring from the amusement of Zuzu's story. "Sure, sure. Please give Jo my regards."

As the group rose to leave, Cosmo leaned close to Aura, his voice low. "You and the others head on to Jo's. I'll catch up. I'll get Murph's thoughts on Finn."

Aura gave him a quick nod before turning to Finn and Zuzu. "Let's give Cosmo and Murphy a chance to spend a few moments alone. He'll catch up to us as we head to Jo's."

As the others began to walk toward Josephine's, Cosmo hung back with Murphy, waiting until they were out of earshot before speaking.

"Murph," Cosmo began, lowering his voice, "there's something we need your thoughts on."

Murphy's ears swiveled forward, curious. "What's going on?"

Cosmo's tail swished thoughtfully. "It's about Finn. Aura and I have been talking..." He glanced at Murphy to make sure he had his full attention. "We're thinking about adding him to our family. As you know, I've been run ragged lately, and I'm the only male cat defending Aura and Zuzu. Finn's a solid cat—clever and a good fighter. But the only way I can bring him in is if he agrees to be a co-alpha with me—just like what I had with you and Ajax."

He paused, watching Murphy closely. "Before we bring it up to Finn, Aura and I need to know what you and Jojo think. If either of you are not for it, then he's out. Simple as that."

Murphy's whiskers twitched as he considered this. "A co-alpha, huh? You think he'll go for that? Most cats want to be the sole alpha."

"That's what worries me, Murph. And as you know, neither I, Ajax, or you would take orders from another male cat. But if he agrees to a co-alpha arrangement, Aura and I think having Finn in the family could really strengthen us. He's got a great place—a big abandoned warehouse where we could all live. Aura says he's got a good heart, and she sees a lot of Karma-like qualities in him. That's high praise."

An impish grin spread across Cosmo's face. "Plus, she's got the hots for him."

Murphy studied him for a moment, his gaze steady. Then, a grin spread across his face, mirroring Cosmo's. "I was hoping she'd have the hots for me, but I noticed her dreamy eyes on him, too." He paused, his tail curling thoughtfully. "I like Finn, Coz. He's got a good head on his shoulders, and you're right—he seems like a solid cat." His eyes met Cosmo's. "Karma once told me that family isn't about numbers but the fit. So, if Finn's willing to share leadership with you and join our peculiar family, I'm all for it."

Cosmo let out a breath he hadn't realized he'd been holding. "That's what I needed to hear, Murph. Thanks. I just hope Jojo finds him acceptable, too. If she does, we'll talk to Finn about joining us."

"I hope Jo doesn't scare him off," Murphy chuckled. "You know how she can be with strangers."

Cosmo smirked. "With strangers? Murph, Jojo's even worse with family."

They both shared a laugh at Cosmo's quip.

Murphy gave Cosmo a reassuring nudge. "You know I'm always on your side, Coz. If Finn joins us, we'll be one step closer to world domination. More cats, more power, right?" His eyes gleamed with mischief.

Cosmo couldn't help but laugh. "You're something else, Murph."

Murphy shrugged, still grinning. "Can't help it. It's my radiant charm."

Cosmo bid farewell to Murphy and dashed down the alley to catch up with the others, reaching them just before they arrived at Josephine's house. Aura glanced at him, and Cosmo gave a subtle nod and smile to signal Murphy's approval. She returned his smile, visibly relieved.

Then, it hit her—Murphy had been the easy sell regarding Finn. Josephine would be far more challenging...

22

IN JOSEPHINE'S BACKYARD, COSMO let out the secret call. Moments later, she burst through the cat door and bounded toward them, her whole body quivering with excitement.

"Oh, happy day!" she bellowed, her tail flicking rapidly.

She skidded to a halt when she noticed a stranger in their midst. "Who he?" she asked, her eyes narrowing.

Aura stepped forward. "Jo, this is Finneas. He was kind enough to offer us shelter when we had to leave Murph's cat cave. Get this—we used to play together as kittens, and Finn remembers Karma!"

The suspicion in Josephine's eyes melted at Aura's words. She scrutinized Finn, taking in his unique fur color and patterns.

"Well, ain't you a hunky burst o' orange sunshine!" she exclaimed. "I thanks you fo' lookin' after my friends. I be Josephine—Jo."

Finn, taken aback by her forceful personality, nodded cheerfully, recalling Cosmo's words: *"Let's just say she's different—in every sense of the word."* He offered a tentative smile. "Hello, Jo. Pleased to meet you."

"You sho' be a good-lookin' cat!" she said, casting a sly glance at Cosmo. "You now gots competition for them females, Coz—real competition."

Cosmo's ears flattened, and he stiffened for a brief moment. Her innocent comment stung more than she knew. Within him, the alpha problem reared its ugly head. Beside him, Aura's whiskers drooped, mirroring his reaction. Jo's words had sparked a disquieting thought—the possibility of Finn pursuing other females. It was a notion that hadn't occurred to her, and the casual observation struck her with sudden, sharp clarity.

Oblivious to the impact of her words on both Cosmo and Aura, Josephine touched cheeks with them and Zuzu. Something about Zuzu's demeanor caught her attention, but she didn't let it dampen her enthusiasm. "I be so happy y'all okay. So happy. I needs to hear mo' 'bout how you been. Follow me—I knows a nice grassy spot where we can talk."

Without waiting for their response, Josephine darted away, leaving them scrambling to keep up with her energetic pace.

A block later, she slipped into the vacant backyard of a house with a prominent "For Sale" sign.

"It be quiet here. Sunny, too. Y'all sit."

As the group settled onto the warm grass, Josephine sprawled out facing them, stretching her legs and letting the sun warm her fur. "Now, tells me everthin'. How y'all end up with Finn?"

Aura's whiskers twitched with a gentle smile as she recalled the story. "After leaving Murphy's cat cave, we had an awful night, sleeping in a culvert in Sunnyside Gardens Park. The next day, we searched for shelter but didn't find anything. So, we went looking for food at an eatery."

She glanced at Finn and smiled. "Finn was digging through a trash can there, and he didn't take kindly to us moving in on his territory. He and Cosmo squared off, ready to battle. But then, I remembered Finn's fur from when we played together as kittens. I called out and told him I recognized him. At first, it surprised him, but then he remembered me, Cosmo, and Karma. After that, things cooled down, and he invited us to stay at his spacious, abandoned warehouse."

Jo's ears perked. "Sound like y'all get lucky," she said, studying Finn with approval. "Ain't be often you finds a male street cat offerin' shelter to strangers."

Finn's expression softened as his gaze met Aura's. "I wouldn't have if I hadn't remembered them—and Karma..." He glanced at Cosmo. "I've enjoyed their company. It's been... easy, you know? We all get along fine."

Zuzu's tail twitched, her eyes narrowing.

Josephine caught Zuzu's glare—and Aura's warm, approving look in response to Finn's words.

Cosmo changed the subject. "Before we came here, we visited Murph, and Finn got to meet him." He gave Jo a lighthearted smile. "I prepared Finn in advance about Murph's ample girth. Let's just say Finn was duly impressed by our friend's full-bodied dimensions."

Josephine gave Cosmo a derisive look. "I knows you, Cosmo. I knows you enjoy seein' the look on Finn's face when he get a good look at Murph."

Cosmo feigned hurt. "I'll have you know I told Finn that Murph is sensitive about being overweight, and I admonished him not to joke about it."

Finn burst out laughing. "Yeah, and then you ripped into him, asking how things were in fat city!"

Jo rolled her eyes. "You a bad cat, Cosmo. A bad cat."

A strained expression crossed Cosmo's face. "Murph knows I'm just being me, so he took no offense."

"Uh-huh." She sighed heavily. "I be scared for Murph. He eatin' hisself to death."

The amusement faded from Cosmo's face as he met her gaze with rare seriousness. "I know," he said quietly. "I know..."

Josephine turned her attention back to Finn, her head tilting with curiosity. "So, why a handsome cat like you be fancy-free? Why you ain't got no partner and a bunch o' young'uns?"

Finn's eyes darkened, and his ears drooped as he struggled to find the words to respond.

Aura stepped in, her voice gentle. "Finn lost his mate last year. She passed away while giving birth... and the kittens didn't survive. Jo, like us, he knows what it's like to lose everything..."

Sadness flickered in Jo's eyes as she touched him gently. "I so sorry fo' you, Finn. I lose my kittens, too. Aura lose hers. We knows such pain. We knows."

Finn's gaze moved between Jo and Aura, his expression softening. "For a while, life didn't seem worth living. But then, for the lucky ones..." His eyes found Aura's. "You might meet someone special again."

Sensing the weight of the moment, Cosmo shifted. "Hey, we still need to find something to eat, so we should probably head back soon."

Josephine's tail swished as she glanced at Zuzu. "Y'all head back to my place. I gots some private talkin' to do with little kitten here."

Surprise flickered across both Zuzu's and Aura's faces.

"Go on now, y'all. Zu and me not be here long." She turned to Finn, her expression softening. "I likes you, Finn. I looks forward to seein' yer handsome face ag'in."

Finn smiled. "I like you, too, Jo. You should visit us sometime."

She smiled. "That sound mighty good."

After the others departed, Jo turned to Zuzu, her expression gentle but firm. "Okay, Zu, what wrong?"

Zuzu's ears flattened against her head as she met Jo's gaze. "Nothing..."

"Little kitten, we ain't gots time to pussyfoot 'round. What be troublin' you?"

Zuzu sighed. "This morning, when I woke up, I saw Aura and Finn looking funny at each other. They... they touched noses and rubbed their faces together." Zuzu's eyes dimmed as she glanced at Jo. "I know Aura doesn't want me anymore. She wants Finn." She lowered her head, her voice heavy. "What will happen to me now, Jo?"

Josephine pressed her cheek against her troubled friend's. "Look at me now, Zu. You looks hard at me."

Zuzu raised her eyes, meeting Jo's steady gaze.

"You wrong, Zu. Wrong, wrong, wrong. Aura, she love you powerful—powerful love she have fo' you. But here the good thing—here the good thing: you can love mo' than one thing—that what make love so special. I loves Cosmo, I loves Aura, I loves you. Iffin' Aura love Finn, that don't mean she not love you anymo'. Understand me, little kitten?"

"I suppose..."

"No—ain't no supposin' 'bout it. Aura—she die for you—that how much she love you. Lovin' Finn don't change her love for you. That the way it is."

Zuzu nodded, looking relieved.

"Zu, Aura, she... she love Ajax so much. I know she miss him bad—she miss the love only a male cat can give. Male cat love. It a diff'rent love than female cat love. You understands me?"

"I think so."

"Good. Now we talkin'." Her gaze intensified. "I hopes in yer heart you feels happy that Aura might get male cat love again. Her bein' happy make her love fo' you grow even mo', 'cause when you happy, it easier to love other things." She touched her cheek to Zuzu's. "Trust yer friend Jo—everthin' be good; everthin' be fine. You one lucky kitten to have Aura love. You one lucky kitten to haves my love, too."

Josephine paused, her whiskers twitching thoughtfully. "Zu, I hopes, one day, you haves male cat love too. It a special kind o' love. Special kind..."

Zuzu pressed against Jo, warmth flooding through her. "Thanks for telling me how it is, Jo. I love you, too."

"That be good to hear, Zu." Jo's eyes softened with affection. "If anythin' happen to Aura, you haves me. We tight. We be best friends now. Cool?"

Zuzu's tail lifted happily. "Best friends."

"Okay, now. You put a smile on yer cute face, 'cause you be loved and wanted. We join the others now."

As they trotted to Jo's place, the genuine smile on Zuzu's face never wavered. Life, for her, had brightened considerably.

When they joined the others, Aura looked at the two of them with concern. "Is everything all right?"

Jo purred and pressed against Zuzu. "We had some good girl talk. Everthin' fine, right, girlfriend?"

Zuzu nodded enthusiastically. "I love being with Jo." Her gaze met Aura's. "I love being with you, too."

The young cat's sudden lightheartedness surprised Aura. Whatever Jo had said to her had noticeably elevated her spirits. "I feel the same about you, Zuzu." She turned to the others. "Please give me a few moments with Jo."

"Take your time, Aura," Cosmo murmured, understanding what their conversation would involve.

Jo led Aura to the side yard of her house, far enough away to ensure privacy. Her whiskers lifted in a playful expression. "My, my, my... that Finn be a cat I could curl up with on a cold night. I make a lot o' heat with him." She gave Aura an impish grin. "You been makin' heat with him, girlfriend?"

Aura couldn't help but laugh at Jo's trademark brashness, a quality that always endeared her to Aura. "No, no, not yet. But I like him, Jo. He has a kind heart."

Jo nodded knowingly. "He do."

Aura's tail swished nervously. "Before joining the others, Cosmo and I wanted to ask if you'd be okay with adding Finn to our family."

A sigh escaped Jo. "Yeah... and no."

Aura looked at her, puzzled. "What do you mean?"

"Finn, he a good cat. I sees it plain as day... but him and Cosmo? That spell trouble."

Aura nodded in understanding. "Cosmo and I talked about it. If Finn would agree to be a co-alpha with him, he'd be okay with it."

Jo's whiskers twitched as she considered Aura's response. "Like what he have with Murph and Ajax, right?"

"Right. We haven't talked to Finn about any of this until we got your and Murphy's okay to add him to our family." Her eyes held a hopeful gleam. "Murphy's all for it. That... that leaves you."

Jo nodded. She took in a deep breath and sighed. "Cosmo—he need help. One male cat ain't enough to protect you and Zu. Finn, he look like a good hunter and fighter..." Her gaze met Aura's. "If Finn and Cosmo say it be good—you knows—them workin' together, then I votes yes to have him be part o' us."

Relief washed over Aura's features. "Thanks, Jo." She paused, her tail lowering slightly. "Did Zuzu tell you about Finn and me?"

"She do. She see you and Finn lovin' on each other this mornin'. Scare her bad. She think you don't wants her anymo'—says you wants Finn now, not her. She scared. Scared bad. But I sets her straight—tells her they be plenty o' love to go 'round—and yer love fo' her be powerful. She cool now."

"Thanks for talking to her and reassuring her, Jo."

She nodded. "So, don't think we be ignorin' the main thing here—you be lovin' on that handsome male cat. Tell me what goin' on."

"It's all new, Jo. For all I know, he could have plenty of females giving him attention."

"Sound like you gots lots to talk 'bout with Finn."

"I do." Aura's whiskers drooped slightly. "We need to get going before it turns dark. Hopefully, we'll find some good eatery food on the way home." Her gaze softened as she met Jo's eyes. "I love you, Jo. You're my dearest friend."

"Same fo' me with you."

The foursome made their way home, each wearing a smile that reflected their heart: Zuzu's smile reflected the warmth of being loved, Aura's held the quiet hope of a second chance at love, Cosmo's spoke of a strengthened family and shared responsibility, and Finn's radiated a newfound sense of belonging. In their own ways, the day had been deeply satisfying for each of them.

23

As they headed home, their contentment gave way to growing hunger. Cosmo's ears perked up as he turned to Finn. "We're in my part of town now. I know some great places to eat."

"Sounds good to me," Finn replied. "Do you have a hankering for anything?"

Cosmo's tail lifted with excitement. "There's this one food I can never resist—tender strips of meat bathed in a sweet and spicy sauce, perfectly caramelized with crispy edges. Just thinking about it makes my mouth water."

"Well, here's hoping their trash cans overflow with it today."

Cosmo nodded. "There's only one way to find out—follow me!"

The streetlights flickered on as dusk settled in, casting shadows across their path. They padded past neat rows of houses, the maple trees standing like sentinels with bare branches reaching toward the darkening sky.

Soon, the residential area gave way to shops and eateries. Cosmo led them down an alley, weaving between buildings until he stopped at a familiar eatery. He paused by one of the trash cans, rising onto his hind legs to sniff the air, his whiskers quivering with anticipation.

He glanced back at the others, who watched expectantly. "There's food in here, but not what I'm looking for." Moving to the next can, he inhaled deeply. His eyes brightened. "Oh yeah—this is it!"

With practiced ease, he leaped atop the adjacent trash can. Reaching over, he pried open the lid, careful not to let it clatter to the ground. Once he'd created enough space, he slipped inside.

The rich aroma of his favorite food hit his nose immediately. Following the scent, he dug through the contents until he found his prized meat strips! Without hesitation, he gathered several pieces and dropped them to his waiting companions.

"Feast away," he purred, watching their eyes light up at the offering.

Back in the can, Cosmo devoured a few tasty pieces before resuming his search. His nose led him to more meat, which he licked, savoring the sweet and sour flavor. "Yum!" he whispered to himself. Grinning, he gathered more to share with the others.

Soon, everyone had eaten their fill. Cosmo emerged from the can, clearly pleased with their successful hunt.

Finn licked the leftover sauce from his paws. "Your taste is impeccable, Coz. We'll definitely have to come back here."

Zuzu purred, her tail swishing in time with her words. "I know what two-legs call this food. Mrs. Chen ate it all the time, and I loved how she always shared it with me. She called it Mongolian beef. Like you, Cosmo, it's my favorite food."

Aura, sitting next to her, nodded eagerly. "I like it, too."

Cosmo's chest swelled with pride. "Mongolian beef, huh? It's a weird name, but I'll remember it. I'm glad you all liked it." He glanced down the alley, his ears twitching as he scanned for any signs of trouble. "We should get moving before we run into other cats looking for a meal."

The others nodded, and Cosmo led them away from the dangerous alleyways and toward the safer sidewalks. They passed more storefronts and crossed into another tree-lined residential area, heading toward Finn's warehouse.

Two blocks later, a menacing growl tore through the peaceful night. Cosmo's fur bristled, his senses on high alert. A thunderous bark echoed through the dark—a primal sound that resonated with every cat's deepest fear. A demon hundfang erupted from the shadows, jaws snapping.

"Scatter! Up the trees!" Cosmo screamed, his voice tight with panic.

He launched himself up a nearby maple, claws sinking into the rough bark.

The others reacted instantly. Aura sprang up another tree, her movements fluid and practiced. Zuzu hesitated, then scrambled toward a nearby trunk. Her claws slipped as she climbed, and with a terrified cry, she fell, hitting the ground with a sickening thud.

"Zuzu!" Aura's screech tore through the night.

The hundfang spotted her and charged, jaws gaping.

Cosmo launched himself from his perch, hurtling toward Zuzu.

"Run!" he wailed as the hundfang closed in.

Zuzu lurched to her feet and sprang aside just as the beast's jaws snapped shut.

Cosmo hurled himself at the beast with a piercing battle cry.

The hundfang whirled from Zuzu toward the attacking cat. Cosmo slipped past its snapping jaws but slammed into the tree trunk. The impact drove the air from his lungs, and he collapsed.

He lay there gasping, dazed but aware enough to know his life was about to end.

As the hundfang lunged for the killing blow, an orange blur struck.

Finn flew through the air with a feral shriek, claws slashing. He raked the beast's face, tearing deep gashes across its muzzle and eye. The hundfang howled and reeled back, blood streaming.

Finn darted to the beast's blind side, his claws striking its sensitive nose again, opening deep wounds. The hundfang yelped and stumbled, but rage replaced pain. It lunged at Finn with a thunderous snarl.

Aura leaped onto the hundfang, landing on its shoulders. Her claws shredded the tender flesh of its ear. As she sprang clear, Finn struck again, his claws slashing its muzzle.

The hundfang howled in pain and fled into the darkness. As its footsteps faded into the night, Cosmo struggled to rise. To his amazement, he and the others were alive.

"Aura," he wheezed, "are you okay?"

Still trembling from the adrenaline, she nodded. "I couldn't leave you there, Cosmo."

Zuzu crept to Cosmo's side, shaking. "I... I thought he'd kill you."

Cosmo touched his nose to hers. "I'm fine." His gaze shifted to Finn. "Thanks to you and Aura."

Finn stood, his sides heaving from the exertion. "That was too close—way too close..."

Aura pressed her face against his. "You were incredible, Finn. You saved us."

Finn dipped his head slightly, a hint of a smile playing on his face. "As I always say, demon hundfangs are all bark and no bite."

Cosmo eyed him with admiration. "Damn, Finn. There's more to you than your good looks."

"Same to you—how you charged that hundfang to save Zuzu—let's just say there's more to both of us than our good looks."

Aura flicked her tail, shaking her head at their banter.

Cosmo's muscles trembled. "This is enough excitement for one night. Let's head home."

"You sure?" Finn's whiskers twitched. "I'm up for terrorizing a few more hundfangs tonight."

Aura marveled at Finn's cheekiness after such an ordeal. "You hundfang terrorizers need rest. We've all earned it."

They crept home through shadow-filled streets, every sense alert for danger. Each knew how close they'd come to death.

In the resting area of their warehouse, exhaustion crept over them. Zuzu pressed against Cosmo's side, still trembling.

"I'm sorry," she whispered, her voice barely audible, thick with guilt. "I almost got you killed..."

Cosmo shook his head. "Zuzu, you've had only one lesson in climbing trees. That's not enough, and that's on me." He met her gaze, his eyes steady. "It wasn't your fault." He paused, then spoke with conviction. "Street cats don't have the luxury of dwelling on what might have happened. We learn, and we move forward. Understand?"

Zuzu stared at him, fear still lingering in her eyes, but his words sank in. She nodded slowly. His reassurance didn't erase the weight of what had almost happened, but it helped ease the tightness in her chest. For the first time since the attack, her racing heart began to slow.

Aura watched Cosmo comfort Zuzu, her eyes soft. "He's right, Zuzu. What matters is that we protected each other. That's what family does."

Cosmo turned to Finn. "You didn't hesitate for a heartbeat to protect us. Thank you."

Finn looked away, still processing what had happened. "I just did what needed doing."

"You were fearless, my friend," Cosmo said softly. "You're a demon hundfang slayer."

Finn's whiskers twitched at the praise. After a moment, he met Cosmo's gaze. "I couldn't bear to lose another family—" He caught himself, and his ears flattened. "I mean... it felt like you all were my family today."

Cosmo's expression softened. "About that." He glanced at Aura. "We want to talk to you about something important."

Zuzu lifted her head from Aura's side, her curiosity piqued.

"Finn," Cosmo began, "the trip to see Murph and Jo today wasn't just about you meeting them. As you know, even though they live with two-legs now, they're still part of our family. We wanted their thoughts about you—whether they could accept you as one of us. They both like you and gave their enthusiastic approval."

Cosmo's whiskers twitched with emotion as he continued. "What you did tonight—how you fought for us—it proves that you belong with us."

Aura's eyes shone with affection. "We want you to be part of us, Finn. We'll fight for you like you fought for us tonight."

Finn blinked slowly, studying their faces.

Cosmo seized the moment to address the final hurdle. "There's one more thing," he said, his voice carrying the weight of his words. "In our family, we don't have a single male alpha—we share the leadership. Murphy, Ajax, and I called it being co-alphas. We worked as a team, with no one cat making all the decisions. When it came to important matters, the whole family got a vote, and it worked well for us. So, if you want to be part of this family, that's how it has to be."

Finn tilted his head. "Co-alphas?"

"Yeah," Cosmo confirmed. "You and me as co-alphas. If that doesn't work for you, we'll stay friends. But not family."

Finn's tail swished thoughtfully. The concept of shared leadership was new to him, but as he turned it over in his mind, it felt right. Still, he had his principles.

"I can live with that," he finally said, "but there are some things I won't go along with—even if I get outvoted."

Cosmo's ears pricked. "Like what?"

"For example, if everyone voted to attack a hundfang for sport, I'd refuse," Finn said firmly. "That's idiotic and reckless. I won't risk lives without reason. If a decision feels wrong in my gut, I won't follow it."

Understanding flickered across Cosmo's face. "I get what you're saying, and I'd do the same. Trust me, in this family, we're not all day dumb. We make smart choices by weighing everyone's thoughts and opinions. Karma taught us that when we were kittens, and it's always worked well for us."

"We don't take foolish risks, Finn," Aura added, her eyes warm. "We think things through."

Zuzu lifted her paw. "Even though I don't know much about life on the streets, I love how everyone still listens to me and values what I say."

Cosmo nuzzled her before turning to Finn. "So, what do you say?"

Finn looked at Cosmo and winked, his whiskers twitching with a mischievous grin. "I only thought one of you was all day dumb."

Getting Finn's subtle jab, Cosmo rolled his eyes.

Finn's face softened into a smile. "I'd like to be part of this family."

Cosmo's expression turned serious for a moment. Then he grinned. "Excellent. Well then, let's take a vote. All those who'd like to have Finn be part of the family, raise a paw."

Aura and Zuzu's paws shot up immediately, their faces glowing with relief and excitement. Finn raised his paw as well, his eyes bright.

Cosmo lifted his paw, his gaze meeting Finn's. "Welcome to the family, Finn." An impish glint appeared in his eyes. "As senior co-alpha, how about you go fetch me a rat and fluff my resting spot before I turn in?"

Aura groaned, burying her face in her paws.

Without missing a beat, Finn chimed in. "I'd like to take a vote to make Cosmo eat a bowl full of Murph's food balls. All those in favor, raise a paw."

With matching grins, he, Aura, and Zuzu shot their paws upward.

Amused, Cosmo's tail whisked back and forth. "Well, Finn, to invoke your words, that's idiotic and reckless. I'd be putting myself in harm's way for nothing. So, my gut feeling—literally, my gut's dictate—is to not go along with the group vote."

They all burst into laughter. Cosmo and Finn exchanged grins, enjoying the easy banter between them.

In this moment, the terror of the hundfang encounter faded, replaced by the warmth of camaraderie and the comfort of belonging. They had each other. They were family. And as they faced the unknown ahead, that was all that mattered.

24

SPRING HAD SETTLED OVER Queens, wrapping the city in warmth and new life. Aura sat alone in a patch of grass near their warehouse home, her body at peace but her mind restless. Sunlight soaked into her fur while the sweet scent of early blooms drifted on the breeze. The calm morning stood in contrast to the chaos they'd weathered just months before. Today, the world pulsed with promise all around her, yet she remained quiet, lost in thought.

Memories of Karma filled her mind, as tangible as the scent of wildflowers—sweet yet bittersweet. His wisdom, his boundless love... The loss still carved an empty space in her heart, sharp and present despite the passing days. But alongside the ache of missing him, gratitude bloomed for how he had shaped her, molded her into the strong, capable cat she was today. His lessons still whispered to her, guiding her as she stepped into this new chapter of her life.

A soft rustle drew her attention. Finn approached, his head tilted and ears forward.

"You okay?" he asked softly, his voice full of concern.

Aura's whiskers lifted with her warm smile, though sadness lingered in her eyes. "I'm just remembering Karma," she said quietly. "He was such a good cat—so wise and loving. I think about him every day." She exhaled slowly, the weight of her words hanging in the air for a moment.

Finn settled beside her, his tail curling thoughtfully around his paws. "I only have faint memories of him, but I can see how much of him lives on in you."

Aura nodded, feeling a surge of warmth in her chest. "He taught me about love and life." She touched her cheek to Finn's, lingering in the contact. "Like Karma, you bring the same comfort when you're by my side..." Her voice softened, barely more than a whisper. "It feels right... you feel like home."

Finn's whiskers quivered at her words, and his ears tilted forward with affection. "I'm glad I can be that for you." He paused, letting out a contented purr. "I'm happy too, Aura. Having you with me makes everything feel better."

She leaned into him, feeling peace settle over them. For the first time since losing Karma, she felt at ease, complete and whole again. "Finn," she murmured, her heart fluttering, "there's something else I want to share with you." She met his gaze, her eyes bright with joy. "I'm going to have kittens."

Finn's breath caught in his throat. His eyes widened as a wave of emotions washed over him. He drew back slightly, just enough to look at her properly, his expression transforming from surprise to pure delight. "Really?" he breathed, a smile spreading across his face. "That... that's wonderful."

"I'm excited. There's much to look forward to." Her paw moved instinctively to her belly, where new life stirred. "I never imagined I'd feel this way again. But now... with you, Cosmo, and Zuzu... we're a perfect family."

"We're an expanding family," Finn purred, gently touching his nose to her.

Aura's face glowed with contentment, her feelings for Finn deepening like roots finding fertile soil. "For the first time in so long, life feels good."

As spring crept into Queens, Cosmo and Finn grew closer, their friendship built on shared hunts and quiet trust. They challenged each other daily—racing up trees, stalking rats, and watching for threats. Each contest or round of friendly banter deepened their bond as co-alphas.

One evening, after another successful hunt, he and Finn lounged on a rooftop, the sky stretching above them, its colors bleeding from rose to deepening blue. Cosmo spoke of his earlier days, when Murphy and Josephine still roamed the streets alongside him, Aura, Ajax, and Karma.

Finn's whiskers twitched with amusement. "Josephine, Josephine, Josephine. If she ever had a partner, I pity that poor cat having to deal with her..."

Cosmo's tail curled as he shot Finn a sly look. "Um, that poor cat would be me."

Finn's ears shot forward in surprise. "You—no way!"

"Yep." Cosmo's whiskers lifted in a gentle smile. "She was my partner. Still is, in her own way."

Finn stared at him, jaw slack. "Okay, okay—give me a moment to process this..."

Cosmo exhaled, then began to share their story—how everything changed after they lost their kittens and how their relationship suffered after the two-legs cut on her.

"Damn, Coz," Finn sighed, his voice heavy with sadness. "Damn..."

"Yeah," Cosmo replied, barely above a whisper. "I blew it with Jo by seeking the pleasures of other females. So, if you want to keep Aura, stay faithful..."

"I get it," Finn responded softly, a thoughtful pause following his words. "I really do..."

Cosmo's tail swished as he gazed into the darkening sky. "Finn, I know Josephine is... well, who she is. But underneath that hard, brash exterior, she's got the softest, most tender heart you'll ever meet. Back in the old days, ours was an epic love..." He turned to Finn, his eyes softening with quiet regret. "It still is."

Finn nodded. "I've seen that tender heart of hers, especially with Zuzu. Jo adores her."

"You're right. I think Zuzu reminds Jo of the kittens we lost," he said softly, then smirked. "But that's Jo for you—gentle as a spring rain one moment and fierce as a demon hundfang the next. You never know which side you'll get, but that's what makes her special. She keeps life interesting—and fun."

Finn laughed, his whiskers twitching. "I'll bet you'd rather face a pack of rabid masked hundfangs than Jo's ferocity."

"You'd win that bet," Cosmo chuckled.

A comfortable silence settled between them as they watched the night claim the city. After a while, Cosmo turned to Finn, his expression softening. "How are things with you and Aura? Expecting cats can get pretty feisty, too."

Finn thought about it for a moment, his whiskers twitching in quiet contemplation. "I can handle it. Like you said about Jo, Aura's special. Her kind heart... I'm sure it's every bit as big as Jo's."

"It is," Cosmo agreed, giving Finn a playful nudge. "But need I remind you how quickly she shredded that hundfang's ear?"

Finn's laugh echoed across the quiet night, deep and genuine, carrying equal parts amusement and healthy respect. "Oh, it's crossed my mind more than once."

Zuzu's ears perked up as Cosmo and Finn rejoined the others back in their home. "If everyone's okay with it, I'd like to visit Jo tomorrow."

"Of course," Aura replied, her whiskers twitching with gentle concern. "You've been spending quite a bit of time with Jo lately. Is everything all right?"

"It is," Zuzu said, her tail lifting happily. "I really like being with her."

She had come far from the pampered house cat who'd first stumbled into their lives. Confidence now propelled her forward, a marked difference from the uncertainty that once defined her movements. She hunted regularly with Cosmo and Finn, her skills growing sharper with each successful hunt. Having learned from the older cats, she'd become a valuable part of their family—a part that now felt the stirrings of independence.

Cosmo touched her paw gently. "Just remember to head home before sunset, Zu. Hundfangs love prowling at night, looking for easy prey."

"I will," she promised, her eyes bright with understanding.

The following morning, she set out for Jo's, her movements quick and precise as she darted through the streets of Queens. Her eyes constantly scanned her surroundings, mapping escape routes and staying sharp for any sign of hundfangs.

At Jo's Roosevelt Avenue home, Zuzu gave their secret call. Moments later, Josephine burst through the cat door.

"Zu! I be thinkin' o' you!"

Zuzu bounded forward, warmed by Jo's enthusiastic welcome. "I've been thinking about you, too, Jo—that's why I'm here."

"C'mon, we sit awhile and catch up!" She led Zuzu to the side yard of her house, where the shade offered relief from the spring warmth.

They settled into their usual spot, enjoying the cool breeze beneath the shadows of overhanging branches.

"How you is, little kitten?"

Zuzu's ears drooped. "Soon, you can't call me little kitten anymore—not after Aura has hers."

"Zu, you always gonna be my special little kitten. Don't matter what comes."

Unconvinced, Zuzu shrugged.

"I sees Aura havin' kittens be eatin' at you. It time for us to be talkin' ag'in. Serious talkin'."

The young cat frowned. "I know when the kittens come, Aura won't have time for me anymore."

Josephine's tail flicked as Zuzu spoke. When she finished, Josephine nodded. "That be true, Zu. That be true. When she ain't tended to them kittens, she be tired—fearsome tired. So, yeah, you right 'bout being ignored. But that don't mean you is not loved, or won't be needed. Aura—she need you bad—she need yer help whens the young'uns be tiny and helpless. You watch 'em when Aura need sleep, keep 'em outta trouble. And when they big enough, you be their mentor. You teach 'em everthin' you learns, and they love you fo' it. You gonna have more attention than you knows what to do with!"

Zuzu's eyes softened as she listened to Jo, the weight of her earlier fears starting to lift. She had been so afraid that Aura's new kittens would push her aside that she would become invisible in their family. But Jo's words painted a different picture—a future where Zuzu had an important role in the group.

"You're right," Zuzu said, her voice quiet yet more confident now. "I guess I never thought of it that way. I thought I was losing something, but maybe... maybe I'll gain something new." She felt a flicker of excitement as the idea of mentoring the kittens transformed from a burden into a gift. "It could be fun—having kittens to play with."

"Now you gettin' it!" Jo grinned, her tail swishing excitedly. "You be loved like crazy. But first—you gots to be patient. Won't be long fo' them helpless kittens be runnin' all over, playin', gettin' into mischief. And trust me—you be sayin', 'Jo, them kittens be so much fun to be with!'"

Zuzu couldn't help but laugh at Jo's unbridled enthusiasm. Maybe this new chapter wouldn't be so bad after all. "Jo, you have an amazing ability to see what I can't see."

Jo chuckled. "That what experience do fo' you, Zu. Years teach lessons that the days can't."

Zuzu smiled to herself as she made her way home, her thoughts now buzzing with new possibilities. Being a big sister didn't feel so scary anymore. It felt like an adventure. An opportunity to teach, to protect, and to shape the next generation of their family. She was ready for it. Ready to give her love to the new kittens and grow even closer to the family she had found.

As she navigated through Queens, Zuzu's thoughts swirled with images of tiny kittens tumbling after her, all looking up to her. She imagined teaching them everything she'd learned from Aura, Cosmo, and Finn—how to hunt, climb trees, spot danger before it spotted you, and the proper way to dispatch a rat. The thought made her whiskers quiver with pride.

Back home, Zuzu found Aura resting in their usual spot. She settled beside her, touching her nose to Aura's cheek.

"Did you have a good visit with Jo?" Aura asked softly.

"The best," Zuzu purred, settling in closer. "She helped me understand something important."

"Oh?"

"That I'm going to be the best big sister ever."

25

SPRING DEEPENED INTO SUMMER in Queens as new life stirred within Aura. She often dozed in patches of sunlight, dreaming of the kittens to come. Her heart overflowed with love for her family—Finn, Cosmo, Zuzu, Jo, and Murphy—each one a cherished part of her life. With the tiny lives growing inside her, that circle of love would expand even further.

One evening, as she and Finn sat on the roof of a nearby shed, watching the city street lights in Queens come alive, Aura gently touched her rounded belly. "I'm excited," she murmured, her whiskers trembling slightly. "Excited... and a little nervous."

Finn leaned in, his voice steady and soft. "Me, too. But let's focus on all the joy ahead, not the worries."

Aura nodded, her gaze wandering to the cityscape. The setting sun brushed the sky with brilliant strokes of orange and pink, its dwindling light reflecting off distant windows. "A future full of possibilities, Finn." She sighed contentedly, her heart full of love and quiet hope for what lay ahead.

As daylight faded and the first stars began to glimmer overhead, they padded inside to join the others, settling in for a peaceful night in their warehouse home.

The following morning, Aura woke and stretched. Beside her, Finn stirred at her movement and opened his eyes. "Good morning, Aura," he whispered, careful not to wake the others.

She pressed close to him, whiskers lifting in a smile. "Don't laugh, but I woke up craving pizza... you know, from our favorite eatery."

His tail curled in amusement. "I'll suggest to Coz and Zu that we head there today and see what we can find. While we're gone, you can catch up on some rest."

At the mention of pizza, Cosmo and Zuzu's ears perked up.

"Oh, yeah!" Cosmo's whiskers quivered with excitement. "I'm always up for pizza."

"I like the cheesy ones best!" Zuzu chimed in eagerly.

After saying goodbye to Aura at noon, the trio set out. The alley behind the eatery was narrow and shadowed, wedged between rows of buildings—the kind of place that most two-legs typically avoided. Trash cans lined the passage, their contents giving off the pungent scents of grease, rotting food, and the unmistakable urine smells left by rats and cats who claimed it as their territory.

Cosmo's nose twitched as the delicious aroma of pizza wafted toward him. His whiskers quivered with curiosity, and he soon spotted the source—a half-eaten pizza lying abandoned on the ground. That it wasn't in a trash can but on the pavement seemed odd and should have raised suspicion. Yet, the tempting aroma overwhelmed both his and Finn's usual caution.

"Oh, yeah!" Cosmo whispered. "Plenty for everyone—let's eat our fill and take the rest home!"

The three cats dove into their feast like starved rats.

Above them, a drop trap waited, its large rectangular frame blending with the building's walls. The pizza below served as bait—a trick two-legs had mastered to catch strays. None of the three cats sensed how this moment would come to haunt them.

Finn leaned forward for another bite, his paw pressing a hidden plate beneath the pizza. A soft click whispered through the alley.

The trap slammed down with a deafening clang.

Cosmo and Finn arched their backs and hissed, fur bristling. Their claws scraped against the metal, desperately trying to escape, but the trap held firm. Their yowls of panic and fury echoed off the alley walls. Zuzu crouched, frozen in fear, knowing they were trapped.

Then came the sound of two-leg footsteps—quiet at first, then growing louder. The cats couldn't know it, but these two-legs were the ones who had set the trap. They were part of a city program to control the feral cat population by spaying females, and Zuzu was their target.

Cosmo and Finn hissed and slashed as the two-legs stopped in front of the cage, their muscles coiled with fury. One of the two-legs pointed at Zuzu—the lone female.

One of the two-legs jabbed a metal pole at Cosmo and Finn, forcing them to the back of the trap. In that instant, the other two-leg, his hands protected by thick gloves, reached in and grabbed Zuzu by the scruff of her neck. She fought and twisted, but he yanked her out and stuffed her into a carrier. He then walked to their moving box, placed the carrier inside, and returned to the cage holding Cosmo and Finn.

As the two-leg with the pole kept Cosmo and Finn occupied, the other lifted the trap. Seeing their chance to escape, Cosmo and Finn bolted. From a safe distance, they watched helplessly as the vehicle pulled away with Zuzu inside.

"Let's go after her!" Cosmo cried out, his voice cracking with desperation. They sprinted after the vehicle, but it accelerated away, disappearing around a corner with Zuzu.

Cosmo and Finn froze, their sides heaving as they gasped for breath. The reality slammed into them like a physical blow—the two-legs had snatched Zuzu away, and they couldn't stop it.

"We need to head home," Finn panted, his voice heavy with defeat. His tail flicked with anger, underscoring his frustration, and his shoulders slumped as if the weight of their failure was too much to bear. He turned to Cosmo, whiskers drooping. "How... how do we tell Aura? This will devastate her."

Cosmo remained motionless, his whiskers trembling with emotion. Finally, he exhaled a shaky breath. "We failed her, Finn. We walked right into that two-leg trap like fools. A pizza just lying there... we should've known something was off."

Finn sighed deeply. "You're right. Our stupidity is going to make telling Aura even harder..."

With heavy hearts, they turned and made their way home.

As the moving box sped away, each bump made Zuzu's heart pound harder. When it finally stopped, a two-leg opened the door and lifted her carrier with practiced ease, carrying Zuzu into a building filled with smells and sounds that overwhelmed her senses. The two-leg, wearing thick gloves, placed her into a sterile cage—cold, impersonal, and utterly unwelcoming.

Still dazed from the shock of being trapped, Zuzu stiffened in fear, realizing where she was: a room full of other animals, all locked in cages, just like the place she'd been taken to after her two-leg had died. Around her, other animals shifted in their cages, their distress thick in the air. Her eyes darted around, searching desperately for a way out.

A short while later, the two-legs took her from her cage and brought her to another part of the building, placing her on a cold metal table. One of them approached with a gentle demeanor, carefully placing a soft mask over her nose and mouth. A sweet-smelling gas filled her lungs, and though her body tensed, the two-leg's soothing murmur calmed her panic. Slowly, the gas took hold. Her racing heart slowed, her muscles loosened, and the world around her dimmed as unconsciousness crept in.

The procedure was swift and precise, with the team working efficiently as they removed Zuzu's ovaries and uterus while monitoring her vital signs. Once finished, they stitched her closed with dissolving sutures, cleaned the area, and moved her to a recovery cage. A warming blanket was draped over her small form, helping to maintain her body temperature as they continued to monitor her vital signs.

As the sedatives wore off, Zuzu's mind churned, frantically trying to make sense of the chaos. The sharp crash of the trap, the angry hisses of Cosmo and Finn, being yanked away from them—it all felt like a nightmare she couldn't escape. She had been so sure they would come for her—that they would find a way to get her out of this. But now... now she was alone.

Her limbs felt heavy and disconnected as if she no longer knew how to move them. The cage felt like a prison, the bars a suffocating weight on her chest. The air was thick with a strange, biting scent, overlaid with the lingering aromas of other creatures. Every breath felt like a struggle. The aching in her belly screamed of a loss she couldn't name but felt with every beat of her heart.

Cosmo, Aura, and Finn... she clung to the memory of them, though they felt farther and farther away with each passing moment. They were the ones who always knew what to do, who always made things better. But now, in the strange stillness of this cage, that sense of safety vanished. The deafening silence tormented her, heightening her fearful thoughts. She blinked, trying to clear the fog in her mind, but the images of what had happened danced in awareness like a mirage—real, but maybe not real...

She called out for her family, but her cries went unanswered. Would they ever come for her? Or would she be doomed to live forever in this cage, abandoned and alone? These questions gnawed at her insides. She yearned for the world outside the cage, which now seemed so distant, so foreign.

A two-leg reached into her cage and carefully lifted her out. Zuzu stiffened, her heart racing, but the two-leg's voice sounded soft, almost comforting. They placed her on a cold metal table, and before she could react, a sharp sting shot through her ear. It didn't hurt as much as everything else, but the sensation made her pull away instinctively.

Her ear tingled with pain, but she couldn't do anything about it. The two-leg returned her to the cage, leaving her confused and disoriented. She tried to make sense of what had happened but couldn't.

What Zuzu didn't know was that they had marked her as spayed so other two-legs would recognize her and release her if she were trapped again.

A day later, after checking her condition one final time, a two-leg removed the cone from around her neck and placed her in another carrier. To Zuzu's surprise, they carried her outside and set her down in a moving box. A short while later, the moving box stopped in the alley where they had trapped her earlier. The two-leg opened the carrier door and motioned for her to step out.

Zuzu hesitated before stepping into the blinding sunlight. Her eyes barely registered the familiar sights of cracked pavement and scattered debris. The two-leg who had carried her stepped back, offering a soft murmur before returning to the moving box and driving away.

Now alone, a dazed Zuzu tried to make sense of everything. Once familiar, the alley felt different—colder, emptier. She looked around, absently searching for Cosmo and Finn, but they were nowhere to be seen.

She sat, forcing herself to think clearly. First, she focused on where she was—the alley behind the pizza eatery. Then another thought struck her—who among her family was closest? Aura, Murphy, or Jo? The answer came quickly: Josephine lived nearest. One thing became clear—she had to get to Jo.

Still disoriented, Zuzu felt an overwhelming urge to flee. Her instincts screamed that she wasn't safe here—not with potential dangers like rats, strange cats, and hundfangs. She rose, remaining motionless for several heartbeats, fear surging through her. Summoning her courage, she took a tentative step, then another. Though her legs trembled beneath her, she pressed forward. The alley felt scarier without Cosmo and Finn, the shadows deeper. The world seemed to close in around her. But there was no stopping now. She had to reach Jo. Jo meant life...

26

Cosmo and Finn trudged homeward beneath the bright afternoon sun, their silence laden with sadness. Cosmo halted and turned to face his friend. "I don't want this to come between you and Aura." He took in a deep breath. "So I'll take full responsibility for this."

Finn's tail shot straight up. "No way, Coz! We both screwed up. We both need to face the consequences."

Cosmo stared at him, words failing. After a long pause, he hung his head. "We... we need to focus on one thing: Zuzu is alive." His eyes suddenly widened. "When we first met her, Zuzu told us that after her two-leg died, they took her to a place where they put cats and other creatures in cages. When they opened her cage door, she managed to escape. She wandered the streets until Aura found her." He lifted his head, a glimmer of hope returning to his eyes. "So, we need to make it clear to Aura that Zuzu is alive, and she's clever enough to get away and come back to us."

"That makes sense," Finn said slowly. "I sure hope it works out that way..."

When they reached the warehouse, Cosmo and Finn paused outside for a few moments, bracing themselves for what lay ahead. Cosmo swallowed hard before stepping inside, with Finn following closely behind. They found Aura curled up in their resting spot. She looked up, her round belly visible, and greeted them with a bright expression. But that brightness faded when she noticed the heaviness in their eyes. Her voice trembled. "Where's Zuzu?"

Finn took a deep breath. "Aura... the two-legs caught Zuzu and took her away." He watched her flinch but pressed on, his voice filled with regret. "We... we couldn't stop it. They set a trap. And we fell for it. They used pizza to lure us in."

Cosmo stepped forward, his voice cracking. "She's alive, Aura. Zuzu is alive. Finn and I chased after the moving box they put her in, but it sped away..." He looked her in the eye. "She's alive—and that's what matters."

Aura sank, anguish in her eyes. "Why didn't you two fight the two-legs to get her back?"

"We couldn't fight them, Aura," Finn said quietly, his voice tight with frustration. "They pushed us away from Zuzu with a stick, and then one of them reached in and pulled her out of the trap. After putting her in their moving box, they returned and let us go. We tried to follow, but..." His gaze, heavy with sorrow, met hers. "We couldn't catch up. Their moving boxes... they move too fast."

Cosmo's voice trembled with regret. "We got caught because we listened to our bellies instead of our heads... and now Zuzu's gone."

"All I could think about was bringing a big slice of pizza home to you," Finn muttered, his head hanging low in shame.

Cosmo raised a paw. "When we first met Zuzu, she told us about the place where they kept creatures in cages... and how she escaped. Zuzu's smart, Aura. She knows how to get away. We need to focus on that."

Aura's whiskers drooped as the news settled in. Her expression was unreadable, and for a moment, she simply breathed. Then, with a barely above a whisper, she spoke. "If I hadn't had that craving for pizza, she'd be here now. So... it's on me, too." She paused, her gaze hardening. "She's alive, and that's all that matters." Her voice shifted from grief to resolve. "And we're going to find her. Let's go."

Finn shook his head. "No, Aura, we aren't. Let's think this through—you're about to give birth any day now, and I'm not leaving you when that happens. Cosmo needs to hunt for food while I stay with you. And we can't just march into wherever the two-legs are keeping her and demand her release."

Aura opened her mouth to protest, but Finn cut her off. "I've already lost a partner and kittens. I won't risk losing you and our kittens by wandering around looking for Zuzu. And this isn't up for a vote."

Aura stared at him, her ears flattening against her head. This wasn't the gentle Finn she knew—the one who always asked what she thought, who valued her input. Her first instinct was to argue, to remind him that she wasn't helpless or in need of protection. But the raw pain in his voice when he'd mentioned his lost family made her pause.

Cosmo blinked slowly, purring in agreement with Finn. "He's right, Aura. If we vote, I'm with him. You and the kittens have to be our focus. But remember—Zuzu isn't the helpless cat she was when you first found her. She knows the streets now, and she'll find her way back when she gets free. If Karma were here, I'm sure he'd say the same thing."

Finn's tail flicked back and forth, grateful for Cosmo's support.

Aura sighed. "You're right, both of you." Her whiskers twitched. "But when our kittens are old enough, we'll all look for her. Together. And that isn't up for a vote either."

She winced in pain.

"What's wrong, Aura?"

"I-I think my kittens are coming." She winced again, her expression tightening. "They're coming!"

Alarm flashed in her eyes as she looked at Finn and Cosmo...

Zuzu stumbled forward in the alleyway, her shaking legs slowly steadying beneath her. The afternoon sun beat down as she navigated the bustling streets of Queens, heat rising from the cracked sidewalks. Junction Boulevard opened before her in a wall of noise and chaos—moving box engines revved, subway trains rumbled, voices murmured and blended. Music poured from a nearby bodega's open door while the scent of frying street food mingled with exhaust fumes.

Zuzu ducked under a nearby bush to catch her breath, seeking some relief from the overwhelming commotion. The frenzied sounds of the busy street heightened her desperation to get to Jo. She closed her eyes for a moment, gathering her thoughts.

With renewed determination, Zuzu darted across the street. A moving box screeched to a halt, barely missing her. Its blaring horn pushed her onward, dodging pedestrians absorbed in their own worlds. A block later, she reached 37th Avenue, alive with the energy of Queens—small shops, street vendors, and the constant hum of the city. The smell of fresh bagels and hot dogs mixed with the warm air of the afternoon. She continued weaving through the bustling crowds as the subway rumbled above, its screeching iron wheels cutting through the air.

Her heart raced as she neared Jo's block, the familiar sights grounding her. She padded down the alley until she reached Jo's backyard. Zuzu weakly imitated Cosmo's secret call to get Jo's attention. Though it was faint, it worked.

As Jo squeezed through the cat door, her face lit up with an enormous grin. But the smile quickly morphed into shock as she saw Zuzu collapse before her. "Zu—what wrong! What happen to you?"

"Two-legs, Jo—two-legs trapped Cosmo, Finn, and me. They took me away and cut me!" Zuzu panted, her voice trembling.

"Cuts on you where, Zu?"

"On my ear and my belly."

Jo's eyes widened in horror. "Sho' me—sho' me where they cuts you."

Zuzu tilted her head to show the missing chunk of her ear.

Jo struggled to speak, her voice trembling. "Roll over an' sho' me yer belly."

Zuzu complied, rolling over as Jo asked.

Jo's body went rigid as she viewed the shaved fur and cut marks on Zuzu's belly. Her breath hitched. Then, a gut-wrenching wail tore from her, echoing in the backyard. She pressed her head to Zuzu's, her voice trembling. "Oh, little kitten—little kitten—look what they does to you!"

Panic flashed in Zuzu's eyes. "Am I gonna die, Jo?"

Jo pulled back, her voice raw as she shook her head. "No! You ain't gonna die, Zu. You be fine. You be sore fo' a few days, but you ain't dyin'. I knows this 'cause the two-legs done the same to me, and here I is, alive and kickin'."

Zuzu's eyes widened at what Jo said. "Does this mean I won't be able to have kittens or have those... urges?"

Jo swallowed hard. "Zu, we ain't talkin' 'bout that right now. That a conversation fo' another day. Another day." She paused, thinking. "We gots a problem that need fixin' right now."

"What?"

"You in no condition fo' me to takes you home, and I ain't never been to your home, so I don't knows the way." She paused again, and then her face lit up. "Zu, my two-legs, they good creatures. I gots an idea—maybe they lets you stay here until you be better. What you think?"

Zuzu recoiled slightly, her expression darkening. "I hate two-legs—look what they've done to me!"

Jo nodded solemnly but remained firm. "It easy to feels that way, Zu. I gets it. Some two-legs be good, some ain't. But my two-legs—they diff'rent. They good ones, hear?"

Zuzu hesitated but nodded meekly.

"I gots a plan, Zu, but I needs yer help."

"What kind of help?"

Jo lowered her voice, her tone gentle but insistent. "I needs you to follow me inside. You give my two-legs a sad look that say, 'Help me, help me.' Two-legs can't resist when you looks at them like that. You knows what I mean?"

Zuzu sighed. "Murphy taught us how to look at two-legs with pitiful eyes. You sit down and stare at them, looking all mournful."

"Good. That be good. Now you shows me what Murphy teach you."

"He said you first have to sit and then do this..." She sat and stared at Jo with the saddest eyes one could imagine. She didn't have to pretend—her eyes reflected her physical and mental pain.

"Oh, Zu, Murph teach you good—real good." Jo nuzzled her gently. "We go in now, and you give my two-legs that look. Cool?"

Zuzu nodded. A wary hesitation lingered in her eyes. "Okay."

Jo smiled, her voice warm with determination. "You be all right, Zu. I promise."

Together, they moved toward the house, and Jo led Zuzu through the cat door, hoping her two-legs would see Zuzu's desperation—and maybe, just maybe, they would help her dear friend.

They padded into the living room, where an adult male and female two-leg sat on the couch, their eyes widening upon seeing Jo with a strange cat. On the carpet in front of them, two young female two-legs played, giggling and tumbling over each other.

Jo leaned close to Zuzu's ear. "We sit now and look mournful. Mournful..."

27

"Six kittens!" Cosmo exclaimed, his voice filled with wonder. Taking in the sight, he turned to Finn with a playful grin. "Say goodbye to your carefree, fun-loving days!"

Finn smiled, beaming at his kittens. "The fun will still be there, Uncle Coz, just a different kind of fun."

Aura smiled at their banter. "Do you want to hear their names, Cosmo?"

He nodded eagerly. "I sure do."

Aura gazed at her brood—all still without fur, their skin soft and pink—and gently touched one with her nose. "I'll start with the girls. This is Cece, she's Kali, and this cutie is Josie."

Cosmo choked up when Aura said Josie. "Thanks, Aura. Josephine will be thrilled."

"I had to name one after her." She took a deep breath, trying to steady her voice. "Okay, here are the boys. This is Karma, and this is Murf."

Cosmo laughed heartily. "Murphy will love it! Let's hope little Murf doesn't get addicted to food balls." His gaze turned to the last kitten. "So, what's his name?"

Finn smiled warmly. "This handsome little fellow is Cozzy."

Cosmo's whiskers twitched as a smile formed on his face. "Wow, you two. I'm honored."

"Hey, you're my best friend, Coz. We had to name one of our kittens after you."

Cosmo gave Finn a smirk. "I look forward to teaching my handsome namesake how to hunt."

Aura sighed deeply, her voice barely above a whisper. "I wish Zuzu could be here, sharing in our joy. Karma, too."

A week went by, and feeling cooped up, Cosmo grew restless. He looked at Aura and Finn. "If you don't mind, I'd like to visit Murph and Jojo tomorrow to share the good news about you having the kittens."

"Good idea, Coz," Finn agreed. "In the meantime, let's rustle up a few rats for dinner."

"I'm up for that."

Back at Josephine's, Zuzu slowly adjusted to her new surroundings. Over the last week, her physical pain had eased, but her heart still carried the weight of her trauma. She clung to Josephine, seeking comfort in her warmth and gentle companionship. Even tough the two-legs' cruelty haunted her, Josephine's love and patience helped her begin to heal.

Despite her initial fear of Jo's two-legs, Zuzu found herself warming to them—especially the young females. They doted on her, bringing her treats and showering her with affection, and Zuzu couldn't help but feel a sense of peace in their presence. Still, a small part of her tensed at their touch, a reminder of what she'd been through.

The delicious food the older two-legs fed her and Jo was another source of comfort. Not having to scramble for every meal reminded Zuzu of the amenities she once had when she lived with Mrs. Chen in Skyline Towers—a time before there were hundfangs, rats, and brutally cold temperatures to contend with.

Zuzu wasn't the only one fighting demons in her head. Josephine had gone through the same thing earlier in her life. She purposely avoided discussing with Zuzu what the two-legs had done—things that would affect her life from then on: no kittens, no urges, none of the physical joys that came with being female. For now, Jo felt that Zuzu needed to focus on positive things, not anything that would bring her down.

In one bitter way, Jo thought Zuzu was luckier than her—she'd never known male physical love, so she'd never know what she was missing. She, on the other hand, knew all too well what she had lost. On countless days, she'd sit on the windowsill of her two-legs' home, gazing out, lost in memories—remembering the hot, steamy times with Cosmo, being madly in love, aching for him, needing him. She'd give anything to have those times back, but they were gone, nothing but ancient memories. Still, she'd often fall asleep dreaming of being curled up with him, even without sex—just curled up, feeling his heartbeat, listening to his calm breathing, feeling his love in other ways...

The following day, as Josephine and Zuzu napped on the soft cushion of their living room couch, a sudden, shrill cry pierced the air from the backyard. Their heads shot up in unison.

"That be Cosmo," Jo murmured. "You stays here and let me talk to him fo' a while. When we done, I be callin' you."

Without waiting for Zuzu's response, Jo darted out of the house.

In the backyard, she raced past Cosmo, surprising him. "Follow me!" she yelled, her voice sharp with urgency.

Puzzled by her odd behavior and the agony in her tone, Cosmo chased after her.

A block later, Jo slipped into the same vacant backyard where she had taken them before. There, she stopped and let out a wail that seemed to come from the depths of her soul.

Cosmo, stunned, stared at her, his mouth agape. "Jo, what's wrong?" No response. "Jo! What's wrong!"

Josephine collapsed to the ground, writhing in sadness. "They—they cuts her, Cosmo. They cuts her!"

"Cut who, Jo? What are you talking about?"

She looked at him with the same sad eyes he remembered when she lost her kittens and when the two-legs had altered her body. "They cuts Zuzu. Zuzu!" Her voice cracked with anguish.

Cosmo's fur bristled. "What do you mean they cut her? How do you know?"

"Coz, Zuzu with me—she with me. The two-legs cut on her and then dumps her back in the alley where they trap you and Finn. Since I be closer, she comes to me."

Cosmo gasped, feeling as if a mighty blow had struck him. "Are... are you sure?" he blurted.

"Yes, I sure! I sees the cuts on her belly. I sees it, Cosmo!"

"Damn those two-legs—damn them!" His voice shook with rage. "We were minding our own business, not hurting anyone, and they trap us, grab Zuzu, and take off. Then you say they cut her and dumped her back in the alley—what kind of creature would do such a thing to another creature!"

"They bad two-legs out there, Cosmo. Bad. Po' Zuzu—now, she never know male love, never know it. And she never be a momma. Po', po' Zu." She wailed again, her pain deep and heartbreaking...

Cosmo pressed against her and lingered for a long moment. "My love for you is as strong as it's always been, Jo—and that will never change. I'll love Zuzu just as hard—we all will."

"I loves you, too, Cosmo—just as hard. I tries to love Zu just as hard as I loves you." With sad eyes, she looked at him. "I ain't told Zu how the cuttin' mess up her future. I can't brings myself to do it, not yet. But I thinks Zu already know. I thinks she know..."

He paused, then looked at her. "Jo, I came today to tell you and Murph that Aura gave birth to six kittens—three females and three males."

Jo's mood lifted ever so slightly. "Aura okay? Kittens okay?"

"All are fine, and Finn's with her." He inhaled deeply, feeling as though sharing good news was inappropriate, given what had happened to Zuzu. Still, Jo had to know. "Jo, they named their females Cece, Kali, and..." He looked into her eyes. "Josie."

Josephine let out another wail, this one of joy. "Josie. Tell Aura I loves it. What be the male names?"

Cosmo smiled. "Karma, Murf, and..."

"What—what be the last male name?"

"Cozzy."

Another wail of delight. "It perfect. Cozzy—it perfect!"

"They're all cute as can be, Jo—they'll probably all have orange fur like Finn."

Jo's heart melted. "They precious. I knows they precious."

After the brief warmth brought by the joy of Aura having the kittens and sharing their names, the weight of Zuzu's ordeal came crashing back.

Cosmo's gaze met Jo's, and the levity vanished from his voice. "Jo, Aura's heartsick over losing Zuzu. If she's able, I want to take her home with me."

Jo paused, her expression filled with concern. "Cosmo, she ain't right—she ain't right. She powerful sad, and fragile—she still processin' it all. My two-legs take her in. They treatin' her right, lovin' her, feedin' her. She need time, Coz. She need time to heal. And she need lovin'—lots o' lovin' that Aura can't give with all them kittens..."

"If Aura finds out Zuzu's here, she'd crawl through the streets to get her. You know that."

Jo's eyes filled with pain. "I do. Cosmo, you listen hard to me. Hard. Iffin' Zu see them kittens, and she know she can't haves any o' her own..."

Her whiskers quivered in sadness. "Coz—she need full-time love to gets better. I got that kind o' time to gives her. She need that kind o' love..."

He paused, inhaling deeply. "You're right. Can I see her while I'm here?"

Jo nodded. "Seein' you do her good. She been wonderin' how y'all is."

"What should I tell Aura?"

"That be easy. You tells her Zuzu be safe with me, and I lovin' her powerful. You tells Aura her best friend be givin' Zu ever bit o' love she gots."

Cosmo nodded. "When I see Zuzu, what should I say? I mean, saying, 'sorry I screwed up your whole life' doesn't seem like the right way to raise her spirits."

"Just ask how she doin'. Just say you be missin' her—and tells her Aura miss her bad. Real bad. Tell her when she feel up to it, she come and see them little kittens."

"I can do that."

She touched her face lovingly to his, her voice soft and gentle. "What happen to Zu stir feelin's up in me, Cosmo. Powerful feelin's o' you and me together. I misses them times. Misses them deep in my bones. Cuttin' change my body, but not hows I feels 'bout you. I so wants to curls up with you—how I misses it."

"I miss it every day, Jo. Every. Single. Day. You're welcome to join me again."

Her twitching whiskers revealed her sadness. "Cosmo, we knows I can't be a street cat no mo'. I is too old fo' street cattin'..."

Sadness filled his eyes. "I know. Still, the offer will always be there."

She nodded. "I knows. And it mean a lot to me." She sighed. "C'mon, we see Zu now."

Back in Jo's backyard, Jo gave their secret call. Cosmo's heart tightened as Zuzu timidly stepped out through the cat door. Seeing her, a wave of emotions crashed over him—relief that she was safe, guilt for not protecting her, and a deep, aching sadness that she'd been robbed of something precious.

He stepped closer, gently brushing his whiskers against hers, offering the only comfort he could. "I've missed you so much—all of us have. We all love you so much." As he looked into her eyes, something unreadable flickered in her gaze—something tired and distant, leaving him uncertain of what she was truly feeling.

"I... I've missed all of you, too."

Her half-hearted reply troubled Cosmo.

Jo stood nearby, watching intently. Seeing Zuzu struggle, she stepped in. "Zu ain't ready to talk much yet, Cosmo. She just need to know y'all still cares for her."

Cosmo looked at Zuzu, his heart heavy with guilt. He opened his mouth to speak, but the words seemed to stick in his throat. Finally, he managed, his voice barely above a whisper. "I can't begin to tell you how we've all ached for you and missed you." He paused, taking a deep breath. "Finn and I chased after you, but that moving box was too fast. Not being able to rescue you... it broke our hearts." He sighed. "Finn and I should've known something was wrong with that pizza lying on the ground. What happened—what happened was our fault. I'm so very sorry."

Zuzu looked at him, her eyes showing no expression. "Did Jo tell you what the two-legs did to me?"

Cosmo's throat tightened, and words seemed to lodge in his chest. He lowered his gaze, unable to meet hers at first. The weight of her pain felt suffocating, and a sharp sting of regret pierced him.

He exhaled slowly, gathering the courage to meet her gaze. "She did..."

Jo's whiskers quivered. "She get through this, Cosmo, 'cause she got us."

"I know." Cosmo looked at Zuzu, his gaze soft. "I came to tell you that Aura had six kittens. When you're ready, we'd like you to see them. Aura aches for you, Zuzu. She'll be so delighted to know you're okay."

Zuzu's lips quivered. "But I'm not okay... and I never will be..."

Cosmo's heart felt like it shattered into a thousand pieces. "You will, Zu. Just... give it time."

Jo looked at Zuzu, her eyes filled with compassion. "Zu, I survive what happen to me, and I be fine now. You be fine, too. Like Cosmo say, give it time. Time be a good healer."

They lingered for a few moments longer, and then Cosmo gave Zuzu one last nuzzle. "When you're ready, come see us. There's much love waiting for you." He hesitated for a moment, wishing he could do more, but instead slinked away.

At Murphy's house, he shared the news—both good and bad.

28

COSMO PADDED SOFTLY INTO the warm, cozy den where Aura and Finn were nestled with their kittens. The sight of them—Aura, tired but glowing, curled protectively around her new brood—tugged at his heart. Finn was close by, watching over them with quiet vigilance.

He cleared his throat. The news he carried pressed down on him. He took a slow, steady breath before speaking. "Aura... Finn... I have news about Zuzu."

Aura's ears perked up, her gaze sharp and filled with hope and fear. "Is she... is she okay?"

"She's alive. But... she's not okay. Not in the way you'd hope." He sat, his tail curling tightly around himself. "The two-legs... they cut her—just like they cut Jo. She'll never be able to have kittens."

Aura's breath hitched. A soft sob escaped her lips. "Why did the two-legs do this!" Her voice cracked, the pain of the question almost too much to bear. "Why...?"

Cosmo's whiskers drooped, and his shoulders slumped as he struggled to find the right words. "I don't know, Aura." He swallowed, his voice thick with sorrow. "The two-legs Jo lives with—they've let Zuzu stay with them. She has food and shelter, and Jo's giving her all the love she needs. But... her spirit is broken, Aura."

Aura's face filled with anguish and frustration. "I have to see her, Cosmo. I need to tell her I'm here for her, to curl around her. I can't stand the thought of her suffering alone."

Cosmo shook his head. "She's not suffering alone. Jo never leaves her side, and she's safe in her two-leg's home. It's what Zuzu needs right now. I invited her to see us and the kittens when she's ready."

Finn's eyes filled with anger. "I can't begin to imagine if such a thing happened to one of our kittens. Zuzu didn't deserve this," he muttered, his voice strained. He exhaled slowly, trying to regain his calm, and looked at Aura. "We'll be here for her when she's ready, but Cosmo's right—we need to let her heal on her terms, and she'll see us when she's ready. The main thing is, she's safe, and you know Jo's loving and caring for her."

A troubled silence settled over them as Aura sat, too lost in her thoughts to reply. But then, softly, her voice broke the stillness.

"I'm her family," Aura whispered, her tail flicking restlessly. "I can't help her from here."

Cosmo's gaze softened. "You're with her, Aura. You hold a place in her heart."

Aura buried her face in her paws, a quiet, sad sigh escaping her. "She'll never experience the joy of having kittens. All I ever wanted was for her to be happy... and now, that may never happen."

Cosmo's voice faltered as he tried to offer comfort, his words falling short. "Zuzu's strong, Aura. Stronger than you think. She just needs time and love... and maybe, when she's ready, she'll join us again." He met Finn's eyes with a helpless look that said he didn't know what else to say.

Finn took charge. "Aura, Zuzu knows we all love her. Somehow, I know she'll get past this." He turned to Cosmo, his voice deliberately brightening. "So, what did Jo say about Aura having the kittens?"

Cosmo's eyes brightened with relief at Finn's change of subject. "She's so happy—especially about you naming one of them Josie. And she's equally delighted that you two have chosen Karma, Murf, and Cozzy. She can't wait to see them when Zuzu's ready to see us."

Aura's whiskers twitched as a small smile came to her face. "Thank you for bringing me the news, Cosmo. I know it wasn't easy. I'm so glad she's with Jo, especially since Jo's already gone through what Zuzu's going through now."

Cosmo nodded, trying to look upbeat. He leaned closer to study the squirming kittens. "Which one is Cozzy?"

Several weeks later, Zuzu, curled tightly against Josephine, stirred from her deep sleep as the morning sun's rays filtered through the window and landed on her face. The comfort of the two-legs' home had become familiar, and the soft sound of Jo's breathing beside her had become a comfort. But a restlessness fluttered in her chest, a subtle whisper saying something was missing.

She opened her still-groggy eyes and gazed at Josephine, noting her glossy, impeccably clean fur. Jo had been nothing but kind, offering her warmth and love in every way possible, but Zuzu's heart ached. She missed her other family, especially Aura.

Slowly, Zuzu stood and padded to the window, where sunlight filtered through the half-open curtains, casting soft patterns on the floor. She leaped onto the sill and gazed at the quiet morning, the calm of the world outside contrasting with the chaos inside her. For a moment, she closed her eyes and let herself imagine forgetting—forgetting the pain, the helplessness, and everything the two-legs had done. But the memories always came rushing back, sharp and overwhelming, flooding her like a wave.

Her body had healed, and she could move freely now. The tight, burning ache that once gripped her had faded to a memory. But her spirit, though improving, remained fragile.

The thought of seeing Aura, of seeing her family again, twisted in her chest. She missed them—missed their warmth, their presence, the way they had always cared for her. But what if they looked at her and saw only the scars—physical and mental—the two-legs had left behind? What if they saw the emptiness she couldn't hide, especially Aura?

Zuzu flicked her tail, frustration tightening in her gut. She couldn't stay here, wrapped in this cocoon of safety and sorrow forever. She had to go to them. She needed to see if they could still see her—the Zuzu who had once bounded through life with joy and innocence.

But what if they didn't? What if the pain of seeing her changed was too much for them to bear?

She felt a pang of unease in her chest, the familiar ache that had settled there since she'd left Aura behind. If only she could go back in time, back to when things were simple and uncomplicated.

But she knew, deep down, that she wasn't the same cat anymore. And maybe—just maybe—that was okay.

With a soft sigh, Jo stirred, blinking a few times before seeing Zuzu perched on the windowsill.

"Hey, Zu." Her voice was thick with sleep but filled with warmth. "You okay?"

Zuzu turned to face her, her voice low, almost a whisper. "I... I want to see them, Jo. I want to see Aura and the kittens."

With eyes filled with compassion but also a touch of concern, Jo's whiskers twitched. "I understands, Zu." She paused, thinking... "How 'bout this? We waits until this evening, and when the two-legs be sleepin', we sneaks out and go sees them. We spends the night with them, then we hurries back here befo' our two-legs wakes up—they never know we be gone." Her eyes brightened. "I can curls up with Cosmo all night. How do that sound?"

Zuzu's eyes lit up as a spark of happiness ignited within her, the first she'd felt since this ordeal began. "That's a great plan. Thank you, Jo."

She nodded and stretched. Taking a deep breath, she looked at Zuzu with a mischievous glint in her eye. "Let's go pester our two-legs fo' a mornin' treat. Then we refines this plan of ours."

Throughout the day, Zuzu shared her knowledge of the route to Finn's warehouse with Jo, detailing the best path, travel time, and potential dangers—especially near eateries where hostile cats and hundfangs scavenged. Jo reminded Zuzu that she might struggle to keep up. Zuzu reassured her, promising to set a comfortable pace and how they could rest if needed.

That evening, when the adult two-legs shut their bedroom door, Jo and Zuzu silently slinked downstairs. After a long drink, they slipped out through the cat door. Pausing on the patio, Jo scanned the darkened yard to ensure everything was clear. She turned to Zuzu and flicked her tail excitedly. "You ready?"

Zuzu leaned close to her ear. "I am. Follow me."

With that, the two cats melted into the night.

Zuzu kept a slow pace along Roosevelt Avenue, making sure Josephine conserved enough energy for the busier section ahead, with its shops and eateries. "Are you comfortable with this pace, Jo?"

Jo's breathing remained steady as she replied, "I is."

"Okay, good. Remember, if a hundfang appears, we immediately scramble up the nearest tree—no negotiating, no hesitation."

"I hears you."

Under the cover of night, Zuzu and Josephine moved silently, their eyes glowing in the moonlight. Jo, used to the comforts of her quiet life and infrequent night outings, flicked her tail nervously as Zuzu scanned the shadows for any sign of danger. With admiration, Jo watched her navigate the street with fluid confidence, and a realization struck her: despite being younger, Zuzu was far more capable in these streets than her.

As they approached Junction Boulevard, the air changed, filled with the aroma of fresh bread and a faint hint of moving box exhaust. Neon signs illuminated the streets in vibrant blues and reds, casting peculiar shadows on the sidewalk. The buzz of late-night two-leg chatter, the sizzle from open kitchens, and the fragrance of stir-fry permeated the atmosphere, marking the transition from the quiet residential neighborhood to a lively hustle and bustle.

Zuzu's ears twitched as she glanced at Jo. "We need to pick up the pace through here."

Jo nodded and matched Zuzu's hurried pace. The area around them pulsed with danger, from moving boxes to two-legs, some with hundfangs on leashes.

With every step, Zuzu stayed alert, her instincts razor-sharp as she scanned for danger and plotted escape routes.

The blinding storefront lights frightened Jo. Her breath came harder—not just from the physical exertion but from the overwhelming sensation that the city was trying to swallow her whole. She pressed closer to Zuzu, silently regretting her impulsive decision to travel at night.

Finally, mercifully, the frenzied scene faded as they entered another residential area. Zuzu spotted a large flowering bush tucked in the corner of a front yard, its branches sprawling out, offering the perfect hideaway. She slowed her pace and tilted her head toward Jo. "Let's rest under this bush."

Jo nodded, her breath still coming in quick bursts. "That—that a good idea."

With a quick flick of her tail, Zuzu ducked under the sheltering bush where they could rest in peace.

Zuzu watched as Jo's sides heaved. "We'll wait here until you catch your breath. We're getting close—it's just a few blocks more."

Too winded to reply, Jo gave a nod.

When Jo's breathing calmed, she looked at Zuzu. "Now you sees why street life ain't fo' me anymor'. I likes my home comforts." Her eyes widened with realization. "Zu, we haves to do this ag'in befor' the sun come up. Girlfriend, I too old fo' this."

"Sorry, Jo, but we're doing fine. If you're ready to move again, I'll set a slower pace." She paused. "This is a dangerous area—a demon hundfang attacked us near here not long ago."

As soon as she said it, Jo's panicked expression made Zuzu regret mentioning it.

A short while later, Zuzu stopped at a metal pole gate blocking a dead-end driveway between two industrial buildings. She turned to Jo. "We're here," she whispered. "Follow me."

Jo followed as Zuzu ducked under the gate and navigated the narrow, pot-holed driveway. Soon, a large, secluded warehouse loomed ahead. Zuzu smiled at Jo. "Come on. I'll show you how to get in."

Zuzu scurried through a small opening that had once been a loading dock door. Inside, the moonlight filtered through the windows, casting a dim glow over the large space.

Josephine, who had never been there before, found the place foreboding. Zuzu paused in the cool, musty air, her heart racing as she wondered if she was ready to face her family again.

A mischievous grin spread across Zuzu's face as she leaned close to Jo's ear. "Will you summon them with your trademark 'Yoo-hoo—y'all in here!' bellow?"

Jo glanced at her, eyes wide. "Zu, if I do that, I be wakin' the dead."

Zuzu chuckled. "That's what I'm hoping for."

Jo caught onto the mischief in Zuzu's tone and whispered, "I be picturin' Coz leapin' in the air like a scared fool!"

Zuzu's tail flicked eagerly. "Do it, Jo!"

Jo inhaled deeply and let loose a thunderous, "YOO-HOO—Y'ALL IN HERE!"

29

AURA'S SIX KITTENS ENTERED the world utterly dependent on her. Their tiny bodies instinctively clung to her belly, blind and deaf to their surroundings. Survival consumed them—every moment focused on staying close to their mother—their source of warmth, food, and safety. The warehouse that sheltered them remained beyond their awareness, an undefined space they had yet to perceive.

By the end of their first week, the kittens' eyes began to open, though their vision was still clouded and unclear. At first, all they saw was a blur of shifting shadows. As the days passed, their sight grew sharper. They could make out the forms of their siblings, wriggling beside them in search of warmth and nourishment.

Aura's gentle purr filled the air, a steady presence. Finn's deep, soothing voice and Cosmo's coarser tones drifted nearby, comforting and familiar. The once-distant world began to take shape—each day brought fresh discoveries: new sounds, sights, and feelings. Slowly, the kittens began to form memories, their tiny minds weaving together a sense of understanding.

At three weeks, the kittens staggered to their feet, lurching sideways with their heads tilted in confusion. With practice, their steps steadied as curiosity led them farther from their sleeping area in the warehouse. Their whiskers twitched, testing the unfamiliar air, while Aura watched with vigilant eyes. Having survived a rat attack as a kitten and being aware of the dangers lurking in the shadows, she, Finn, and Cosmo kept a constant watch, determined to protect their precious brood.

By the fourth week, the kittens had grown bolder. What had once been their safe zone now felt small.

They ventured farther, exploring the edges of their territory in the warehouse. There were new smells, new textures—new things to discover.

They wrestled and tumbled, chasing one another in a blur of fur, their movements full of exuberance. It wasn't long before the towering crates in the corner caught their attention.

At first, there was hesitation—small, unsure paws reaching toward the unknown. But that fear soon gave way to daring.

One by one, they scaled the crates, sometimes with an awkward wobble, sometimes with triumphant leaps. They collapsed in tangled heaps, their play turning the warehouse into an endless playground of possibilities.

Cozzy, always the first to test limits, darted and pounced, his energy infectious. Murf, ever the hungry one, was never far from Aura's belly, and when he wasn't nursing, he was always rummaging around for something to nibble on. Josie, quieter than her siblings, watched from the sidelines, taking in every noise and movement, her large eyes tracking her brothers' and sisters' actions with quiet curiosity. Karma, clumsy but persistent, often stumbled over his paws, but his missteps only added to his charm as he dove into each new adventure. Cece, fearless and full of energy, plunged headfirst into every challenge, often leading her siblings in wild chases. Sweet Kali followed Cosmo around, nuzzling him whenever she could, always by his side, her affection softening his typically gruff demeanor.

By six weeks, they raced through the warehouse, weaving in and out of each other's paths and tumbling over one another in a swirl of fur and paws. They scaled the highest piles of debris, leaping from one surface to the next with surprising agility—even if a few of them sometimes missed the mark. Their chatter filled the air with simple words and excited meows, expressing their curiosity and joy.

Cozzy, the ringleader, led the others, his voice ringing out with every daring move: "Big jump! I do it!" Ever the adventurer, Cece bounced at his heels: "I jump too!" Her eyes sparkled with excitement, always up for the next challenge. Murf, being Murf, followed right behind them—just as eager but constantly sidetracked by sniffing the air: "I hungry now!" Karma's initial clumsiness had improved, but "Oops. I fall again!" echoed frequently. Kali never missed an opportunity to weave in and around Cosmo's legs, her voice always ringing out with "Caamo, Caamo!" Josie, quieter than the others, seemed most entertained by Karma's antics, often whispering to herself: "Kaama fall. Kaama fall..."

Except for Murf, they nursed less now, but the security of their mother's presence kept them grounded. Soon, they'd stop nursing, and the outside world would no longer be a distant concept—it would become something they had to face, whether they were ready or not. But Aura, driven by maternal instinct, dreaded that inevitable day.

Beyond the warehouse walls, the city both beckoned and threatened. Aura could see it in their eyes: the same spark of curiosity she and Cosmo once had as kittens burned fiercely in them. They wanted to explore, to learn everything they could. But she knew the dangers too well. Demon hundfangs prowled the streets, rats lurked in the shadows, and rival cats defended their territory with ruthless tenacity. Still, she couldn't shield them forever.

For now, though, they remained her little kittens—safe within these walls, innocent to the world's ways. Aura held these precious moments close, knowing all too soon they would fade into memory...

That evening, something suddenly upended their small, familiar world.

"YOO-HOO—Y'ALL IN HERE!"

The sharp, unexpected call pierced the quiet night, sending Cosmo leaping into the air, landing with a thud on top of Finn. Realizing it was Jo, his hearty laughter rang out as Aura darted toward the noise. The curious kittens charged after her, with Cozzy leading the pack, his tail held high with excitement.

To the kittens' amazement, two cats stood silhouetted in the shadows. Until now, the only cats they knew were in their warehouse. These newcomers—strange, yet familiar—took a moment to process. Before they could fully understand what they were seeing, their mom let out a joyous scream that echoed through the warehouse, louder than any sound they had ever heard from her before.

"Zuzu! Zuzu!"

As their mother called out, she rushed toward the smaller of the two cats, her body trembling with joy. The kittens could only stand there, wide-eyed, watching as their mother lovingly touched this new figure, a creature that looked like them but wasn't part of their world.

"Zuzu, oh Zuzu!" Aura purred, nuzzling the smaller cat with a deep, affectionate rumble. Zuzu chuckled softly, her tail flicking in delight. But as Aura gazed into Zuzu's eyes, something felt off. Gone was the carefree, energetic cat she remembered. Her eyes seemed dim, her movements hesitant, as if uncertain of her place in this once familiar space. Yet, it was *her*. Zuzu. Back.

Next to them, Jo's voice rang out, full of warmth and excitement. "Well, look at all you little fluff balls!" Her eyes widened as she took in the sight of the kittens. "Ain't you the cutest things I ever sees!"

The kittens, still recovering from their shock, blinked in wonder at the two newcomers. Then, curiosity overcame their fear. They charged forward, sniffing and circling, their fragmented chatter filling the air. Cozzy bobbed his head as he inched closer to Jo, then sniffed her with curious eyes. Cece, as always, followed his lead, fascinated by the new scent. Murf pressed his nose to Zuzu's belly, surprised to find no milk scent. Karma tripped over his paws, crashing against Jo's body with a soft thud. "Oops!" Kali, observing with wide eyes, pressed against Cosmo, frightened. He looked at her. "It's okay, little shadow—Zuzu and Jo are our friends." With his reassurance, she touched Zuzu's tail to make sure she was real. Josie stepped closer and peeked shyly at Zuzu. "You pretty."

Zuzu chuckled, a little nervous as she watched the kittens tumble over each other in excitement. "Wow, I didn't expect such a warm welcome."

Aura stepped back, feeling her heart swell with pride as she watched her kittens surround Jo and Zuzu. With delight in her eyes, she glanced at Finn and Cosmo before turning back to her curious brood.

"Okay, kittens, listen up—let me introduce you to your Aunt Zuzu and Aunt Jo!" She touched Zuzu gently with her paw, her eyes gleaming. "This is Aunt Zuzu. She's family, just like you. And this is Aunt Jo—she's my best friend, and she's like a sister to me."

With wide eyes, the kittens looked surprised that the strange cats had names. "Zuzu! Jo!" they clamored, still unsure but eager to understand. Their words were clumsy, but there was no mistaking the excitement in their voices as they continued to sniff and investigate their new family members. Their chatter spilled over one another in joyful bursts.

Aura reached out and nudged the closest kitten. "Jo and Zuzu, this is Cozzy." She touched Cece with her paw. "And this is Cece." She pointed out the others, saving Josie for last. She looked at Jo with shining eyes. "And this is Josie—our quietest kitten."

Jo laughed heartily, her eyes softening as she gazed at her namesake. "Hey, they ain't nothin' wrong with bein' quiet." She paused, beaming at the energetic, orange-colored fur balls. "You all precious. Precious little orange balls o' sunshine." She looked at Cosmo, her whiskers twitching. The melancholy in her eyes spoke of their long-lost kittens. Cosmo understood and nodded slightly, sharing her silent sadness.

Cece dashed around Zuzu's legs in a playful circle. "We play now!"

"Yeah, we play!" Cozzy belted out.

Wide-eyed and overwhelmed, Zuzu had never encountered such a whirlwind of motion and nonstop chatter. As she glanced around the warehouse, she viewed it with fresh eyes. What had once been a welcoming refuge now felt squalid compared to Jo's cozy home. The difference between street life and home living struck her deeply.

"Okay, everyone, settle down!" Aura shouted to make herself heard. "I'm going outside with Zuzu to talk for a bit. You all stay here with your dad and Uncle Cosmo."

Jo leaned down and gently nudged Cece with her paw. "You is a curious one, ain't you?"

Cece looked up at Jo, startled at first, but then a grin spread across her face. The other kittens circled Jo, excited. Jo beamed, her joy infectious. "C'mon, y'all—we play!"

As Aura watched her kittens tumble around Jo, their excitement filling the room, a smile tugged at her lips. She turned to Zuzu. "As you can see, quiet is rare around here. Let's go sit on the shed roof—it's peaceful there."

Outside, Aura climbed up the side of the neighboring shed, with Zuzu following closely behind. Once on the roof, Aura sat, her gaze lingering on Zuzu.

A flood of emotions washed over Aura—relief, joy, and deep heartache. Her heart beat faster as she studied Zuzu's face. Questions crowded her mind: *Is she okay? Really okay?*

With a deep breath, Aura leaned in, brushing her cheek gently against Zuzu's. "So many emotions are swirling in me that I don't even know where to begin," she murmured. "I've been so worried about you, Zuzu. I've hoped for this day—hoped I could look into your eyes and finally say... 'Welcome home.'"

Zuzu's eyes met hers—soft, uncertain, and shadowed with doubt. "I... I'm not sure if this is my home anymore, Aura."

"No matter what has changed, this will always be your home," Aura replied, her sincerity evident in every word. "You're part of our family. We all love you."

Zuzu hesitated, her gaze dropping. "Jo said she told Cosmo what happened to me, so... you know what the two-legs did to me."

Aura nodded, her heart heavy. "It broke my heart, Zuzu. I'm so sorry. So very sorry..."

Zuzu met Aura's eyes. "Jo's been so good to me. I love being with her, and I feel safe in her house."

Aura's heart tightened, and she let out a soft sigh. "Zuzu, I know I can't give you what Jo can. Not with the kittens relying on me." She gazed into the darkness, her thoughts swirling. "Jo has always been there for me in my times of need, and now she's giving you the same care and comfort she once gave me." She paused for a long moment. "I trust Jo to look after you the way I can't right now. Just know you'll always be part of this family."

Zuzu nodded. "I'm not saying I want to live with her permanently, but for now, being with her is good for me. She knows what it's like... the two-legs did the same thing to her as they did to me..."

Aura leaned into her friend, her voice soft but steady. "If your heart tells you that being with Jo is where you need to be, I accept that. Just know that no matter what happens, you'll always have a place here—with me and us. A place where you're loved. And that's always waiting for you, Zuzu."

Zuzu nuzzled her cheek against Aura's, a wave of relief washing over her. "Thank you, Aura. You have no idea how much that means to me."

A sense of peace settled between them as the wind whispered through the trees. Zuzu closed her eyes, and in that quiet moment, she realized something deep within her—a gentle truth. Aura had given her the space she needed to heal in her own way, to find herself again. And Zuzu knew, in that stillness, that this gift was more meaningful than she could ever fully express.

As Aura sat on the roof, feeling the cool night air on her fur, she realized just how much had changed. Zuzu was no longer dependent on her. Despite her maternal instinct to keep Zuzu close, Aura felt a deep sense of peace, knowing that she would find her way with Josephine's gentle love and guidance instead of her own. And somehow, that felt okay.

EPILOGUE

ON A RARE COOL summer day in Queens, afternoon sunlight streamed through the open living room window, bathing the space in golden warmth as the sweet scent of blooming flowers drifted in. Jo and Zuzu lounged on the couch, content in their shared peace. Lost in thought, Zuzu watched Jo drift between sleep and wakefulness. When Jo caught her staring, an impish smile spread across her face.

"What?"

Zuzu's whiskers twitched. "I be thinkin' 'bout how happy I is here—and how much I likes bein' with you."

Josephine studied Zuzu for a moment before touching her nose to Zuzu's with heartfelt tenderness. "Zu, you the reason I gets up ev'ry mornin' now with a smile. You is precious to me, little kitten, and I so happy you stayin' with me. We sure gots it good here, don't we?"

"We do," Zuzu nodded. "I at peace with my decision to stay. And I likes living with yer two-legs. They takes good care o' us and makes us feel safe."

"They do. Our two-legs good creatures. Good creatures."

A sharp, familiar call from the backyard shattered their peaceful moment.

"That Cosmo!" Jo bellowed.

She bounded off the couch, paws tapping a quick rhythm on the floor as she zipped through the cat door, with Zuzu close behind—both thrilled by Cosmo's unexpected visit.

In the sunlit yard, he stood with his tail joyfully swishing. "Hello, my two favorite cats!"

"Cosmo! What you be doin' here?" Jo called. "Everthin' okay?"

"Everything's fine. Are you two up for an evening family gathering at Sunnyside Gardens Park? I just came from Murph's place—he's joining us."

Jo glanced at Zuzu, who nodded eagerly. "Yeah, Zu and I up fo' it!" Her eyes filled with concern. "But I ain't sure Murphy be able to come. He too heavy to travel."

Cosmo's whiskers twitched with amusement. "Jo, you won't believe this, but Murph's finally embraced the concept of portion control. I wouldn't call him buff, but his belly no longer drags on the ground!"

"That be mighty good news! I can't waits to sees him! 'Buff Murph'—never thinks I be sayin' them words together!"

"Me neither," Zuzu added. "How be the kittens?"

Cosmo laughed. "Wait until you see them! The males are all bigger than you now."

Zuzu's eyes widened. "Seriously?"

"It's true. Cozzy's already talking about striking out on his own, and Cece wants to join him. They're both skilled hunters now."

"I can't waits to see them all—Aura and Finn, too," Zuzu replied, her tail flicking with excitement.

"They're at the eateries now, scrounging for dinner. I'll head back and let them know we're good for tonight." Cosmo's whiskers twitched as he looked at Jo. "You know where the community gardens in the park are, right?"

Jo nodded. "Yeah, I knows it well."

"Great. I'll go back to Murph's, and then we'll join the others at the eateries. From there, we'll head to the park together and meet you there."

Jo touched her cheek to his. "Zu and me be lookin' fo'ward to it. We sees you there after the sun go down."

Heading down Jo's alley, Cosmo made his way back to Murphy's house. He called his friend, who ducked through the cat door to join him. "Good news, Murph—Jo and Zuzu will meet us at the park."

"Cool!" Murphy replied, his tail swishing energetically. "Want to head there now?"

"Not yet—it's too early. Let's meet up with Aura and the others at the eateries first, then we'll all go to the park together. I might grab a quick bite while we're there."

With that, they padded off toward the eateries. Murphy, even with his limp, moved with newfound grace beside Cosmo. The trip to Josephine's house months ago, where he had nearly collapsed after minimal exertion, had served as his wake-up call. Through sheer determination, he'd shed enough weight that movement no longer burdened him. Now, his fluid stride and lifted chin spoke of pride, of rediscovered strength in a body that finally felt like his own again.

As they turned onto the alley lined with eateries, the scent of food wafted from nearby kitchens. Up ahead, Cosmo spotted familiar faces: Aura perched atop a stack of crates, always watchful, while Finn lounged next to her. The kittens—now nearly grown—bounded around them in a joyful swirl.

"Uncle Coz!" Cozzy called out, bounding over. "We saved you a nice, half-eaten slice of pizza!"

Cosmo's whiskers twitched with amusement. "Thanks, Cozzy. I hope there's something for Murphy, too."

Murphy shook his head. "I'll pass—I'm trying to eat less than half my weight each day."

The other young cats bounded over. Kali dropped a half-eaten slice of pizza at Cosmo's feet and smiled. "I made sure no one would eat your share, Uncle."

Cosmo's eyes softened. "That was thoughtful of you, Kali. Thanks for looking out for me."

She glanced at Murphy. "I can try to find some food for you, too, Uncle Murphy."

"Thanks, Kali, but I already ate."

As she scampered off with her siblings, Murphy joined Aura and Finn while Cosmo ate his meal.

Aura's eyes sparkled. "You're looking mighty good, Murph. I'm proud of you for getting fit again."

Murphy's tail swished appreciatively. "Thanks, Aura. I realized boredom used to drive me to eat. Now, when I feel restless, I go for a walk or climb the backyard tree instead of hitting the food balls."

Aura glanced at her energetic brood with a wry smile. "Since they were born, 'boredom' has been a foreign word to me."

Finn chuckled. "Me too." His whiskers twitched with mischief as he looked at Murphy. "You know, I'll miss teasing you about your weight. Cosmo and I had a lot of fun trying to outdo each other with subtle 'ample you' quips."

Murphy grinned. "Yeah, yeah, but I knew you two teased me out of concern—and brotherly love." He paused, chuckling. "Hey, Aura, remember when you all stayed at my cat cave and we snuck into my house to eat some of my food balls?"

Aura nodded. "Yeah, I remember. Why?"

Murphy's whiskers twitched with barely contained glee. "Do you also remember I had a special pile of food balls just for Cosmo?"

She thought for a moment. "Yeah, I do. Karma ate from it, too, if I remember right."

Murphy nodded, his eyes dancing with mischief. "Well, as revenge for all Cosmo's weight razzing, I whizzed in his pile of food balls. Nearly doubled over laughing as he munched away—until Karma joined him."

Aura burst out laughing. "Little did you know, Cosmo returned the favor—he snuck into your home and peed in your food bowl. If you remember, you said you thought your two-legs switched to a different kind of food balls because they tasted gamey."

Knowing that Cosmo had pulled one over on him, Murphy flicked his tail with rueful amusement. "I always wondered about that—since later batches tasted fine." He smirked. "But unlike Cosmo and Karma, I didn't spend the night in a snowdrift having a gastrointestinal meltdown."

Aura shook her head, grinning. "You, Finn, and Cosmo—in many ways, you're still young cats at heart."

Cosmo heard them laughing and padded over, ears perked. "What's so funny?"

Finn beamed, his face lit with amusement. "I was just saying how much you and I will miss razzing Murph about his weight."

Cosmo's face lit with an impish grin. "Yeah, Murph, you were our chief source of amusement."

Murphy glanced at the playful young cats and smiled. "Well, Finn and Coz, I'm sure their antics far outshine me for amusement. Look at them."

As the fading sunlight stretched long shadows across the alley's pavement, they watched the young cats milling about. Cozzy and Cece sprang off a diner trash can, their mouths stuffed with French fries.

"You got more than me," Cece grumbled through bulging cheeks.

Unable to speak with his mouth full, Cozzy's eyes sparkled as he darted off to enjoy his treasure.

Nearby, Murf gnawed contentedly at the meat still on a discarded bone, eyes half-closed in dreamy satisfaction. Karma, preferring seafood, rummaged through another trash can while Kali stretched out in a patch of remaining sunlight.

Josie, ever the observer, stood slightly away from the others, her body relaxed but her sharp eyes watching her siblings closely. Satisfied that all was well, she padded over to her mother. "Mom, shouldn't we head to the park if we want to meet Aunts Zuzu and Josephine before sunset?"

At the mention of the park, Cozzy's ears perked up. "I love Sunnyside Gardens Park!"

"Wanna race?" Cece's eyes sparkled as she issued the challenge.

Before he could answer, she took off. "Hey, no fair!" he shouted, streaking after her.

"Watch out for moving boxes!" Aura called after them, her voice mixing amusement with concern. She turned to the others. "C'mon, everyone, we don't want to be late."

At the park, as the sun painted the sky with hues of red and orange, the young cats bounded through the entrance, their movements sleek and confident. Cozzy led the way, darting between the community garden's raised beds, reaching Josephine and Zuzu first. Cece skidded to a stop beside him, nearly colliding with Zuzu. As Zuzu let out a startled meow, Josephine laughed with delight.

"Hi, Aunts Jo and Zuzu!" Cozzy panted, grinning. "As usual, I beat Cece."

Cece's tail twitched with annoyance, but she grinned proudly. "Yeah, but not by much. Cozzy and I are always the fastest."

Jo swished her tail. "You two is lightnin' fast. I be pityin' the po' rat y'all be chasin'—they ain't got no chance, no chance at all!"

Murf and Karma joined them, sniffing the fragrant garden air. "Hi, Aunt Zuzu," Karma said, smiling. "It sure smells good here—much better than where we ate dinner."

Murf nodded enthusiastically. "I found a bone with a lot of meat on it tonight—yum!"

Zuzu laughed, her whiskers rising as she smiled. "Leave it to you to finds the best thing to eat."

Always near Cosmo, Kali trotted up with Josie bringing up the rear. "Hi, Aunt Zuzu. I found a big piece of pizza for Uncle at the eateries," she said proudly.

Zuzu smiled at Cosmo before turning to Kali. "Thanks fo' lookin' after Cosmo. He very dear to me."

"I look out for everyone," Josie said softly, her gaze flicking between Zuzu and Jo, hoping for recognition.

Zuzu touched her cheek to Josie's. "I knows you do. You everbody's protector, and you quite good at it."

Josie beamed with pride, her tail lifting high as she soaked in the praise.

Murphy padded over to them, a wide grin spreading across his face. "Hey, Jo and Zuzu. Notice anything different?"

Jo's eyes went wide. "Murph—you be one lean and mean cat! Lean and mean. I is so proud o' you!"

Murphy's face lit up. "Yeah, well, as you clearly let me know, I had to make some changes."

Zuzu touched her face to his. "Jo be right—you look great, Murphy."

Jo nudged Cosmo. "It be good to see you, Coz. Mighty good. Since they ain't no two-legs 'round, let's move to the grassy area."

As they moved toward the grass, they met Aura and Finn, who had lingered back, enjoying a rare quiet moment together.

"Hey, Zuzu and Jo!" Aura called warmly. "I see our kittens are happy to see you."

The three cats pressed together, purring affectionately.

"It be too long since we get together," Jo said. "Way too long."

"I always feel the same way." Aura looked at Zuzu with tender eyes. "You look happy—it's good to see."

"I is happy, Aura. Bein' with Jo is where I is supposed to be."

Aura smiled, thinking how Jo's dialect appeared to have rubbed off on Zuzu. "I agree. You two are good for each other."

"Let's sits a while and catch up," Jo said, tail swishing briskly. She turned to the males. "You males gives us girls some time to catch up. Go on, now."

Cosmo's whiskers twitched with amusement. "Try to finish your reminiscing before dawn comes."

Jo flattened her ears and narrowed her eyes at him. Cosmo grinned in response and then scampered off with his friends.

As the night settled in, Aura, Jo, and Zuzu watched the young cats frolicking in the moonlight.

"Look at 'em," Jo said softly. "They be changin' so much. I hardly be recognizin' them."

Zuzu followed their fluid movements, flicking her tail thoughtfully. She spoke with a hint of awe. "They all grew into themselves. Cozzy got that sure-footed pace of a hunter now. He and Cece ain't just playin' anymo'—they is ready fo' the world."

She watched them race up and down trees with accomplished grace. "Looks how they carry themselves, their boundless confidence." Turning to Aura, her gaze softened. "You, Finn, and Cosmo has done an incredible job raisin' them to be street-smart cats with good hearts."

Zuzu paused, her throat tightening as she struggled to find the right words. "And you does a terrific job raisin' me, too. I'll never forget the day you found me—alone and terrified on the streets. You takes me in, expectin' nothin', and shows me I is more than just a helpless, naïve young cat. You shows me the importance of family and how to survive on the streets."

She inhaled deeply. "Before you, I be lost in so many ways, but like a flower, I bloom under your care. I loves you, Aura."

"Zu be right," Josephine nodded. "You teach them young'uns good, Aura. And you teach Zu good, too. I so proud to calls you my dear friend."

Aura's heart warmed at their words. "Thank you both. You mean the world to me." She sighed softly, watching Cozzy and Cece. "Cozzy's already talking about living on his own, and of course, Cece wants to go with him."

As she watched them play, a quiet ache formed in her chest. "It won't be long before the others want to head off on their own, too... I'll miss them so much."

Jo pressed her shoulder to Aura's. "I knows you will. How things be with you and Finn?"

Aura's tail swished gently. "How I love that orange cat. We're good together."

Jo's eyes twinkled. "I still see them dreamy eyes when you looks at him."

Aura chuckled. "I have to admit, a part of me looks forward to Finn and I just being a couple again." She winked at her two friends. "Hopefully, I won't have another litter right away."

Their conversation continued with light and easy banter. After a while, Cosmo and the others joined them, bringing their lively conversation full circle.

As the night deepened, Cosmo glanced at the moon and sighed. "Jo, I hate to say this, but we need to head out soon, or you, Zuzu, and Murph might be missed by your two-legs."

Jo exhaled slowly. "You right, Coz." She turned to the young cats. "I could stays here fo'ever, jus' bein' with my family."

She leaned close to Cosmo's ear and whispered, "There be a full moon this week, so I expects you to be stayin' the night with me at my place."

Cosmo's whiskers twitched as he winked at her in reply.

Cozzy nuzzled against Jo. "When can we meet again, Aunt Jo? I like our family gatherings."

"I likes them too, Cozzy. We needs to meet mo' offen."

Josie darted in, uncharacteristically bold, and touched her cheek to Zuzu's. "I always think about you, Aunt Zuzu. I wish I had pretty white fur like yours."

"Ha!" Murf laughed. "On the street, if you had white fur, it'd be dirty in no time. Our orange fur hides dirt!"

"Murf be right, Josie," Zuzu chuckled. "Besides, yer fur be gorgeous—I loves how brightly it shine."

Kali pressed against Cosmo, her eyes gleaming in the moonlight. "Uncle says it will be cold soon—too cold to travel. Maybe we can meet again before the cold comes."

"That's a great idea, Kali," said Finn. "Let's take a vote. All those in favor, raise a paw."

Without hesitation, every feline's paw shot into the air.

Finn laughed. "The vote is unanimous—we'll all meet again before the cold arrives."

As they headed for the park entrance, a peaceful silence enveloped them. The warm summer air, filled with the chirps of crickets and the occasional call of birds settling in for the night, surrounded them. For a few splendid moments, they savored the simple comfort of being together, not worried about finding their next meal, the changes ahead, or the challenges of life in Queens. For now, the ties that bound them muted all worries, and family, to them, was the most beautiful word in their world.

ACKNOWLEDGEMENTS

To Carmen, my German wife, I'll use your language to describe my feelings for you: *Du bist meine größte Liebe* (you are my greatest love).

To my readers, your support means the world to me. I deeply appreciate you embracing my stories and offering such encouragement for my writing. Though we may not have met directly, your presence is felt in every word I write. May the light of God always shine on your path.

ABOUT THE AUTHOR

James Randall Miller was born in Germany and has traveled and lived throughout the world. After thirty years in Alaska, he now lives near the White Tank Mountains in Arizona. Other books by James include *Julius*, an illustrated children's story, and the inspirational novels *The Healer And Me, Park Bench Stories, Howling Across Bridges, Knock on the Sky, After the Purple Heart, Gus and Billy, Untangling Claire,* and *Because of You*.

Hearing from his readers always delights James. You can reach him at JamesMillerBooks@gmail.com

ADOPT A PET

Every year, millions of animals in shelters and rescues across the country are in need of loving homes. Stray and abandoned animals—whether cats, dogs, rabbits, or even exotic pets—often find themselves without a family, waiting for a second chance at life. With an estimated 3.2 million shelter animals being adopted annually in the U.S., the need for adoption continues to be urgent. This is where *Petfinder* steps in, offering a platform that connects potential pet owners with these animals in need.

Petfinder is a non-profit organization that has been helping animals find homes since 1996. Its mission is to make it easier for people to adopt pets by providing a comprehensive, user-friendly website where over 11,000 animal shelters and rescue groups can list adoptable animals. Through *Petfinder*, prospective pet owners can search for pets by breed, size, age, and location, making it easier to find the perfect companion. Although *Petfinder* doesn't directly facilitate adoptions, it partners with organizations across North America to provide a central hub where people can connect with local shelters and rescues.

As a non-profit, *Petfinder* is dedicated to promoting animal welfare and increasing the adoption rates of homeless pets. The organization works by supporting shelters and rescue groups through its platform and offering resources to help educate the public on responsible pet ownership. *Petfinder*'s focus on adoption not only helps to reduce the number of animals in shelters but also gives these pets a chance to experience the love and care they deserve. If you're interested in adopting through *Petfinder* or need more information, you can visit their website at petfinder.com or contact them directly via email at *info@petfinder.com*.

FINAL THOUGHTS

In ancient times cats were worshipped as gods; they have not forgotten this. — TERRY PRATCHETT

I have studied many philosophers and many cats. The wisdom of cats is infinitely superior. — HIPPOLYTE TAINE

A cat is a puzzle for which there is no solution. — HAZEL NICHOLSON

In a cat's eyes, all things belong to cats. —ENGLISH PROVERB

You cannot look at a sleeping cat and feel tense. — JANE PAULEY

The cat is the only animal that has managed to domesticate man. — MARCEL MAUSS

A street cat's life is a lesson in survival, but it's also a celebration of independence. — UNKNOWN

Be content with what you have; rejoice in the way things are. When you realize there is nothing lacking, the whole world belongs to you. — LAO TZU

There are some things you learn best in calm, and some in storm. — WILLA CATHER

When you learn, teach, when you get, give. — MAYA ANGELOU

A bird does not sing because it has an answer. It sings because it has a song. — CHINESE PROVERB

How far can you go down the wrong path before you can't get back on the right one. — CAROLEE DEAN

If you don't like something, change it; if you can't change it, change the way you think about it. — MARY ENGELBREIT

Happiness is not something ready-made. It comes from your own actions. — DALAI LAMA XIV

Not all those who wander are lost. — J.R.R. TOLKIEN

The darkest hour has only sixty minutes. — MORRIS MANDEL

You never know how strong you are until being strong is your only choice. — BOB MARLEY

Rivers know this: There is no hurry. We shall get there some day. — A.A. MILNE

The soul that sees beauty may sometimes walk alone. — JOHANN WOLFGANG VON GOETHE

Difficulties in life are intended to make us better, not bitter. — DAN REEVES

The rain taps softly on my window, but its sound feels like a thousand words I wish I could say. — UNKNOWN

The primary cause of unhappiness is never the situation but your thoughts about it. — ECKHART TOLLE

A flower does not think of competing with the flower next to it. It just blooms. — SENSEI OGUI

We do not remember days; we remember moments. — CESARE PAVESE

Goodbye? Oh no, please. Can't we just go back to page one and start all over again? — WINNIE THE POOH

www.ingramcontent.com/pod-product-compliance
Lightning Source LLC
Chambersburg PA
CBHW022105170626
46808CB00002B/612